Parade of Pugin

a novel by
Nick Corbett

TRANSFORMING CITIES

TRANSFORMING CITIES

'A compelling historical novel
about a remarkable man'

Lady Wedgwood

Palace of Pugin

Nick Corbett was born and raised in Sutton Coldfield. He studied city planning at Manchester and Oxford Brookes Universities, with a stint at Amsterdam University. Most of his working life is split between London and Birmingham. *Palace of Pugin* is his first historical novel.

Also by Nick Corbett

Arden (sequel to *Palace of Pugin*)

Revival in the Square

One

The old Palace of Westminster is the stage and London itself is the vast theatre. It is seven o'clock in the evening, Thursday, 16th October 1834. Thousands of spectators are on the streets. Every balcony and parapet is crammed with people. It is the most astounding scene since the great fire of 1666.

At Old Palace Yard, a stooped, hooded figure pushes his way to the front of the crowd. He inhales the smoky air and coughs violently. Underneath his arm he carries an unwieldy sack. He can already feel the heat upon his face. His pulse quickens. Looking down Margaret Street, he can see the full extent of the fire. A police officer presses against him. 'You ain't going no further, sunshine,' he snarls. His blue uniform is blackened by soot and ash.

The man pulls back his hood, revealing a distinguished face. He has high cheekbones and thick, white hair tumbling down to his large, brown eyes. He raises a hand. 'Braidwood! Braidwood! Will you let me through, Mr Braidwood?'

James Braidwood is the Chief Superintendent of the London Fire Establishment. He is thirty-four and has whiskers from his ears to the corners of his mouth. His face reveals a flicker of recognition. 'Let him through! The artist never misses a catastrophe.'

Braidwood walks off briskly towards the conflagration. A black dog follows him like a shadow.

'Go through then,' says the police officer, 'but stay close, we've just 'ad a flashover. The biggest fire ball you'll see this side of 'ell.'

The artist passes under the police officer's raised arm. He places his sack on the ground and stands for a moment, awestruck, on the edge of Old Palace Yard. He pulls himself together, opens the sack and sets up his easel. The canvas is placed in position.

The artist's hands move quickly. A few brush strokes reveal the jumble of old buildings being consumed by the fire. The Classical stone frontage by Wyatt, the artist's former employer, melts into oblivion. Washes of paint reveal the flames rising high into the sky, distorting the atmosphere. Men are painted climbing onto the roof of the Great Hall. They are removing tiles so that water can be poured in and toxic gases released. At ground level, furniture, books, paintings, and other valuable salvage are piled high on the edge of Old Palace Yard. Soldiers are loading stuff onto the back of carts pulled by excited horses. As soon as a cart is loaded the driver whips his horse into a gallop and another horse and cart takes its place. The salvage is being offloaded a few streets away in safe houses.

The artist looks up at the hazy, full moon. It has conspired with the Thames to leave a vast expanse of thick, oozing mud, where earlier there was filthy water. The fire hoses are too short to reach what is left of the river.

Chief Superintendent Braidwood orders the opening of the fire hydrants. The underground wooden conduits are plugged. The result is several gushing fountains, six feet tall, and the creation of a pool of water along Margaret Street, which dozens of hoses feed into. There are great splashes as wild-eyed horses, soldiers, and firemen wielding axes charge through the water.

'Save the hall!' The crowd is desperate to save Westminster Hall, the eleventh century seat of government, the very heart of England. The hands of firemen, Members of Parliament, lords, and the public,

3

are all at work with the pumps. The Attorney General is bent double. He has fallen off a ladder and dislocated his knee. He whacks it back into place and hobbles off. Buckets full of water are being passed along lines of volunteers, but they are having little impact.

The heat is now too intense. The lines are breaking up. People flee in all directions with soot-blackened faces, coughing and gasping for air. The smoke is overwhelming. James Braidwood climbs on top of a pump and shouts a command. 'Abandon all but Westminster Hall!'

The artist wraps up his work and runs towards Westminster Bridge. He catches his breath and approaches a red-coated soldier. 'I've got permission from the Superintendent to paint the fire from the bridge. Will you let me pass?'

'You'll be roasted alive if you go onto this bridge, sir.'

The artist persists. 'Well, how can I get to the other side?'

'There's a waterman. I wager he'll take you to the other side, if you pay him.'

The artist finds the waterman and agrees to pay the inflated fee. The waterman grabs a slimy rope and drags his little wooden boat, through the mud, towards the distant water. The artist follows him. The mud sucks at his feet, soon it is over the top of his boots. At last they reach the water, glowing with the reflection of fire.

It is difficult to row across the river because of a flotilla of vessels carrying sightseers. Several contain London's wealthiest residents, who have paid for the best seats in the house. After several near misses, the artist arrives at the other side of the river. He clambers out of the boat and squelches his way through the disgusting sludge. He joins the large crowd gathered on the shoreline, finds the best vantage point, and erects his easel in soft grey mud. The wind is hot on his face.

4

He pulls his hood down and gets on with his work. The lapping water is some distance away.

The sight of the inferno is even more impressive from this south side of the river. The south-westerly wind blows the flames into the trees and across Westminster Bridge. The artist must paint the boats quickly as the heat is causing them to retreat. The vessel closest to the fire is a steamer belonging to the Sun Fire insurance company. Mounted upon it is a mighty fire engine, with a long hose and powerful pump, but it is of no use. It must wait for the tide to come in before it can reach Parliament.

The artist's attention is drawn to an animated figure. A young man in his early twenties with long, thick dark hair is standing up in a swaying rowing boat. His black clothes suggest he might be a priest. The young man raises his arms with abandon and joins the chorus. 'Save the hall!' The young man is Augustus Pugin. His heart is pounding with excitement. 'George! It's the end of an era!' His companion turns away from Parliament and stares at Pugin, captivated. He can see the fire in his eyes. Pugin raises a fist to the conflagration. 'We *will* have a new Parliament!'

Behind the artist a man puts his arm around his sweetheart's waist. 'Mabel, are you all right, girl?' Tears are streaming down her face. 'I just want them to save the hall,' she whimpers. An old man is shouting beside her in a hoarse voice. He is so close to Mabel she can feel the heat of his breath. 'It's Robert Peel and the Catholics who are to blame for this!' His rants continues, 'It's the wrath of God against the Poor Law!'

A woman screams. 'It's the end of the world!' She collapses in a heap beside the artist. He continues painting.

At that same moment in time, the architect Charles Barry returns to London from Brighton aboard a packed stagecoach, pulled by two sweating black horses. Barry's large frame is crammed into the seat beside the window. Sitting next to him is another large man, Major Henderson, aged forty, back from military service in India. He has retired early due to an injury. 'I shall certainly be pleased to see my parents, again,' he adds, twisting his moustache. 'It's been nearly two years.' He pulls a face. 'I say, are you all right, Mr Barry?' For the last few seconds Barry has been ignoring Major Henderson. He is staring out of the window. 'Oh, sorry, Major. Take a look at this, would you? What do you make of the luminous haze over London? The sun went down hours ago. It's not just the lights being reflected is it?'

They hit a large pothole and the carriage sways, alarmingly. Major Henderson steadies himself. 'I told the driver he was top heavy. He's got far too much on the roof. It wouldn't surprise me if we topple over.'

'Oh, Major, please don't say that!' exclaims the nervous woman sitting opposite as she reaches for her bonnet. They are not far from London and she is anxious for the journey to be over. Major Henderson leans over Barry and looks out of the window. 'Oh, no, I don't like the look of that, not one little bit, reminds me of a scene in the Punjab. It's a fire!'

'Good gracious!' says the woman, placing a hand over her mouth. Her young daughter looks up at her, wide eyed. 'Mamma, do you think our house is on fire?'

'Of course not, Catherine, dear,' she replies with a worried look.

The major scowls and turns to Barry. 'Give the driver a prod, see if he can get some information.'

'Good idea, Major.' Barry prods the roof with his cane and lowers the window. He pops his head out. 'Driver!'

A boy's upside down face appears outside the

window, illuminated by the carriage lamp.

'What's happening in London, boy?'

The boy's face disappears. The driver pulls the horses up and then he waves down a Hansom cab approaching in the opposite direction. All is silent within the carriage as the passengers try to make out what is being said. Outside the drivers are talking in their coarse cockney accents. It is impossible to make out what they are saying. The driver gees the horses on. 'What's going on?' yells Major Henderson. The reddened face of the boy appears again beside the window. 'It's Parliament, sir. It's burned down!'

'Good God!' exclaims the Major, 'I heard the Poor Law reforms were unpopular, but have they started a revolution?'

'Surely not,' gasps the woman, 'could we have misheard the boy?'

Barry is staring out of the window mulling over these questions. Uppermost in his thoughts is that the disaster has created a unique opportunity. What a chance for an architect.

Two months earlier...

Thursday, 28th August 1834, at five o'clock in the afternoon. There is a pleasant breeze over the becalmed English Channel. Looking out to sea, Pugin admires the clouds on the horizon. He is reminded of Turner's seascapes. He likes Turner's work and shares the artist's wonder of the sea. The sun has begun its descent. Underneath it, the town of Ramsgate is blissfully unaware it is on the edge of an epoch. The docks are heaving with humanity as yet another steamer disembarks.

Amongst the hustle and bustle a young man wearing small round spectacles observes Pugin from a distance. He considers him to be a curious but handsome fellow. Pugin's attire is eccentric. He is wearing a sailor's jacket and his trousers are too short, revealing fluffy socks. The young man decides to speak to him.

'Hello again, Augustus, there's a lot more shipping in the English Channel these days, isn't there?'

'Hello again, Arthur. Yes, I suppose we should thank Louis-Philippe for that. He has at least provided some stability for France.'

'Damn frogs.'

Arthur is a student of antiquities. The garrulous Pugin was delighted to have met him earlier, on board ship. He is always pleased to find someone who is prepared to listen to his theories about Gothic design.

'Excuse me a moment, Arthur,' Pugin rushes over to the porters who are mishandling his baggage. 'Gentlemen! The content of these trunks is precious to me. Please take care of them. Keep them the right way up!'

'Begging your pardon, sir!' The flustered porters continue with more care. The trunks are full of architectural treasures that Pugin has collected on his extended three-month tour of France, Germany and Holland. The trunks also contain the drawings he has produced of cathedrals, abbeys, and ancient towns, all to be used in his new book, *Contrasts*.

Arthur spots the porters are mishandling his baggage. Inspired by Pugin, he decides to intervene. 'You, there! Porter! Could you put my trunk on the quayside without dragging it? The porter rolls his eyes, drops the trunk and walks off. Arthur chases after him.

Pugin turns his back to the commotion. He is alone again, looking out to sea. The sun catches ripples on the surface of the water. His eyebrows rise. There is a shoal of fish out there. The ripples disappear and Pugin's smile drops. His pleasure at seeing the shoreline of England is tinged with sadness and doubt.

Having remonstrated with the porters, Arthur returns and picks up on an earlier conversation. 'Augustus, surely you know it was Classical architecture, not Gothic, that was the preferred style of the Catholic Church in Rome, *prior* to the Reformation. You have been to Italy haven't you?'

Pugin is stumped. 'I'm afraid not, Arthur.

'Where were you educated?'

'I attended Blue Coats for a while, but my parents mostly taught me at home, in Bloomsbury. Our house included an architectural studio and a boarding school. Every summer we'd all go on tour, to the cathedrals of England and France. We didn't need to go to Italy, Arthur.'

'Do you all still go on these tours?'

'No,' replies Pugin with a far away look. 'I went to Wells with my mother, two years ago, that was the last family trip.'

'What's Wells like? I'm ashamed to say I've never been.'

'In Wells, Arthur, the scales fell from my eyes.'

'How do you mean?'

'The cathedral and the medieval streets spoke to me of a better world. They stirred thoughts within me, about art, society, God… The trip gave me the idea for my new book.'

'Oh, yes, you told me, *Contrasts* isn't it?'

'That's right.'

'You mentioned your mother, why didn't your father go to Wells?'

'He was too ill to travel. He stayed at home, in Bloomsbury.'

'Is he still a headmaster?'

'He'd never used that title. He's an architectural artist and a teacher.' Pugin omits to say that his father and mother are dead. He also doesn't share that his father was a French émigré who narrowly escaped the guillotine. Perhaps it is his French blood that explains Pugin's bonhomie and his unique sense of style. He is enthusiastic, friendly and naïve. He turns to Arthur. 'Remind me, where are you studying?'

'Oxford.'

'Of course, you're getting a proper education, and you're much better travelled than I am.' Pugin feels exposed but he does not lose one ounce of his enthusiasm. He rallies. 'I haven't been to Italy, but I've just visited some of the sacred, Gothic buildings of northern Europe. Shouldn't we admire these, Arthur, rather than Classical temples devoted to pagan idols?' Pugin continues. 'You see, Arthur, I believe the Reformation was a historical aberration. It destroyed sacred places like Tintern Abbey.'

Arthur nods and draws breath, but Pugin doesn't stop. 'The Reformation diverted England from her true architectural path.'

Arthur rolls his eyes. He heard all of this on board ship and doesn't want to hear it again. He changes the subject. 'Will you see your parents in Ramsgate?'

Pugin's countenance changes. He decides to be honest. 'My father died shortly after we returned from Wells. My mother died a few months after him.'

Arthur is clearly shocked. 'I'm so sorry, Augustus. It must have been a very difficult time for you.'

Pugin can see that Arthur is genuinely concerned for him. 'I went to stay with my Aunt Selina for a time, after my mother passed on. My aunt's very kind. She'd retired from London to a cottage in Ramsgate, so I moved my family here to be near her.' Pugin gives a nod towards the town. 'Ramsgate is home, for now. I wouldn't have been able to do the three month tour without my aunt's support.'

'I wish I had an aunt like that. Hang on a tick, that bloody porter's dragging my trunk again.'

A ship is about to leave port. Steam ejects from its funnel and its whistle blows. Pugin is left to his thoughts.

After the death of his parents the days lengthened and England turned green. Summer blossomed and the railways opened up the country. Pugin met Louisa and within weeks he married her. She was his second wife. Even though he was newly married, a sense of loss settled upon Pugin. He followed in the footsteps of the poets along the Wye Valley, until he reached Tintern Abbey. Whilst searching for meaning amongst the ruins and imagining the monastic life, he decided to become an architect. He also decided to become a Catholic.

Pugin sighs. The three-month tour of Europe has confirmed everything that Wells and Tintern Abbey suggested to him. The Gothic style of architecture truly represents England's Christian identity. He is convinced it needs to be applied to the nation's burgeoning industrial towns.

Pugin is suddenly distracted. He is pleased to see that his old friend, George Dayes has come to meet him. George is a thin fellow of medium height, with a profusion of black hair, not unlike Pugin's. He is always well turned out in a tailored suit that belies his poverty. George is alone and he looks rather lost.

'George! George!' Pugin calls out with abandon.

A young girl stares at Pugin as he waves his arms wildly in the air. Her chaperone, an elderly aunt, frowns aghast and ushers the girl away. George spots Pugin. He smiles and slowly half raises a hand. Pugin stops in his tracks. He feels his shoulders drop. He knows that look on George's face, too well. Something has happened. Pugin elbows his way through the crowd.

'Is it Louisa?' Pugin asks cautiously, referring to his wife. They have only been married for a year and a half. Louisa was ill before he left for his tour. In fact, she hasn't been well since she gave birth to their son, Edward, nearly six months ago. Pugin was concerned about leaving his family, but the travelling was essential for the research needed for his book, which he hopes will bring in an income.

George shakes his head, but he doesn't speak. Pugin is becoming frantic. 'It's not my son is it? Is anything wrong with Teddy?' George remains silent and shakes his head. His face is turned down and he is staring at his feet. Pugin grabs hold of George's lapels.

'Tell me, what is it?'

George's large, watery brown eyes stare into Pugin's transparent, grey eyes. 'It's your Aunt Selina. She's dying.'

Pugin's body begins to sway. George grabs hold of his shoulders before he falls. 'Come on, Augustus! You're going to be all right. Can you stand up?'

'Give me a moment,' he mumbles, 'let me lean against your shoulder.'

'You've had a shock, catch your breath.'

'I'm going to be utterly lost without her, George. I'll be totally orphaned. But you say she's still alive?'

'You should go to her straight away…'

Six weeks later…

Wednesday, 8th October 1834. Pugin is in London to meet with Aunt Selina's solicitors. The sky is a metallic grey. Aunt Selina's body has been buried in the family vault in the village of Islington, Middlesex. After visiting his aunt's memorial, Pugin takes the opportunity to inspect a new grey brick church built by Charles Barry, also in Islington. The church is in the Perpendicular Gothic style. It intrigues Pugin. After producing some sketches of it, he takes a Hansom cab to Holborn.

The horse trots from Islington's golden lanes, along the edges of ploughed fields, and surprisingly soon, they are passing through new London streets. Behind scaffolding made from wooden planks and ropes, gangs of men from Ireland are building ranks of brick terraced houses.

The cab pulls up in front of a fine Queen Anne building in Holborn. Pugin feels tense. A clerk shows him into a musty smelling office where a huge, walrus of a man struggles out of a chair. Pugin has dark shadows under his eyes; he has not been sleeping well. Since the death of his aunt he finds it difficult to take in what people are saying, so he concentrates hard. The walrus catches his breath and wipes his whiskers. He booms in a slow, baritone voice. 'My dear sir, may I offer you my condolences? Now, I also have the duty to inform you the bulk of your aunt's estate, over £3,000, is bequeathed to you, her beloved nephew.'

Pugin is confused; 'Did my aunt really have such a fortune?'

'Indeed she did, sir.'

Aunt Selina always provided for Pugin. When his mother and father died, it was she who gave him the emotional support he needed. She did the same for him when his first wife, Anne, died shortly after childbirth. In times of turmoil, Aunt Selina's cottage in Ramsgate has provided Pugin with a safe harbour. She was a central figure in his life, this dear, spinster aunt.

Pugin was the long awaited, only child of middle-aged parents. He was spoilt by them and by his doting aunt. Now they are all gone. It may be little consolation, but he does now have sufficient funds to fulfil his ambition of building a family home for Louisa and his children, Anne and Teddy. The house will serve as a model for the Gothic Revival. He can also publish his book, *Contrasts*.

Pugin walks from Holborn towards a coffee house in Covent Garden, where he has arranged to meet George. The streets are becoming shabby. The tightly packed terraces are dotted with gin houses and brothels. Gangs of menacing youths stand on street corners.

When Pugin arrives at the coffee house he is so

relieved to see George's familiar face, he embraces him. Pugin's recent bereavement has left him in an emotional state. He keeps reaching out to steady himself, grabbing hold of the back of a chair, as if aboard a ship in a storm. They decide to pay a visit to the Covent Garden theatre, where George works as a stagehand.

They stroll across the cobbled piazza, weaving between finely dressed, high society couples promenading under the colonnades. Then they go down an alley and knock on the back stage door.

When he was a teenager, Pugin made a name for himself as a furniture designer and manufacturer. He set up his own little studio in a less fashionable part of Covent Garden. His most enjoyable work came from designing theatrical stage sets. He loved creating the scenes that transported people to different places and historical periods. From the theatre community he gained a unique education in design and life. It was a heady place for an eighteen year old. He was also passionate about collecting medieval furniture and making imitations of it. The Revolution in France meant there were bargains galore on the Continent, of the finest quality. Pugin got himself a little boat and regularly sailed across the English Channel, sometimes with George and Anne. He would stock up with treasures and then sail back.

They wait for the doorman to open up. Pugin turns to George. 'Are you still enjoying your work here old man?'

'Oh, yes, Augustus, this is where I belong. Front of house is still a strange place though.'

'How'd you mean?'

'You know, dukes rubbing up with tarts. It's hard work for me during the day and debauchery at night. You know how it is, Augustus.'

Pugin frowns. The doorman ushers them through.

They walk through an array of back stage spaces, full of props, ropes, curtains, and whispering actors. Tailors and seamstresses are working on costumes. There are wig makers, carpenters, writers, choreographers, and beautiful, voluptuous dancers. One of them, Kitty, grabs hold of Pugin. She won't let him go until he tells her all his news. Anne was her good friend and fellow dance troupe member.

Anne was Pugin's teenage sweetheart, his first love. She was George's half sister. George was the one who introduced them. Anne was a lovely looking, down to earth girl, who was enthralled by the theatre. Pugin made love to her in the Royal Box once; they stayed there all night. There are tears now from Kitty. She holds onto Pugin's arm. He kisses her on the cheek, and walks away slowly, an arm outstretched towards her.

Pugin steps out into the opulent auditorium, richly decorated in red and gold. Even now he is collating design ideas. Since deciding to become an architect, he has been thinking about how his theatre experience, and his reverence for Gothic design, can be taken to a much bigger stage.

By the time Pugin and George leave Covent Garden theatre, night has fallen. The stars are dim above the flickering gaslights. There are a lot of people out on the streets, much more than usual.

'Is there something going on tonight?' enquires Pugin.

'I don't know. Come on let's get to the river. My little boat's moored there.'

'Are you sure your landlady won't mind me sleeping in your garret?'

'We don't need to tell her.'

Down at the river the watermen, dressed in their white costumes, are excited about something. Groups of them are huddled together pointing to the southern sky.

Pugin turns to George with a look of alarm.

'What is it?' asks George.

A waterman interjects. 'God save us, sir! The House of Lords has gone up in flames.'

'Come on George. Get into your boat. We've got to see this!'

Two

Thursday, 27th March 1837. It is pleasantly spring like this morning. The young farmer stops in his tracks, wipes the sweat from his brow and smiles expectantly. He will let the enormous Shire horse rest for a minute. Now the farmer steps keenly over the rich loam ridges and furrows, freshly sown with barley seeds. He is headed for the highest part of his four-acre field. There is no mistaking the sound of it. It is definitely coming. Looking up the track, he sees the new red brick bridge, gleaming in the misty morning light. There are already a few people on it, watching and waiting.

'Here it comes!'

Puffs of white smoke appear above the treetops. A few seconds later, leaning out of the window and waving wildly is Augustus Pugin, aged twenty-five. He is one of the first passengers to be travelling on the new London to Birmingham railway line. The sun has broken through the cloud.

Inside the little train carriage it is a jewel box, with its red leather padded seats, primrose silk wallpaper, and blue velvet curtains. It is packed full with five men and a tall, thin woman with a large beak of a nose. She is draped in black feathers and finery and looks rather like a cormorant. Every now and again she speaks and throws her neck back as if swallowing a fish. Now she flaps her wings excitedly. 'Do sit down young man and close the window!'

Pugin cannot sit. He is too excited.

The passengers continue their conversation oblivious

to Pugin. A man who looks like a penguin with a monocle leans forward. 'So, do you think it's been worth the wait? It's been a long time coming.'

'And there's the cost, six million pounds!'

'They've had to build so many bridges. There's even a viaduct,' says the cormorant throwing back her neck.

'It'll open up the markets,' adds a Birmingham manufacturer.

'Rest assured, it's one of the greatest engineering achievements the world has ever known,' says a red-faced parson.

'Reverend, do you really consider it to be on a par with the pyramids?' asks the penguin with disbelief.

Pugin pulls his head back in from the window. He turns around to face his travelling companions. 'We're coming to Rugby. We'll have to get off for the stagecoach in a minute.'

Due to delays with numerous Acts of Parliament, protesting landowners, and difficulties with company finance, the new London to Birmingham railway line has not been finished on time. At several points the passengers will have to disembark and continue in horse drawn stagecoaches.

It is a horse drawn stagecoach that finally delivers Pugin to Curzon Street station in Birmingham, just after four o'clock in the afternoon. The new station edifice is still covered in rickety scaffolding, ropes, and Irish builders. The journey has taken eight hours but Pugin feels invigorated. He has been looking forward to seeing Birmingham. His commercial clients have told him all about this booming manufacturing town. From what he saw on the approaching turnpike, it is bursting at the seams. He notes there are many smoking chimneys, but few church spires.

There is some time for exploring. Pugin isn't expected at Oscott College until six o'clock. It is less than a seven-mile ride in a Hansom cab. Pugin notices the familiar smell of animals and the groaning of cattle at market, but this is mixed with the smell of metal and the sound of clanging and hammering. He collects his bag from the roof of the coach and throws it over his shoulder. He asks the driver for directions to New Street. He makes his way down a smart avenue flanked by town houses owned by wealthy merchants and industrialists. Occasional gaps reveal views of gardens and orchards. In the distance are green hills.

Pugin arrives at New Street and his spirit is lifted within him. He has found what he is looking for. It dominates the street like a cathedral, with great bays and buttresses. King Edward's School was the first project he assisted Charles Barry with. It is in the Gothic style and it is magnificent. Residents and visitors consider it to be the town's most impressive building. Pugin has designed its interior furnishings and Gothic detailing. His pace quickens. He knocks keenly upon the front door. Eventually, a young clerk opens it. He is officious in manner. 'Yes, what is it?'

'Good afternoon, sir, I'm Pugin, the architect. I assisted in the building of this school. I don't have an appointment, but I wondered if it might be possible to see the interior.'

'Ah, but you don't have an appointment, you say?'

'I don't, I'm just passing through.'

'I'll have to check with the Master. Naturally, he's a very busy man. Please wait there, sir.' The clerk disappears before Pugin can answer.

Pugin is left to wait in the bustling street. He sits down on the doorstep. A man gallops past, dangerously close, testing a grey mare. The clerk reappears. 'The Chief Master says he's never heard of you, sir. Mr Charles Barry was the architect. Good day to you, sir.'

Deflated, Pugin walks towards the clanging sound of industry. The houses become narrower and cheaper.

BANG! Pugin jumps and clutches his chest. He shouts out loud. 'What was that?'

'Ha, ha, ha...' cackles an old woman, 'it's just them testing a gun. Are yow new in town, sweetheart?

'Yes, ma'am,' replies Pugin, raising a finger to his hat.

'I live down 'ere,' she says pointing towards a dingy alley, ''wanna come in and freshen up?'

'Er, no thank you, ma'am,' replies Pugin with a half smile. The whole street is under a pall of smoke. People are everywhere, with handkerchiefs held to their noses. There is a strong smell of gunpowder. BANG! Another gun is tested. 'This place is dangerous!' says Pugin.

The smoke clears, revealing tiny workshops in the front rooms of cheaply built terraced houses. 'You don't know the half of it!' replies the old woman, who is following him. 'Each gentlemen who owns one of these workshops employs a gang, and they're the roughest men you could meet. Take care of yourself around 'ere, don't go down them back alleys.'

The workers are bustling, going back and forth, between the buildings. 'All right, cocker!' says one of them. Pugin responds by doffing his hat.

Amongst the bravado, Pugin notices tiny waifs playing in the gutters. They are the children of recent arrivals from Ireland, conspicuous by their rags, gaunt faces, and coarse accents. Their parents go from door to door, touting for work. Pugin wonders what arrangements exist for their relief. He prays under his breath that they be spared from the Work House.

Pugin continues to the end of the street. Two women wearing rouge stand beside the entrance of a corner shop. They wave and give him a vacant smile. ''Ello, I'm Nancy, I've got something for you,' says one of them. Pugin nods and smiles, for a moment he toys with the idea of speaking to her.

'I should leave them harlots alone, young man,' says

an old man in overalls, with a paternal wink.'

Pugin is not shocked. Theatre people, such as he was, are frequently exposed to many kinds of degradation. When he was a set designer in Covent Garden he would have to circumnavigate dozens of prostitutes to enter the theatre. He knew some of them well. Now he thinks of his daughter, Anne, and the fact that Nancy is someone's daughter too. He offers her a warm smile and walks on.

Before he leaves for Oscott there is one other building Pugin wants to see. He turns to a young man who has just walked out of the corner shop. He is wearing a distinctive baggy cap pulled down over one side of his face. Pugin has never seen such a cap before today; a number of these Birmingham men are wearing them.

'Pardon me, sir, I'm looking for Paradise Street.'

'Ha! What the 'eck are yer wearing? Yuse not from around 'ere are ya, mate?'

Unfazed by the lad, Pugin persists. 'I'm looking for John Hardman's manufactory, do you know it?'

'Yeah, it's just around the corner, that way, at the top of the hill. Hey Nancy! What do yer make of this fella?'

Before Nancy can give her opinion, Pugin is off. He does look odd. Physically, he's stout, of medium height, strong and good-looking, but he is wearing a self made wide brimmed hat, a sailor's jacket, and his trousers are too short.

Standing tall and proud at the top of Paradise Street is John Hardman's manufactory. The building has a certain style. An architect has clearly designed it. The windows are generously proportioned. Pugin is observing John Hardman's business because Hardman is on the committee that will be interviewing him tomorrow.

Pugin received the invitation to attend for interview from Doctor Weedall, the president of Oscott College.

His letter explained the committee would also include John Talbot, the 16th Earl of Shrewsbury; Bishop Thomas Walsh; and John Hardman, senior, the industrialist. The men on the interview committee all take their position in public life seriously.

The Earl of Shrewsbury, who is addressed as, *my Lord*, or, *Lord Shrewsbury,* has already exchanged correspondence with Pugin. When *Contrasts* was published, Pugin energetically distributed copies of it to eminent persons, including the Earl, who read it with interest.

Oscott College is a new seminary building that is nearing completion. Joseph Potter has designed it under the very close scrutiny of Lord Shrewsbury, who is providing the funding. The commission that Pugin is to be interviewed for is to design the furnishings and stained glass windows for the chapel.

Pugin is eyeing the Hardman manufactory on Paradise Street, looking for clues about John Hardman's character. His attention is drawn to an elegant young lady with a group of children, leaving the front entrance. After a moment, a young gentleman, dressed in a black business suit, joins her. He is of a similar age and stature to Pugin. The man, the woman, and the children, board a waiting carriage. The driver gees the black horse on to a trot. They come level with Pugin. One of the children points at Pugin and laughs at him. The woman scolds the child. 'Powell! Don't be so impolite!'

It is time for Pugin to leave for Oscott College. He makes his way towards the high street where it will be easier to find a cab.

It is a pleasant spring evening, and the shadows are lengthening. The hood is partially pulled down on the carriage. Sweeter air, orchards, and hedgerows aglow with early blossom replace the urban streets. When

Pugin blows his nose he is a little alarmed to see black soot deposited in his handkerchief. Birmingham is smaller than he had imagined, much smaller than London, but it is dirtier. The surrounding countryside is similar to what he saw to the south of the town, it is like a garden, but there are some differences. The oak trees are not as big. It feels more stretched, as if the soil is perhaps not quite so fertile. 'This is still Warwickshire isn't it?' he asks his driver.

'Yes, but only just, sir.' The driver cranes his neck so he can see Pugin. 'Do you see the Bar Beacon up there to the north?'

'Oh, yes, you mean that hill?'

'You have it, sir. Well, that's Staffordshire. It's as wild as you like. Nothing up there for you, sir, unless you like a spot of hunting. Although Lichfield Cathedral is very fine.'

'Ah, so I hear. It's the resting place of Saint Chad, isn't it?'

'It was.'

'Was?'

'It was until the Catholics pinched his bones.'

'Why did they do that?'

'Something to do with the Reformation.'

'They will have taken them for safekeeping.'

The cabby laughs through his nose. 'If you say so, sir.' He gives the reins a shake as they approach a little hill. 'Giddy up, Ned!' Now he turns and steels another glance at Pugin. 'What line of business might you be in, sir, if you don't mind me asking, the navy is it?'

Pugin is lost in his thoughts. He doesn't know Staffordshire. He'd like to run up that Bar Beacon and see what lands and opportunities lie beyond it. He should answer the cabby's question. He would normally describe himself as an architect, although he holds no professional qualification and he has no desire to join the new Institute of British Architects. He is a gifted architectural designer, as his father was. His father served in the French Court, before having to flee to England to escape the Revolution. When Pugin was just fifteen, he and his father worked together for George IV at Windsor Castle, giving expression to their passion for medieval design and the King's desire to recreate Camelot.

Pugin wonders if he should tell the cabby he is an author, now that his book has been published. He gives it a go. 'I'm an author,' he replies after a long delay.

The cabby is impressed. 'An *author*, what kind of books do you write, sir?'

'Well, my book, *Contrasts*, is a treatise on medieval Gothic design, contrasted with ostentatious classicism and bland utilitarianism.'

The cabby scratches his head. 'Oh, I see, and how many copies have you sold, sir, if I might ask?'

This question remains unanswered. The countryside is rolling by and Pugin is engrossed in his thoughts. He hates the lack of civility he has witnessed in Birmingham. It is the antipathy of everything he stands for in *Contrasts*. The reason he wrote the book was to halt the despoiling of his beloved England, to prevent it being covered in industrial sprawl.

A Red Admiral butterfly, the first Pugin has seen this year, lands on the Hansom cab. It flutters off before he can touch it. The vivid red colours remind him of the theatre, of Anne. Now his thoughts are fluttering between places. When he left Euston early in the morning, he had been excited by the thought of Warwickshire. He has been in the county a few times before, to see Mrs Amherst of Kenilworth, a client when he was in the furniture making business. He found Warwickshire to be a romantic county. Having designed many theatre sets at Covent Garden for Shakespeare's plays, he was interested in Warwickshire's connections with the Bard. Pugin is also a great fan of the Waverley novels by Sir Walter Scott, including *Kenilworth* with its theme of ambition versus love. Pugin's business dealings with Mrs Amherst enabled him to join thousands of other Waverley pilgrims who visit Kenilworth Castle every year. Now he turns around in the cab and looks back at the smoking town of Birmingham.

He has to admit to himself, there is something about it that is appealing. It is how he imagines America to be, a new frontier. It seems to be where all of the manufactured goods needed for the Empire are being made. Pugin sighs and shakes his head. He recalls how he was forced to give up his furniture making business due to mounting debts. He even had to spend a few nights in the debtor's prison. He has great respect for entrepreneurs and craftsmen who can make things that people want, and at a profit.

The youths of Birmingham act as if the world is their oyster. Pugin likes that. Although they are less sophisticated, they remind him of his friends in Covent Garden. They are low society and yet in their own little worlds, they are lords. Pugin laughs out loud. The driver turns his head and gives him a nervous half smile.

The lane follows through a dark copse and then out again into a wide-open country. 'What's that hall over there to the left,' Pugin asks the cabby, 'it's one of the grandest Jacobean houses I've ever seen.'

'Oh, that's Aston Hall, sir.'

'Which lord lives there?'

'No lord lives there, sir, it's the home of James Watt, who makes the steam engines.'

'Really? I should very much like to make his acquaintance.'

To the east, in the distance, stands an edifice on top of a commanding ridge of land. It takes Pugin's breath away. It is a vast, Gothic building, four storeys high, half covered in a wooden web of scaffolding. It greets the sky with pointed gables, chimneys, and a great soaring castellated tower. The reddish brown colour of the brick is the colour of good earth. It could be straight out of *Contrasts*. Pugin rises out of his seat, with one hand holding onto the side of the carriage. He is pointing with his other hand. 'What is that?'

'Do sit down, sir! There's no standing in the cab, it's not at all safe!'

'What is that?' repeats Pugin, taking his seat.

'What is what, sir?'

'That building, on the horizon.'

'Oh, that's Oscott, sir. It's where I'm taking you. They own all this land we're passing through.' He then adds, hesitantly, 'If I might ask, are you one of them?'

'One of what?'

'A Catholic I mean, sir.'

Pugin does not answer, he is astounded at the man's lack of decorum. The cabby takes the silence as conformation that he isn't a Catholic. He speaks in a confidential tone. 'They're all out of the closet now, sir. Catholic emancipation, pah! Where's their allegiance to the Crown? Strange times we're living in, sir.'

'I have recently converted, actually, to Catholicism,' says Pugin aloofly.

'Strange times, sir,' repeats the cabby shaking his head.

They approach the steep hill that leads up to Oscott. The lane meanders through a pear orchard that clings to the western slopes. Pugin can smell the blossom. Young men in cassocks, novices from Oscott, tend beehives in little blue painted timber structures.

'They do make a good pear cider. I'll give 'em that, sir. I'll give 'em that,' repeats the cabby, charitably. The lane narrows and they approach rather mean looking gates. Pugin's heartbeat quickens. His emotions are stirred. Beyond those gates is a resplendent Gothic

Revival building.

Three

The air is fragrant and full of woodland birdsong. The Hansom cab arrives upon a raised terrace alongside Oscott College. Much of the building is shrouded in scaffolding. The cab comes to a halt behind a stately, dark purple carriage. It has the letter *T* engraved upon its doors. In front of this eye-catching carriage is a team of four magnificent white horses; each one has a plume of feathers between its ears. Pugin steps down from the cab and takes a few steps towards the edge of the terrace. From this vantage point he looks over the country they have just driven through. In the distance the smoking chimneys of Birmingham are clearly visible. The sun is descending and casting long shadows over the land.

A curious little man scurries out of the building like a beetle. He is wearing a very old fashioned powdered wig. In his highly polished black shoes he dances around the cabby, waving a purse.

'Mr Pugin I presume?'

'Eh? No, I'm the cabby. The squire's over there.'

'Oh, well, let me settle his account.'

'Right you are, *sir*.'

Pugin walks over and introduces himself. 'Good evening, sir, I'm Pugin.'

'Ah, very good, Mr. Pugin! I'm Doctor Weedall, the president of the college. I am honoured to meet you, my dear fellow, very honoured indeed.'

Pugin's round face is lifted with a smile. 'I'm honoured to meet you, Doctor Weedall. I can't tell you how impressed I am with this building.'

'Oh, you're very kind, but it isn't finished yet, as you can see, and indeed that is why you're here. Do come in, Mr. Pugin. His Lordship arrived a few minutes ago. Congratulations on your book, such an achievement! I hear you're involved with the competition to redesign Parliament. Goodness gracious me, what a busy man you must be, and still so young! May I show you to your room?'

Dinner is served in a large dining hall. It is one of the few rooms to be complete. About thirty boys and young men are seated upon benches at long tables. The younger boys attend a school attached to the seminary. Many of the students are the sons of Catholic aristocrats or are from England's wealthiest families. The hall is illuminated by dozens of candles upon chandeliers. A large fire crackles near the head table. This is where Pugin sits, between John Hardman and Lord Shrewsbury. Doctor Weedall sits in the middle of the table, next to Bishop Walsh. Schoolmasters occupy the other seats.

Doctor Weedall is eccentric and ancient. He has a short, grey, beard, which he likes to stroke. Doctor Weedall knows the most intimate details of everyone's family lives. Pugin and his book fascinate him.

John Hardman, junior, the manufacturer of metal buttons, is twenty-five, the same age as Pugin. He is standing in for his unwell father, John Hardman, senior, who is a good friend of Lord Shrewsbury. Pugin warms to young Hardman immediately. Their conversation is easy, as if they are old friends. Hardman has bushy side burns and he wears small round spectacles. The light in his piercing blue eyes shines forth. Every now and again he fixes Pugin with an intense look that searches his very soul.

Bishop Walsh is an erudite and visionary prince of

the Church. He has thick grey hair and is over sixty years old. He makes a strong impression on Pugin. Since Sir Robert Peel enabled Catholic Emancipation, eight years ago, Bishop Walsh has concentrated upon building Oscott College. The Pope has asked Bishop Walsh and Lord Shrewsbury to make it impressive, to show that the Catholic Church is back in business.

John Talbot, the 16th Earl of Shrewsbury, is aged forty-six. He has fair hair and a pleasant face. He is tall, kind, and has dreamy eyes. He is a legend for his philanthropy. By rank, he is the most senior Earl of the realm. He is the preeminent Catholic in England and he visits the Pope regularly. Although Lord Shrewsbury is the most illustrious man in the room, Pugin finds him to be relaxed; he is easy company. Lord Shrewsbury is impressed with Pugin's book. He made sure he would be sitting next to him during dinner. They enjoy talking together about architecture and society.

As Pugin swallows his final piece of the excellent steak pie, he mulls over the next question he is going to ask Lord Shrewsbury. He knows the Earl will like this. 'My Lord, is it true that one of your ancestors was a councillor to William the Conqueror?'

Lord Shrewsbury's face lights up. 'Yes, that's quite true, Mr Pugin. My family came over with the Duke. Have you been to Normandy?'

'Oh, yes, my Lord, several times.'

Lord Shrewsbury leans forward. Pugin continues. 'My father ran an architectural drawing school. Every year I would accompany him and the students on a European tour. We would go to Normandy to study the cathedrals and monasteries. We would always visit Caen, the Abbaye aux Hommes, where we would pay our respects at the Conqueror's grave. We would visit Rouen; draw the cathedral and the tomb of Rollo, the first Duke of Normandy. Of course, we would also see the Bayeux Tapestry. I believe the Duke of Normandy has bequeathed England with a remarkable legacy.'

Lord Shrewsbury breathes deeply. 'Mr Pugin, it's getting late, we've had a good dinner, and a glass or two of port, but if you're willing, I suggest that we climb the new tower.'

'Oh, no, surely not my Lord,' interjects Doctor Weedall. 'It is late and our guest will be ready for his bed. I do not think it would be at all safe to climb the tower at this late hour.'

'That *is* a pity,' replies young John Hardman.

'It really is quite safe Doctor Weedall,' adds Lord Shrewsbury. 'The staircase is in place, but of course we must not keep Mr Pugin from his bed.'

'I would very much like to climb the tower, if it's possible to do so,' Pugin says without hesitation, and then he adds, respectfully, 'but I don't wish to inconvenience Doctor Weedall.'

'Well, go along then,' says Doctor Weedall, 'I hope you'll enjoy the view, although what you'll see at this hour I don't know. Perhaps an owl will flutter by. But you must excuse me gentlemen, for I do hear my bed calling me.'

'And you must excuse me too gentleman,' adds Bishop Walsh, rising to his feet.

Before they leave the dining hall, Lord Shrewsbury, Hardman, and Pugin each light a large candle. They make their way down the corridor to a part of the building that is still unoccupied. The walls are yet to be plastered. They arrive at the base of the tower where a narrow, circular staircase has been recently constructed.

'Are you sure you're up for this gentlemen?' asks Lord Shrewsbury.

Hardman nods keenly. 'Yes, my Lord.'

'Yes, of course, do lead the way, my Lord,' adds Pugin.

'Good, follow me then. Do be careful of your candles, give each other plenty of space.'

Pugin follows behind Lord Shrewsbury. Hardman is at the rear. They climb the steps slowly and very carefully. At last they reach the summit. Pugin takes a moment to inspect a Gothic arch. He places his candle on the last step to protect it from the breeze, and then he is out in the fresh night air. There is a clear sky and a bright full moon.

After being immersed in the cheerful chatter of the dining hall, the silence is captivating. They dare not break it. There is just the gentle rustling of trees beneath them. An owl hoots. Another owl returns the call. Lord Shrewsbury treads carefully over the sloping lead roof. 'Watch your step gentlemen,' he warns. Pugin and Hardman follow the Earl to the edge of the tower. Pugin steadies himself by placing his hands against the battlements. The three men are looking northwards, over an expansive, dark forest, which stretches to the horizon. All is bathed in soothing, velvet moonlight.

'That's Sutton Park,' says Hardman.

Lord Shrewsbury makes his way to the other side of the tower. He is looking westwards. He beckons to the others. 'Gentleman, do come over and look at this prospect.'

About seven miles away, the twinkling lights of Birmingham are sailing in a sea of shadows. Pugin notices curious bright red pinpricks amongst them. 'What are those red lights?'

'Furnaces. They're working shifts through the night to meet demand,' answers Hardman. 'Orders are coming in from around the world.'

Lord Shrewsbury turns to Pugin. 'If the town continues to grow at its present rate, I'll wager it'll be at the gates of Oscott within twenty years.'

Hardman laughs out loud. 'Surely not, my Lord.'

'I'm not jesting, John,' replies Lord Shrewsbury with a flash of his eyes. He turns back to Pugin. 'I enjoyed reading your book, Mr Pugin. I believe our thoughts have been following the same track.'

'How do you mean, my Lord?'

'We share a respect for sacred architecture, and a desire to see our towns reflect more humane values.'

'I see.'

'Birmingham is growing into a wealthy industrial city, but not everyone finds work. Many just find poverty and hopelessness. The housing is abominable.'

Pugin nods and frowns. 'I wonder if the industrial revolution can be harnessed, like a horse, to plough in a more favourable direction.'

'That's an interesting thought. Now that the Catholic Church is free, we must do something. If we do nothing, England could be shaken by revolution, as in America and France.'

Pugin stares at Lord Shrewsbury. He finds his earnestness endearing. 'But where are the churches, my Lord? They simply do not exist in the manufacturing towns.'

'We must build them, Mr Pugin, and why not in the Gothic style?'

Pugin's eyebrows rise. 'Mr Charles Barry has recently built several churches in the Gothic style, but of course they're Anglican, and now he's preoccupied with the Palace of Westminster. He is a great architect.'

'He's also preoccupied with building country houses for his wealthy clients,' replies the Earl. 'I hear it's a lucrative business.'

Pugin looks again at the Earl, inquisitively. He contrasts him with Charles Barry. They are two of the most impressive men he has met. The Earl is a few years older than Barry but he looks younger. Both men are sophisticated, sociable, well educated and travelled, but there is a difference. Charles Barry is formidable and effective, but the Earl has grace. When Pugin worked with Barry on the King Edward's School in Birmingham, he resolved to learn as much as possible from him. He looks up to Barry, as a student looks up to a professor, whereas he would like to be the Earl's friend, ridiculous though that may seem, given their vastly different social standing.

Lord Shrewsbury continues. 'Let us remember, it's only since 1829 that we've been able to worship openly or hold public office. Oscott College will promote understanding of the old faith.'

'How will it do that, my Lord?'

'Through education. Young Catholic men used to learn about the glory of God at Oxford and Cambridge. After the Reformation, many of the old families sought asylum on the Continent. Oscott has kept the flame alive, hidden, but alive. It seems portentous that the remains of Saint Chad have recently been rediscovered.'

'Really?'

'Yes, we have them here.'

John Hardman coughs, loudly.

The expression upon Lord Shrewsbury's face reveals he has said too much. He changes the subject. 'You've studied Normandy, Mr Pugin. Did you learn about the ecclesiastical revival there, in the eleventh century?

Pugin is still thinking about the remains of Saint Chad.

'Mr Pugin?' repeats Lord Shrewsbury.

'Yes, my Lord, I'm aware the Duke of Normandy built cathedrals and monasteries which revived the arts, government, agriculture, just about everything.'

'Quite so! He rebuilt Normandy, with a praying church at the heart of it. If we are to move the hand of God in the dark places of England, prayer must be the currency of the kingdom.'

The men are silent. At last Pugin speaks. 'When I sail my little boat, the *Elizabeth,* across the English Channel, my thoughts often turn to William the Conqueror. How many ships did he build for the conquest, wasn't it nearly one thousand? They were built in a remarkably short period of time. Then he built the cathedrals of England. Extraordinary!' Pugin looks up at the moon. 'He provided much of the inspiration for my book. I see providence at work in his vision for England. I also see the value of a praying church, my Lord.'

Lord Shrewsbury looks delighted. 'I'd like the chapel here at Oscott to be the first house of prayer we build, and then perhaps we'll build them in the manufacturing towns.'

'I should like to offer you my services, my Lord,' says Pugin with a serious expression. He turns aside. 'So, where, may I ask, are the remains of Saint Chad?'

Hardman coughs and looks at Lord Shrewsbury with some concern. Lord Shrewsbury claps his hands together. 'Well, Mr Pugin, I have enjoyed our conversation. I offer you my best wishes for your interview tomorrow morning. I believe it is time to say good night.'

It is the following morning and Pugin is stroking his chin nervously. He always feels ill at ease in these formal interviews. Lord Shrewsbury, Doctor Weedall, and John Hardman, all sit on the opposite side of the large table in the president's office. They are charming men but they are also erudite and quite demanding in their questions. Pugin grasps the side of his chair. The questions keep coming: *Why do you work for yourself? Why did you cease manufacturing furniture? Why did you convert to Catholicism?*

'And now if we may ask you a few questions about your family, Mr Pugin,' says Doctor Weedall. Pugin shifts uncomfortably in his chair. He is beginning to sweat.

Hardman continues. 'I understand that you've followed in your father's footsteps, your father is an architectural illustrator, is that correct, sir?'

Lord Shrewsbury interrupts. '*Was* an architectural illustrator.'

Hardman looks mortified. 'I do apologise...'

'There really is no need to apologise, Mr Hardman. My papa was an architectural illustrator and tutor. He ran a school from our family house in Bloomsbury. My papa and mamma passed on within a few months of each other, quite recently.'

Lord Shrewsbury understands the pain of bereavement. He quickly changes the subject. 'And I understand that your are married with children, Mr. Pugin?'

'Yes, my Lord, Louisa is my second wife.' There is a slight pause. Pugin wears a pained expression. He finds it difficult to talk about his family, especially given the loss of his father, mother, Aunt Selina, and his darling first wife, Anne. He turns away and looks out of the window. The low morning sunlight shines upon branches adorned with buds.

Doctor Weedall glances at Lord Shrewsbury. The Earl's expression confirms he has nothing to add. Doctor Weedall turns to Hardman, who gives a little shake of his head. Doctor Weedall concludes the interview. 'Thank you for your candour, Mr Pugin, if you wouldn't mind leaving us now to our deliberations, we will send for you shortly.'

Doctor Weedall rises to his feet. 'You may wish to take a short stroll in the grounds, but please don't go too far, for we shall not be long, perhaps half an hour.'

It is a fine, mild morning. The woods around Oscott are full of birdsong. Pugin finds a bench thoughtfully positioned for the enjoyment of the view. He decides to sit down and waits to see what the world will reveal. Beyond the white blossom orchards, he can see Bar Beacon, the distant green hill that was pointed out by the cabby. There are high speckled clouds in the sky.

Pugin hasn't sat still like this for as long as he can remember. It is quite a luxury to be in this idyll. He appears to have the grounds to himself. He removes his hat and cups his face in his refreshingly cold hands. His cheeks are burning. He remembers when Anne held his face in her hands.

Life had been so good back in the hot summer of 1831. Pugin was nineteen and he had fallen in love with the beautiful Anne. She was a dancer and more experienced in love than he was. Anne was the half sister of George, Pugin's best friend. It was George who made the introductions, after several requests from Pugin.

But George and Anne were not from a respectable family and Pugin's parents did not approve of them. Pugin's father may have arrived in England as a penniless French émigré, but his mother was from a well-to-do family in Lincolnshire. There were stormy scenes in the Bloomsbury house in the summer of 1831. Pugin, the teenager, was used to getting his own way and he had packed a lot into his first nineteen years. He already had his own business and a reputation for being the best theatrical set designer, and he had worked with his father and their French cabinetmaker friends for George IV.

Now Pugin pulls his hands away from his face. He smiles as he remembers the first time he took Anne away, to Christchurch. It was to show her the Priory that had so impressed him. This romantic trip was the happiest day of their lives. It was a summer of love, but there was a price to pay. Anne became pregnant. They married in secret, in Whitechapel, lying about their ages so they didn't need to get parental consent. When Pugin's parents realised there was nothing they could do to change events, they were surprisingly accommodating. Pugin and Anne moved in with them. The Bloomsbury house was crowded, with the family, the architectural school, and with the students who boarded with them. Anne died shortly after her baby was born.

On the 12th June 1832, Pugin travelled with Anne's body, back to Christchurch. She had left instructions that she wished to be buried there. In the midsummer dusk, her body was laid to rest. Their baby was named Anne, after her mother. At the age of twenty, Pugin was a widower and a single parent. He returned to the house in Bloomsbury, which had always been so full of people, but was now utterly empty. Aunt Selina stepped in and took care of the baby.

A solitary student strolls purposefully out of the woods. He is headed towards Pugin. 'Good morning, sir, it's a very fine day.'

Pugin stares at the student. 'Good morning, sir.' He is sure he has met this young fellow before, but he can not place him.

The student helps him out. 'I'm Kerril Amherst, you stayed with us at Fieldgate, Kenilworth, when you designed some new furniture for our house.'

'Ah, yes, of course! Kerril, you've grown. It's good to see you. I say, has anyone told you that you look very much like Lord Shrewsbury? Are you related?'

'Yes, he is a cousin to my mother.'

'Ah, I see,' replies Pugin, relieved. He realises it was a foolish question to ask. He continues. 'Are you a student here?'

'Yes, sir. By the way, I'm reading your new book. Doctor Weedall recommended it. Would you be so kind as to sign it for me, if I fetch it?'

Pugin is about to make some excuses, but then he looks into the young man's eyes and he detects some sadness. 'How are your parents?'

'My mother is fine, thank you, sir, but my father died.'

'I'm so very sorry to hear that, Kerril,' replies Pugin with a concerned look. 'Of course, I will sign your book, but you'd better be quick because I'm about to be called back into an interview.'

Pugin waits until Kerril is some distance away and then he cups his face in his hands again. When he removes his hands, he looks through tears at the smoking town of Birmingham on the horizon. He wonders what the future has in store for it, for Kerril, for him. He is surprised by his grief.

Doctor Weedall is approaching in his powdered wig. As he walks along the gravel path he stabs the air, practising swashbuckling sword fighting moves. An herbaceous border distracts him. Meanwhile, Kerril bounds over with his copy of *Contrasts*. Pugin signs the book and shakes Kerril's hand.

'I wish you well with your studies, Kerril. Do give your mother my regards. It was so kind of her to show me around Kenilworth Castle.'

'I will, thank you, sir, you'd be most welcome to visit again, whenever you like.'

Kerril leaves for his next class. Doctor Weedall arrives. He looks very solemn. 'We would like to make you an offer, Mr Pugin.'

four

Tuesday, 5th September 1837. The first scattering of autumn leaves is thrown into the air. The gleaming, black locomotive, with its steaming chimney, chugs passed woods owned by Lord Lichfield, at an exhilarating thirty-three miles-per-hour. Pugin has been looking out of the window since they departed from Birmingham. The Staffordshire fields are dotted with people, waving at the train. It is only a few weeks since the Grand Junction Railway Company completed the line from Birmingham to connect with the Liverpool and Manchester Railway. The trains are still a great novelty.

Pugin is on his way to visit Lord and Lady Shrewsbury. For the first time, he is going to stay with them at their family seat of Alton Towers.

Now Pugin sits back in the soft, upholstered seat. He smiles, feeling very satisfied. The offer from Doctor Weedall has changed his life. He has spent much of the summer at Oscott. He has designed the interior of the chapel for them, and two new gatehouses. Pugin has also taken up a teaching post at Oscott. He is now the Professor of Ecclesiastical Antiquities. All of this and he is only twenty-six.

Over the summer, Pugin has frequently travelled to London on the new railway. He has produced many drawings for Charles Barry, for his submission in the competition to design the new Palace of Westminster. Pugin's long absences from home have placed a considerable strain upon Louisa who has been left to look after the children, Anne, Teddy, and the new arrival, Agnes. The family is living in a new house, designed by Pugin, in Salisbury.

There is a deafening blast from the train's whistle. Passengers cover their ears. The black locomotive emerges out of a cloud of steam and arrives, triumphantly, into Stafford station. There is a roar from the crowd.

Pugin disembarks, collects his bag from the roof, and makes his way through the mass of people.

Emerging into a bright, sunny day, the first thing he notices is an elegant purple carriage led by a team of four splendid plumed white horses. His first thought is, '*Is there a royal visit?*' Then he recognises the Gothic letter *T* engraved upon the carriage doors. It is Lord Shrewsbury's carriage, the same one he saw outside Oscott College back in March. The liveried driver climbs down. 'Are you Mr Pugin, sir?'

'Yes, I am.'

'His Lordship is expecting you at Alton Towers, sir. Are you happy for the hood to be down on the carriage? We can put it up if you prefer.'

'It's fine down. It's a beautiful day. How far away is Alton Towers?'

'About twenty miles, sir, it's a pleasant drive.'

The groom climbs down from his seat between the rear wheels and he lowers the steps for Pugin to climb aboard. He wears the same livery as the driver with the letter *T* embroidered upon it. Talbot is Lord Shrewsbury's family name.

The horses trot on through the ancient town of Stafford. From his elevated position, carried on a suspension system of elliptical springs, Pugin feels as if he is on a flying carpet. Within a few minutes they are passing through attractive, gently undulating parkland. Herds of long-horned cattle are gathered under the shade of enormous oak trees. They approach an ancient stone bridge over the River Trent. The wide river is in spate after heavy rain fell through the night upon the distant moors. The horses trot through muddy water.

Now they drive through a patchwork of little fields and isolated stone built villages. They cross the River Tean, lined with weeping willows and reed beds. They pass over the Roman Road that connects with Rocester. The forested lands of north Staffordshire begin to rise. Pugin is very taken with this romantic, verdant land. He is reminded of the Rhine Valley in Germany.

The carriage climbs up a steep, wooded hill. They are approaching a picturesque little village. The honey coloured stone cottages gleam in the sunshine. They remind Pugin of the cottages he has seen in the Gloucestershire uplands. The driver turns around. 'This is Alton now sir, we're nearly there.'

The road dips into a deep valley. It quickly becomes a steep sided gorge. They pass the three-story Talbot Inn and cross the bridge over the River Churnet. It is a boiling cauldron of tumbling water. After passing the river, Pugin looks up and sees a soaring castle perched on top of a craggy outcrop; it is out of a fairy tale. 'What's that castle up there?'

'Alton Castle, sir! It's the original home of the Earls of Shrewsbury. It's just a ruin now.'

Pugin is excited. They pass between a pair of granite sentry posts, which guard the entrance to Alton Towers. The driver gees the team of horses on to take the last steep ascent, up through the dappled light of Abbey Wood. Metal horseshoes are clattering on the road, echoing through the trees.

They are under the canopy for a long time, and then emerge into a sunburst. Above them is a clear blue sky. The power of the horses is transformed into a gallop across the wide-open parkland. Pugin has to hold onto his hat. There is the smell of fresh meadows and the sight of a bright lake with many swans. The carriage turns a corner and Pugin leans out of the carriage. For the first time he sees it, the majestic grey edifice that rises from the earth, Alton Towers is resplendent. Flocks of noisy rooks fly to their roosts in the ramparts. The moors shimmer on the golden horizon. Pugin has entered another realm, a higher country, an Earldom. He is a little afraid.

The carriage pulls up beside a flight of steps that lead up to an imposing entrance. The doorway is somewhere in the shadows. Standing tall and straight, hidden from view, is Lord Shrewsbury. His large gentle eyes light up when he sees his guest has arrived. As soon as Pugin is out of the carriage, Lord Shrewsbury is down the steps to greet him. They shake hands. They are genuinely pleased to see each other. Their common interests mean they are like old friends, regardless of their disparate social class, and the fact that the Earl is twenty-one years older than Pugin.

'So, it's *Professor Pugin!*' exclaims Lord Shrewsbury, in a mocking tone. 'Welcome to Alton Towers! How was your journey?'

'Fine, my Lord! Thank you for sending me your carriage. I felt like royalty.'

'Did you come directly from Oscott?'

'I did.'

'How are things progressing? Did my paintings arrive?

'Indeed, yes, they're quite magnificent.'

'Is the library in place?'

'Yes, and it's growing. Bishop Walsh is in discussion with the Cardinal about acquiring a splendid collection of books.'

'And how do you feel about teaching?'

'To shape young minds is such a privilege.'

The Earl chuckles. 'The students are only a few years younger than yourself.'

'Indeed! We have a very merry time. Some of them

have offered assistance with my next book.'

'Another one? My goodness, you're prolific, what will it be about?'

'A practical guide to Gothic architecture.'

'Excellent! Please reserve me a copy. Now, how is young John Hardman?'

'An excellent fellow, we've become good friends.'

'I thought you might.'

'He is helping me to create a new museum of ecclesiastic antiquities.'

'How very exciting. Well, do come in, Smithers will take care of your luggage. My wife, Maria, is anxious to meet you. She'll be back tomorrow. If you're not too tired, I would like to show you the west wing, and my paintings, and we must go onto the roof.'

'The roof?' Pugin looks overwhelmed.

'Yes, I want to show you the view before any clouds spoil it.' The Earl notices Pugin's hesitance. 'Do you need to rest awhile?'

'No, no, I should like very much to see everything.'

Pugin follows Lord Shrewsbury up the stone steps. The Earl hesitates for a moment, so Pugin can admire the view of the park. They are standing between two statues of hunting dogs.

'It is a magnificent prospect!' says Pugin, and then he cups his ear with his hand. He can hear a harp playing. It is a haunting sound, gushing out of the house like a tumbling stream. 'Is that music real or am I imagining it?' he asks, 'I feel as if I have entered a Waverley novel.'

Lord Shrewsbury laughs. 'Come along, this is the reception hall and then there is the armoury displaying our instruments of war.'

They proceed down a gloomy corridor that displays the coats of arms of the various strands of the Talbot family, going all the way back to the Norman Conquest. They pause in an octagonal space, immersed in multicoloured light, emanating from stained glass windows. The heavenly harp is getting louder. The Earl glances at Pugin, to gauge his reaction. He is used to hearing gasps of wonder from his visitors at this point. Pugin simply nods. He is giving nothing away. The Earl leads him on.

Now they are bathed in white light as they stroll through the long glass orangery. The source of the music becomes evident. An elderly blind man dressed in a white tunic is strumming a harp. 'I'm just bringing Mr Pugin through, Edward,' says the Earl to the harpist as they walk by. Edward nods and continues strumming.

The Earl leads Pugin through an interconnected sequence of opulent rooms and then they arrive in the newly decorated west wing. They stand at the end of a long picture gallery. At the far end is a large Gothic window, framing a view of the distant moors. The Earl looks at Pugin questioningly. 'What do you think?'

'I'm reminded of Windsor Castle, my Lord.'

Lord Shrewsbury likes the reply; he smiles.

What Pugin is actually thinking, is that he would like to redesign all of it, but he finds it hard to speak his mind. He doesn't like to say *no* and he doesn't like to offend people.

'Come and look at the paintings,' says Lord Shrewsbury, enthusiastically. He leads Pugin towards one of his favourites. 'What do you think of this?'

Pugin is wide-eyed. 'She's very beautiful, is it Mary?'

'Yes, of course, she's holding the infant Jesus. Look at her blue dress. The paint is made from lapis lazuli.'

'I should say I've never seen the colour blue before seeing this painting. It's extraordinary. How enticing the blue mountains are in the background, and the blue sky, it speaks to me of eternity. Who is the artist?'

'Titian.'

'If I had but one tenth, no, one hundredth, the talent of Mr Titian, I would give up architecture and be a painter.'

Lord Shrewsbury smiles. 'You like colour don't you?'

'Yes, very much.'

'Titian devoted himself to colour. The blue of Mary's dress is called, ultramarine. Have you been to Italy, Pugin?'

'Never.'

'You should try to go, especially to Venice, their medieval painters were masters of colour.'

After admiring the Titian, they ascend a grand staircase and walk along a landing lined with more fine paintings. They pass through a small doorway, under a Gothic arch, and climb the narrow, stone steps within one of the many towers. At last they step out into bright sunshine. They are standing upon a high roof. 'Do come over here and take a look,' says Lord Shrewsbury, catching his breath. He gestures for Pugin to move towards the edge of the grey battlements.

Pugin cautiously tests the strength of the stone parapet before he leans against it. Now he takes in the view. Beyond the extravagant, lush gardens, are green, forested hills on all sides, and wild, purple moors rise to the north and west.

'I'm struck by the grandeur of Staffordshire, my Lord. The moors remind me of the sea.'

'The sea? How can that be?'

'They're so, other worldly... I feel as if I've entered into the pages of a beautifully illustrated story book.'

'Could it be one of your own books?'

Pugin laughs. 'Possibly, yes. There isn't a single clue that we're in the nineteenth century. If there was a joust on the lawns down there, it would fit in perfectly.'

Lord Shrewsbury feels at ease on the roofs of Alton Towers. He is on the top of his own world. He owns most of the land they can see. Up here he talks more freely than he might otherwise do. He turns to Pugin, with a sincere look. 'I was so sorry to hear about your bereavements. I offer you my sincere condolences.'

Pugin's pleasant, round face breaks into a half smile. He nods and then he turns back to the view. The Earl is anxious for Pugin to know that he is not a stranger to pain and loss. He continues, as if in a confession. 'I hope you don't mind me saying this, I've been following your work over the last couple of years, and I think it's highly commendable, the way you've continued, even after losing your parents and your wife. I feel rather guilty for wasting my early years in self pity.'

'Self pity, my Lord?'

'Maria and I lost a son in infancy. My own mother died a year after my birth.'

'I'm very sorry to hear that,' replies Pugin, and then he gently moves the subject away from bereavement. 'I'm so pleased to have seen this part of Staffordshire. It's a romantic landscape.'

'Yes, we're very fortunate. I wasn't born to be an Earl though you know? I'm the youngest son of a youngest son. I inherited from my uncle. After the death of my mother, my father remarried. Perhaps not surprisingly, my stepmother sent my brother, Charles, and me away.'

'Where did you go?'

'We went to stay with a great aunt at Lacock Abbey.'

'Is that in Wiltshire?'

'Yes, have you been there?'

'No, my Lord, but I've heard of it. I believe the Countess of Salisbury commissioned it, she also built Salisbury Cathedral.'

'Quite so, the abbey is fascinating, architecturally. It was founded in 1232. The cloisters and some of the quarters survived the Reformation, surprisingly intact.

There is splendid fantail vaulting. You should see it. A new great hall was added in the 1750's in the Gothic Revival style. I grew up amongst ancient Gothic architecture, and Gothic Revival. I found it comforting, somehow.'

Pugin smiles, approvingly. 'Did you spend all of your childhood at Lacock?'

'No, my brother, Charles, and I were sent away to boarding school, in Lancashire, about as far away as they could send us. When I inherited the Earldom, I visited Alton and it reminded me of the friendly village at Lacock. The local stone here is very similar to the Bath stone used at Lacock.

Pugin looks the Earl in the eye. 'It must have been a difficult childhood for you. Do you see much of your brother?'

The Earl's nose twitches. 'I'm afraid Charles died at boarding school. It really was a terrible place.' He turns away and looks across the Churnet Valley. He wipes his eye before turning back to Pugin. He speaks in a defiant tone. 'I led a school rebellion after his death. I was expelled. Only my family knows about that. Don't let Maria know I've told you.'

Pugin is surprised. 'I won't repeat a word of it, my Lord. Did you return to Lacock after you were, er, expelled?'

'No, my great aunt wouldn't take me back, and neither would my father. I was given a tutor and the two of us were packed off to explore Europe and Africa. It was quite an adventure. It seemed everywhere we went the British army had just left. I witnessed the horrors of war and conflict, the casualties, the depravity, the poverty. I longed to be back at Lacock Abbey.'

Pugin asks thoughtfully, 'Is that why you've become a generous benefactor, because of the suffering you witnessed?'

The Earl pulls a face. 'I don't know about that.' He

gathers his thoughts. 'It is true that the condition of our industrial towns concerns me, greatly. The workhouses are despicable places.'

'The harvests are very poor this year,' replies Pugin with a worried look, 'it could add to their intake.'

'Yes, in Ireland the poor are suffering, particularly dreadfully.'

'And yet the landowners horses are well fed.'

The Earl is taken aback by that comment; he takes a moment to digest it. 'Well, Mr Pugin, our prayers have been answered with Catholic Emancipation, now we can be more active in public life.'

'You sound as if you're ready for the challenge, my Lord.'

'Yes, well I've waited a long time. For twenty years, Robert Peel fought against emancipation, but then like Saul on the road to Damascus, he saw the light, and he introduced the Bill himself. Whoever would have thought it possible?'

'It's surely the power of prayer.'

The Earl nods, 'Yes, of course, but we have to work hard too.'

'Indeed.'

'For so many centuries we were inferior to our compatriots, unable even to say the word *Mass* in public. Now the doors have been opened for revival, but the revolutions in America and France show we must be resolute if all is not to be lost.'

'What is your priority, my Lord?'

'Well, rebuilding the Palace of Westminster is most pressing. It should not be in a style used to worship pagan gods.'

'I couldn't agree more, my Lord.'

'Wherever I go, Mr Pugin, your name keeps popping up. It's as if we're both tacking in the same wind. Look, since the Reformation, I'm the first member of my family to take our seat in Lords, as a Catholic. I've been appointed to an influential committee. It will be overseeing the appointments for the rebuilding of Parliament.'

Pugin's grey eyes are widening. 'Do go on my Lord.'

'I think the first time I heard mention of your name, was at a dinner, at Holland House, in Kensington, a few years ago. I've learnt that most of the real business of Government is done at Holland House.'

Pugin laughs but he is anxious for the Earl to make his point. He has to hold himself back from gesturing with his hand to hurry him up.

The Earl continues. 'Amongst the guests was the Prime Minister, Sir Robert Peel, Sir Edward Cust - the King's friend, and the architect Mr Charles Barry, who had recently designed a new house for Sir Edward.'

Pugin is tapping his fingers against the stonework.

The Earl sighs and leans against the battlement, as if he's got all the time in the world. 'I recall that Sir Edward Cust mentioned your name, I think you had dined together, isn't that right?'

'Quite so, my Lord.'

'I thought so, well, Sir Edward gave an impassioned plea to the Prime Minister, that Parliament should not be rebuilt by Smirke, in the Classical style, being proposed. There was quite a debate. There was another fellow there, an old architect by the name of Matthew Habershon, a rather disagreeable man with a large nose. He is openly anti-Catholic. He was all for Smirke's design.'

'Ah, my Lord, I know of Mr Habershon. He wrote a vitriolic review of *Contrasts*, he hates me!'

'I think you should be careful of him. He seemed to be quite friendly with Charles Barry. In fact, I should tell you, I heard Habershon tell Barry that you needed to be put in your place. So, watch out.'

Pugin laughs. 'Thank you for the warning, now, please continue, what was the outcome of your discussion?'

'Well, it was agreed that the public competition would be held to redesign Parliament, and that submissions must be in the Gothic style.'

Pugin is a little agitated. 'My Lord, you may know I assisted Mr Charles Barry with his submission to the competition. A great deal of work went into it. I lost my sight, temporarily, due to working on those drawings throughout many nights.'

The Earl is genuinely concerned. 'You must take good care of your eyes, my dear man.'

'Don't worry, my Lord. I was received into the Catholic Church that summer and my eyes soon became clear again; was there anything to add beyond the competition?'

The Earl is slightly disconcerted by Pugin's directness. 'Well, as you know, Mr Barry beat the competition, with your help, in January last year, that's nearly two years ago, but what do we have to show for it? Absolutely nothing!'

Pugin feels the need to defend Charles Barry, who he admires enormously. When it comes to the Palace of Westminster, Barry is his employer. 'My Lord, I should point out that the newly formed Institute of British Architects has objected to our scheme most vociferously. They have insisted that all the competition submissions be exhibited for public debate. They have come up with no end of legal and financial reasons for cancelling our project.'

The Earl is sensitive to Pugin's anguish. 'I'm aware of their tactics, but listen. Maria and I dined again at Holland House last summer. The new Prime Minister, Viscount Melbourne, was there, and again Sir Edward Cust was a guest. It's always useful to have Sir Edward present because then you have the ear of the King. He tells him everything. Over port, we considered the objectors, and how best to deal with them. It was agreed that Charles Barry and you be given five months to produce detailed drawings to enable accurate building costs to be calculated. We thought this would silence the objectors, because after doing so much work it would be ridiculous not to proceed with it.'

Pugin looks slightly annoyed. 'I've been working on the drawings for several months already.'

The Earl continues. 'I want to help you in the development of your career and reputation. Being the Professor of Ecclesiastical Antiquities may help. Your book *Contrasts* is winning more people over to sacred architecture, even if the likes of Habershon hate it.'

Pugin folds his arms and he looks a little uneasy. 'I'm certainly indebted to you, my Lord, but I'm not sure I deserve such unqualified support from you.'

'Pugin, we share a common cause, do we not?'

'You mean in relation to the Palace of Westminster?'

A warm breeze flows over them. For a moment the Earl looks up at the blue sky and then he turns to Pugin with bright eyes full of light. 'We have an opportunity to use sacred architecture to define the values of our age, at Parliament, and across England's growing cities.

'We could build Jerusalem in England, is that what you mean?'

'You put it in better words than I could.'

'We do share a cause, my Lord.'

The Earl looks delighted. He pats Pugin on the back. 'Now, about church building, we need a new programme, for the industrial towns. I believe we should start with a new cathedral in Birmingham. Would you like to build that?'

'I'm speechless.'

'I would also like to commission you to build a new parish church, near here, in Cheadle, something very special. You won't be constrained by budget.'

Pugin smiles broadly. An unrestricted budget is even sweeter music to his ears than Edward's harp. 'Could we also build a hospital for the relief of the poor, a better model than the dreadful workhouse?'

'As you propose in your book?'

'Yes, my Lord, a medieval style hospital, a place where the poor can live, work, grow their own food, and worship together.'

'Could it be based upon a monastic model, similar to Lacock Abbey, where the nuns always looked after the poor?'

'Yes, and let's enable families to live together. Have you read *Oliver Twist*?'

The Earl looks bemused, 'Yes, of course.'

'Dickens exposes a great evil, that the workhouses separate families, husbands, wives, and their children.'

'That's true. So, where do you propose to build this hospital?'

'Well, my Lord, I was taken by the ruined castle I saw, near your entrance gates. Could we build it there?'

The Earl rubs his chin. 'Well, there's some good level ground that might be suitable. Let's go over there, tomorrow,'

'Now, I should allow you to get refreshed.'

'Thank you. I'm looking forward to meeting the Countess.'

The Earl rubs his chin again. He is contemplating whether to share something else. He speaks in a confidential tone. 'Maria and I married young. We lived for twelve years in a small house near Warwick. It was a very big adjustment for us, to become the Earl and Countess of Shrewsbury, ten years ago. We've invested in this house as a place to bring Catholics and Protestants together, to build bridges. I've doubled the size of the place, for entertaining. Maria might seem a little extravagant, what with the feathers on the horses and Edward playing the harp, but we're quite simple people really... or at least we used to be. Tell me, honestly, what do you think of the house, is it quite right?'

'Well... no, my Lord.' Pugin is taken aback by his own honesty; he has managed to say *no*. He continues. 'It's not quite right. It's in the Gothic style, to be sure, but the interiors do not feel authentic to me. They're rather gaudy.'

Now the Earl is taken aback. Pugin continues. 'We need to refine the medieval crafts for our modern age. I was taken by the iron and brass on the steam engine that delivered me to Stafford. We need to be flexible in the use of such materials, even for use within buildings.'

'I think you could change this nation through architecture, Mr Pugin.'

Pugin nods his head. 'When I started out, I learned how theatrical sets can transport an audience to a different mood. Design can influence people's feelings. The way buildings and towns are arranged affects the behaviour of their inhabitants. If the environment is to lift the soul of a man towards God, we need to design everything in an authentic way.'

'I think I can hear the genius behind *Contrasts*.'

'It's common sense, my Lord.'

'The big picture and the details.'

'Talking about details, I'd be very interested to visit Stoke and the Potteries, to look at the tiles.'

'Oh, any tiles in particular?'

'I'm interested in making encaustic tiles, in the medieval fashion, where the colours and patterns are all fired together.'

'I also have an interest in medieval tiles, Mr Pugin. A pavement of them survives at Lacock Abbey, dating from the mid-thirteenth century. They have inlays of clay of a different colour. I've talked about them to Herbert Minton of Stoke. He's an excellent potter with a large manufactory.'

Pugin's face lights up. 'He's just the man! He makes church paving tiles. So, you know him, my Lord?'

'Yes, of course I know Minton.'

'Could you introduce me to him?'

'Yes, he's not far away. I'll send a messager to him. We'll drive over to Stoke and see if he'll give us a tour of his pottery.

Pugin looks ecstatic. 'Thank you, my Lord! I would like to bring to Alton Towers the same grandeur we're proposing for the House of Lords.'

'Well, as I said in my letter to you, I'm keen for you to work here, but are you sure you're going to be able to handle all of this work?'

'Of course, as I explained in my reply to you, I have an excellent builder, Mr Myers. He is quite the best stonemason in England. I've learnt everything I know about construction from him. As I stated in my letter, I've arranged for him to visit tomorrow, do you recall?'

'Oh, er tomorrow is it, er, right, I look forward to meeting him.'

Pugin looks a little hesitant. 'Whilst Mr Myers is a master builder, my Lord, he might not, perhaps, be a master of social etiquette, but I assure you he's an excellent fellow.'

'Remind me, where's he from?'

'Hull.'

The following day Pugin is awoken from an afternoon nap by a gentle knocking upon his door. He is unsure where he is, or why he is lying upon an enormous bed in a palatial room. His architectural drawings are scattered across the bed and the floor. There is the knocking again. 'Yes, what is it?'

The assured voice of Smithers, the butler, can be heard on the other side of the door. 'Lord and Lady Shrewsbury request the pleasure of your company, sir. Drinks are being served in the music room,' then adding in a rather disparaging tone, 'Oh, and a Mr Myers has arrived, sir.'

Pugin is up on his feet. He opens the door. 'Sorry, who's arrived?'

'Mr Myers, sir, I understand he is your builder.'

'Ah, excellent, he's not just my builder though, Smithers, he's a master craftsman and a genius in realising my schemes.'

'Of course, sir.'

Lord and Lady Shrewsbury stand beside a large, stone mullioned bay window. Through this window is a dramatic view of the park, full of late summer sunshine, and beyond are the bleak moors. Lady Shrewsbury is beautiful. She is wearing a blue satin dress, designed to fit tightly at her waist. Her long dark hair is tied up with lace and ribbons. A gold crucifix adorns her bare neck. She is an exotic bird of paradise.

Sitting at the window seat are two attractive young ladies. Standing next to them a younger, even prettier girl, reads poetry out loud. Her voice is sweet and melodic. Pugin remembers Anne, his first love. He recalls how he would listen to her rehearsing her lines backstage at Covent Garden.

Myers puts his plate down, it is stacked high with sandwiches. He lunges out of his armchair and greets Pugin with a firm handshake. Myers is an enormous man, well over six feet tall. He is thirty-four and has a great bushy beard. He is dressed in his best black suit and waistcoat wrapped around his bulging stomach. He takes Pugin aside. 'Pleased to meet you again, Mr P, I never thought I'd be in a place as fine as this, the guest of an earl and a countess, no less. We've just heard a lovely poem from this young lady, about a *fern*.'

'It's good to see you Mr Myers, thank you for coming,'

Pugin turns around and smiles at Lady Shrewsbury. She speaks first, in an assertive tone. 'Good afternoon, Mr Pugin, I'm pleased to meet you at last. Is your room to your liking?'

'Yes, thank you, my Lady. It's a splendid room.'

'I'm glad to hear it. Now, let me introduce the girls to you.' The three girls dutifully form a line, and they give Pugin a little curtsy. He bows in return. He notices they all have the refined, aristocratic features of the Talbots.

The Countess continues. 'Mary and Gwendalyn are our daughters. Dear Gwendalyn is to marry Prince Borghese from Italy.' She smiles dreamily. Then she looks at her other daughter and her smile drops. 'We need to find a husband for Mary.'

The Earl interjects. 'Maria, my dear, Mr Pugin and Mr Myers need not be concerned about finding a husband for Mary. There is plenty of time yet.' He gives his daughter a reassuring nod.

'We'll have to go to Italy if an appropriate match can't be found,' adds Lady Shrewsbury, defiantly.'

As well as being attractive, the oldest girl, Gwendalyn, also has an air of authority. She speaks up. 'I'm very pleased to meet you, Mr Pugin. This is Miss Mary Amherst, our cousin, she's very good at reading poetry.'

Pugin's face lights up. 'Miss Amherst, are you the daughter of Mrs Amherst from Kenilworth?'

'Yes, sir, I remember you visited my mamma.'

'Indeed, indeed.'

'Are you acquainted with Mrs Amherst?' enquires Lady Shrewsbury.

'She was my client, my Lady, when I was in the furniture making business.'

'I see,' replies Lady Shrewsbury, with a disapproving frown.

Pugin is smiling and his eyes are shining. He turns back to Mary Amherst. 'How is your mother?'

'Very well, thank you, sir.'

'Please do give her my regards. Do you know I

sometimes teach your brother, Kerril, at Oscott College?'

'Oh, yes, he's mentioned you in his letters, Mr Pugin. He says you're a good teacher.'

Pugin laughs. 'Kerril is a very good student.'

Lady Shrewsbury covers a yawn. 'May I ask about your wife, Mr Pugin, is she in good health?'

'Very well, thank you, my Lady.'

'And remind me, where is it that you live?'

'Chelsea, in London.'

The Countess makes an effort to hold her smile.

Pugin notices her disdain and he tries to redeem the situation. 'My father and I designed furniture for George IV. Our family is originally from Fribourg. That's where our family coat of arms comes from.'

The Countess seems a little reassured. 'My husband tells me you're going to be undertaking improvements for us, here at Alton Towers.' Pugin's eyes are too intense for Lady Shrewsbury. She diverts her gaze to George Myers, who has a piece of sandwich caught in his beard. The Countess looks appalled. Myers glances at Pugin for support. Pugin gestures for Myers to wipe his face, which he does with his sleeve. The piece of sandwich lands upon the red Axminster carpet.

'Indeed, yes, my Lady,' replies Pugin, attempting to regain Lady Shrewsbury's attention.

The Countess continues. 'We live a long way from London, Mr Pugin. We have a duty to make Alton Towers an agreeable place for society. I know you're working on the Palace of Westminster, but can you help us too?'

'Yes, I believe I can, my Lady.'

When Lady Shrewsbury smiles she looks so much younger. She continues. 'Bishop Walsh speaks highly of you, Mr Pugin. He says you are a man for our age.'

Pugin winces. 'He's too kind.'

'I'm sure your wife must be a great help to you. Is

58

Mrs Pugin devout in her faith?'

The Earl scratches the back of his neck. He is embarrassed by his wife's cross-examination, but he need not worry, Pugin is quite at ease. 'She is not yet a Catholic, my Lady, but I pray it will not be long before she's received into the church.'

'We will have a Mass for her in the chapel on that joyful day, Mr Pugin.'

There is a loud slurp as Myers takes his tea. His enormous calloused fingers are wrapped around a dainty Royal Dalton fine china cup. There are giggles from the girls. Lady Shrewsbury glares at them. They instantly fall silent. Now the Countess turns to Myers. She shapes each word carefully with her lips, as if speaking to someone who is hard of hearing. 'Are you a Catholic, Mr Myers?'

'Oh, yes ma'am, very devout,' he says glancing at Pugin, who is nodding encouragingly.

Lord Shrewsbury's carriage descends from the forested uplands of Staffordshire. Two liveried outriders provide the degree of ceremony befitting the highest ranking Earl in the land. A team of four magnificent plumed white horses pulls the carriage. They are heading down towards the floodplain of the River Trent. Within the carriage, the Earl, Pugin, and Myers talk eagerly about buildings and railways. Pugin glances out of the window. 'Gracious!' he says, alarmed.

'What is it, Mr P?' asks Myers.

'Look at the colliery! There's a pithead, a great wheel and chimney.'

Myers sucks in air. 'Those black gashes do scar the countryside.'

Lord Shrewsbury is more sanguine. 'They might be scars on the landscape, gentlemen, but there'd be no potteries without the collieries; both keep thousands of people in employment. Stoke is the centre of the world for ceramics.'

'They employ little children too,' mumbles Myers.

'I'm all for legislation there, Mr Myers, it's certainly needed,' replies Lord Shrewsbury, with an earnest look. He turns to Pugin. 'Herbert Minton of Stoke produces the best bone china. He's an excellent fellow, quite a dandy, but don't let your first impressions of him, or the town, put you off his pottery. I think you're going to be impressed.'

The carriage turns a corner and Stoke-on-Trent comes into view. It is an intriguing sight of smoking chimneys, bottle kilns, and redbrick industry. Ranks of terraced houses under blue slate roofs climb the hills.

'You can almost feel the coal beneath us,' says Pugin.

'Scratch the surface and it's there, quite literally,' replies Lord Shrewsbury.

Myers shifts uneasily and retrieves a bag of boiled sweets from deep within his trouser pocket. He offers them to his companions. Pugin takes one. The Earl declines.

As the procession of white horses trot along London Road they create quite a stir in Stoke-on-Trent. Children run alongside the carriage, wearing little more than rags. Myers drops boiled sweets out of the window for them. Lines of men in cloth caps are returning from a shift down the mines, with soot-blackened faces. They stop and stare at the Earl's carriage. Pugin feels as if he has entered another country.

The Minton works consists of a long red brick frontage onto the London Road, with several kilns and smoking chimneys. Herbert Minton has a lad posted at the gate, he now runs into the pottery to announce the arrival of Lord Shrewsbury.

The driver cautiously manoeuvres the carriage horses through the entrance gates. Lord Shrewsbury is the first one out. Herbert Minton is already walking briskly towards him. He looks very debonair, dressed in a navy blue frock coat, bright floral waist jacket and double silk cravat. He is in his early forties, a few years younger than the Earl, with similar boyish good looks.

'My Lord! It's so very good to see you,' says Minton with a little bow.

'It's good to see you too, Mr Minton,' replies Lord Shrewsbury with a shake of the hand. 'May I introduce you to the architect, Mr Pugin?'

'Oh, yes, I've heard all about you, Mr Pugin. I have a copy of your book. I'm very interested in your work.'

Pugin shakes Minton's hand, keenly. 'I'm interested in your work too, sir. It's a great pleasure to meet you at last.'

Myers, who is head and shoulders above the others, stands awkwardly behind Pugin.

'Do come into the studio for some refreshment,' says Minton looking at the Earl. At the mention of refreshments, Myers steps forward and he offers his enormous hand for Minton to shake. Minton looks at Myers curiously. He shakes his hand and quickly looks him up and down as if inspecting a novelty.

They refresh themselves from their journey, drinking tea out of beautiful china cups decorated with scenes of Staffordshire in blue and white. 'Would you like to see the design studio now, gentlemen?' asks Minton, rising to his feet.'

'Yes, lead the way, Minton,' replies Lord Shrewsbury.

Myers takes an enormous bite of cake.

'Bring it with you, Mr Myers,' says Minton.

Minton guides them into a beautiful, bright, spacious studio. The walls are covered in white tiles with a colourful, floral border. There is a high, sloping ceiling, with enormous skylights giving everything sharp definition. There are stylish young artists sitting behind drawing boards. Some of them speak with French accents. Minton places his hand on the shoulder of a young man. 'This is my nephew, Robert. He's working on a fern design.'

'Ah, ferns are very fashionable, aren't they?' comments Myers, 'especially amongst the young ladies.' He scratches his head. 'Why is that?'

Minton smiles. 'It's since Charles Darwin returned from his voyage in the Beagle. That fellow works too hard. He's been staying with his uncle, Josiah Wedgwood, my neighbour, for a rest.'

'Young Darwin is a pleasant fellow,' says Lord Shrewsbury.

Myers pipes up again. 'Botany would be an interesting hobby, if only I had the time.' He searches the faces of the others, looking for agreement, but they are all stony faced. When Myers looks away Minton and Pugin grin at each other. Pugin is fascinated to see how Minton has created an international design studio in the middle of Stoke-on-Trent. He looks as if he would be more at home in Covent Garden.

Minton continues. 'Come and have a look at these display cabinets, Mr Pugin. I think you may find the exhibits of interest.'

The men are all pressing their noses against a glass cabinet containing thickly lustred, medieval style tiles. Lord Shrewsbury turns to Pugin. 'Do you recall I mentioned the thirteenth century tiles at Lacock? They look just like these.'

Pugin nods and then he turns to Minton. 'So, have you been able to make new encaustic tiles in the medieval way?'

Minton stands up straight, with his thumbs resting in his jacket pockets. 'I've been getting up at half past five every morning since I took the pottery over last year, trying to perfect encaustic tiles. I'll show you the chemistry laboratory. We've been working on getting the different coloured clays to bond together in the kiln. If the different clays fire at different times, the tile explodes. We've had a lot of cleaning up to do.'

'Have you resolved the problem?' asks Pugin.

'Yes.'

'How?'

'I've had to do a lot of research on ancient kilns.'

'Where have you found them?'

'Archaeological excavations. The results have been worth waiting for. We can now make tiles in the medieval fashion. This means we can restore medieval tile pavements in churches.'

Pugin is wide eyed. 'Can you go into mass production?'

'Indeed, we can. I thought that might be of interest to you, Mr Pugin.' Minton turns away for a moment. He looks out of the window, over the roofs of industrial Stoke. He continues, as if speaking to the sky. 'My father worked for Spode in London. He moved to Stoke, built these works and pioneered the use of bone china. Now I'm going to open new markets with these encaustic tiles. I'm expanding the business, internationally. I've just returned from Italy.' He turns back to Pugin, 'Have you been to Italy?'

Pugin shakes his head and looks slightly embarrassed. Minton looks surprised. 'Oh, you really must go to Florence. The tiles in the cathedral are exquisite.'

'Is there a market for your tiles closer to home?'

'I came back through Belgium. I was invited to call at the Court and I had the honour of meeting King Leopold, and his nephew, Prince Albert of Coburg. He's a delightful young man, has a keen interest in the arts…'

'He's an anti-slavery campaigner, isn't he?'

'Yes, I believe so. He's moving to London.'

Lord Shrewsbury interjects. 'I suspect King Leopold would like his nephew, young Albert, to marry the Duchess of Kent.'

'Who will become Queen Victoria,' adds Pugin.

'I suspect, if the rumours of the King's health are true, Victoria will soon become Queen,' adds Minton. He continues, 'Prince Albert took a great interest in my encaustic tiles. He asked me to call on him in London. He wants to see more of my work.'

'You must do that, Minton,' says Lord Shrewsbury. 'He would be a great ally to our cause.'

'Cause?' enquires Minton with a quizzical look, 'what cause?'

'For a revival of the Christian arts,' replies the Earl.

'Ah.'

Pugin changes tack. 'Do you envisage the demand for medieval style tiles will come mostly from the church?'

'Churches are my passion, but our tiles will go into schools, libraries, town halls, and houses. Do you have any projects in mind, Mr Pugin?'

Pugin exchanges a furtive glance with Lord Shrewsbury, who nods and smiles broadly. Pugin decides to play his trump card. He turns to Minton. 'You may have heard that there is to be a new Palace of Westminster.'

'Yes, of course.'

'I'm working on the project with Mr Charles Barry, the eminent architect.'

Now Minton is wide eyed. 'Will the palace require encaustic tiles?'

'I can think of nothing better for the interior walls and floors, but would you be able to work to my designs?'

'Yes, of course, I admire your work, Mr Pugin. Perhaps we could produce a new Gothic range together?'

'I'd like that.'

'Please be assured, this pottery can be adapted to meet any level of demand, providing the best quality tiles at a relatively low cost.'

'Don't forget our new church at Cheadle, Mr Pugin,' says Lord Shrewsbury.

'I haven't my Lord, we'll use Mr Minton's tiles there too. We're going to build the finest parish church in the land.

five

Thursday, 28th June 1838. It is fifteen minutes past eight o'clock in the morning. The carpet of the drawing room at Number 3, Prospect Place, Chelsea, is covered in drawings. Kneeling down in the middle of this disorder is Pugin. Sitting beside him, on the edge of a green settee, is his good friend, John Hardman of Birmingham. They are like two schoolboys engrossed in a favourite game. They have already been working for two hours. The household was awoken at the crack of dawn by cannons being fired in the park, to celebrate Queen Victoria's coronation day.

Hardman is counting pieces of paper. 'If you accept all of these commissions, you will be building eighteen churches, two cathedrals, three convents, two monasteries, a school, and there's half a dozen houses.'

'Don't forget the Palace of Westminster, John,' adds Pugin.

'I could never forget the great Charles Barry. He demands more of your time than anyone else!' Hardman continues. 'I wonder why you've had so many commissions in such a short period of time. Is it because of your book or is it just that your genius has finally been recognised?'

Pugin laughs. 'The book has helped, but I have to thank Lord Shrewsbury for many of these commissions.'

Hardman nods. 'Yes, that's probably true.'

'My biggest worry is getting all of the drawings done on time for Mr Barry. He's very demanding, and so he should be, but he does keep changing his mind. I've done two-dozen revisions for one handrail. I've produced well over a thousand drawings for the chamber of the House of Lords so far. I'm beginning to wonder if I should withdraw from this commission.'

Hardman flinches. 'Well, it's a very prestigious commission. Perhaps you just need to stand up to Barry, tell him he can't keep changing his mind. I don't like the way he bullies you. Do you want me to speak to him?'

'Of course not.'

'Well, don't overdo it, you gave everyone quite a scare when your eyesight failed again last month.'

'Don't fret so, John,' replies Pugin with a disparaging look. He climbs to his feet and stands upon a small island of carpet that is free of drawings. 'Listen, there's something I want to tell you.'

'Oh, that sounds ominous. What is it?'

'The foundation stone will be laid today at Saint Mary's, Derby.'

'Yes, so it will. It's going to be a splendid church. Do you wish you were up there for the ceremony?'

'No, Myers is taking care of everything. He's even purchased a silver trowel for the job,' says Pugin with a chuckle.

'I know, I made it for him.'

Pugin steps cautiously between the drawings. Using both hands he pushes the sash window all the way up. He pokes his head through the opening and looks down the street. The breeze is pleasant. He can see the main road where lots of people are already making their way to the coronation procession. A blackbird sings gloriously in a tree, with its own celebration. Pugin smiles and turns back to his friend. 'London is the place to be today, John. Never has a coronation filled me with such expectancy.'

'There's a sense of hope in the air, isn't there? At

last, the Georgian era is over.'

'To think, the new Queen is only eighteen. Seven years younger than us.'

'England will be young again,' replies Hardman with a smile. 'What was it you wanted to tell me, something about Saint Mary's?'

'Ah, yes, Saint Mary's. My concern is I don't want it to be covered in damned blisters.'

Hardman looks puzzled. 'What do you mean by blisters?'

'I mean those memorials that get stuck all over the walls of churches. Some of them are as long as obituaries in *The Times*. And I can't abide those damned memorial statues, a lot of them are quite pagan. Horrible things!'

'How can you stop them?'

'We can give people a better alternative, John'

Hardman scratches the back of his neck. 'How?'

'The answer lies in stained glass.'

Pugin's eldest child, Anne, aged six, appears in the doorway holding Agnes, aged one, in her arms. 'Papa!'

Beside them is Teddy, aged four, waving a Union Jack flag. 'We don't want to be at the back, Papa, can we go now?' All of the children are beautiful, with dark complexions.

Louisa, Pugin's formidable wife, looms up behind the children. She stands, hands on his hips, extravagantly bejewelled. Pugin has designed her black Gothic dress and her jewellery. Her theatrical appearance suggests she might be an actress, but she is not. Louisa is from a much more respectable family than Anne, his first wife, and she does not possess Anne's good looks. Her eyes narrow, 'Come along children. Your papa has reserved us all seats in the stalls. We'll all be able to see Queen Victoria.' Before she takes the children away she gives Pugin an icy look and jerks her head in a way that makes it very clear, she is ready to go.

Pugin looks anxious. 'Don't worry Louisa, my dear. We will be ready in a minute or two. Do ask nanny to give the children some cake.'

'They're not having any more cake!' snaps Louisa from the hallway.

Pugin turns back to Hardman. He speaks in a confidential tone. 'There's wonderful news about Louisa, but you must keep it secret for now.'

'Oh, I will,' replies Hardman, suspecting another child must be on the way.

'She's to be accepted into the Catholic Church.'

'That's wonderful news.' Hardman is genuinely delighted.

'I'm sure it'll make her more… tranquil,' adds Pugin.

'When will the service be held?'

'Next Spring. Lord and Lady Shrewsbury have insisted the service be held in the chapel at Alton Towers. Louisa is quite overwhelmed by the prospect. Another thing, Gwendalyn, the Shrewsbury's daughter, and her husband, Prince Borghese, are coming to stay with us en route to Rome.

'Really? The Prince and Princess of Borghese, staying here?'

'Yes. Gwendalyn is a delightful girl and the Prince is very amiable. I'm designing new apartments for them at Alton Towers.'

'What does Louisa think of them visiting?'

'It may explain her temper. She's very nervous.'

Hardman, ever practical, steers the conversation back to business. 'Now, what was it you were saying about stained glass and memorials?'

'Oh, yes, well, stained glass is becoming so popular. Personal memorials can be discreetly inscribed on the bottom of the glass, rather than putting those vain memorial blisters on the walls. I got the idea from Oscott. The nobility have stained glass windows put in to commemorate the attendance of their offspring in the school.'

'It's a good idea, I like it.'

'The trouble, John, is the quality of the glass. With all of our machinery and modern inventions, I can't find anyone who can match the quality of the ancient glassmakers. Can you keep a secret, John?'

'What, another one?'

'I want to create a new glass workshop, and it's not just for the church work. We are going to be using stained glass throughout the new Palace of Westminster. Charles Barry is proposing to use a company in Edinburgh, but they are wholly inappropriate. They don't understand the first thing of medieval design. So, I'm wondering if you might like to help.' Pugin stops for a moment and gauges Hardman's reaction.

Hardman furrows his brow. 'As you know, my business is metal buttons. We don't make stained glass.'

'But you've turned your manufactory over to many other things. You're not just a button maker, John. You're a goldsmith. You make candlesticks, chalices and all the things you find in churches, everything apart from stained glass, in fact. Everything you turn your hands to seems to prosper.'

Hardman doesn't flinch. 'You say it'll definitely be stained glass for the Palace of Westminster?'

'Quite so.'

Hardman's raised eyebrows reveal his growing interest. 'That'll be a substantial contract won't it?'

'I should say so, one of the biggest.'

'So, do you think I should create a glass works at the factory?'

'That's an interesting idea, John. I would certainly support you in your proposal. If you can create glass with a medieval quality, I'll persuade Mr Barry to use you. We could do some research together, to get that rich effect of the olden days. What an excellent suggestion, John. Together we'll develop windows to improve the meditative qualities of church and state.'

'I'm not saying I will do it.'

Before Pugin can answer, Teddy shouts from the hallway. 'Papa! Let's go!'

'Coming, my boy!'

Pugin walks out of Number 3, Prospect Place with his wife, Louisa, his children, Anne and Teddy, and with John Hardman. Late seventeenth century terraced houses of the kind that fill this unfashionable part of Chelsea, front the street. They turn a corner and stroll through dappled light, under the canopy of enormous London plane trees. They are close to the river. Pugin lifts Teddy onto his shoulders, much to the boy's delight.

After a few minutes, Pugin's shoulders ache. 'You're too heavy now, Teddy, down you come.'

'Will uncle John carry me?'

With that Hardman lifts Teddy up and places him upon his shoulders.

'Please leave my spectacles alone, Teddy!'

'Can I try them on?'

'No!' He raises a hand to reposition his spectacles upon his nose.

Louisa frowns. 'Do hold his legs tightly, John!'

'Don't worry, Louisa, I've got him.'

Pugin nudges Hardman and points across the road. 'That site over there once contained the mansion of Sir Thomas Moore.'

'I wonder if he wrote *Utopia* there.'

They continue towards the wharfs. The river is full of boats. The watermen in their bleached costumes are busy ferrying people upstream to Westminster. Union Jacks are everywhere.

Pugin ushers everyone into a ferry. Two burly watermen row them with the tide towards Westminster Bridge, which is already packed with people.

'It looks so sad doesn't it, Augustus?' Louisa is pointing to the charred remains of Parliament.'

Pugin nods. 'Yes, my dear, that's how the ancient monasteries looked after the Reformation.'

'Saint Stephen's Hall is nothing but a shell,' says Hardman. 'Why doesn't Charles Barry knock it down, and the remains of the Speaker's House while he's at it? They're too far gone.'

'He probably will. But look now, John, to the other side of them, do you see it?'

The ferry progresses and a full panorama of the charred remains of the Palace of Westminster is revealed. Pugin is excited. 'There it is, Westminster Hall!' He puts his arm around Teddy. 'Look, can you see the hall, my boy?'

Teddy is nodding and smiling. Pugin turns to Hardman. 'The roof structure is an architectural wonder, commissioned by the son of William the Conqueror. It's massive, with no supporting columns, and it's survived intact, isn't that remarkable?'

'Indeed it is, Pugin. Indeed it is,' marvels Hardman.

After disembarking, Pugin leads his group towards the temporary grandstands erected beside the Abbey. A million spectators are gathered in London, and most have little Union Jacks to wave. Every balcony and rooftop is covered with people. The streets are also lined by thousands of policemen.

At half past ten o'clock, the carriages of the coronation procession begin to go by. First, are the ambassadors, in their colourful uniforms and smart carriages, and then it is members of the royal family. At last, Queen Victoria's state landau carriage approaches, pulled by a team of six beautifully groomed chestnut horses. Pugin lifts Teddy up so he can get a better view.

'Why are the horses brown, Papa?' asks Anne, pulling at her father's arm.

'Brown is for humility, darling.'

There is loud applause from the crowd and shouts of, 'God bless you ma'am!' Pugin and his family have a very clear view. The young, radiant, Queen Victoria looks directly at Pugin and smiles before turning to her companion.

Pugin is overwhelmed. He gasps. 'Oh, the pressures that must be placed upon those fragile shoulders.'

Thursday, 14th October 1841. It is nine o'clock in the morning. The first chill of autumn has arrived. The sky is patterned with high cloud. Pugin sits alone in Howard's Coffee House. He stares out of the window, admiring the Gothic tracery on Westminster Abbey. Following the fire, the coffee house has been relocated into a surviving corner, off Westminster Hall.

Pugin takes another sip of his coffee. His eyes close tightly. It is surprisingly good. When he opens his eyes he sees an elegant gentleman sitting down beside him. He places his top hat on the table.

'It's the best coffee in town isn't it?' he says with a smile.

Pugin nods and smiles back. 'Good morning, Lord Shrewsbury, yes it is.'

The Earl looks at Pugin's attire and he pulls a face. Pugin looks down at himself. He is wearing the same sailor's jacket he always wears when he is working. The large pockets contain pencils, rubbers, note pads, and a ruler. 'Oh, I'm sorry, I'm not appropriately dressed, am I?'

'Not really, no, not for a meeting with his Royal Highness, and you look pale.

'I've been quite ill, my Lord. The doctors bled me with leeches. Detestable things! I hate being ill, you know I can't stand to lose a minute.'

'My dear, Pugin, has your illness been so serious? I had no idea.'

'I'm afraid so. I really wanted to accept your

invitation to Rome, but I was forbidden from travelling by my doctors.'

'There'll be other times for Rome. Do the doctors know what the cause of your illness is?'

'Rheumatic fever, I think they said, but it seems to change every time.'

'What are the symptoms?'

'Aching joints, fever, it's very unpleasant.'

'Are you taking any medicine?'

'The prescription is a few grains of mercury, every four hours, to reduce the swelling. It left me as weak as a kitten. I thought my teeth were going to fall out. I'm a lot stronger now though. I'm really quite recovered. I worked straight through last night, preparing drawings for Mr Barry.'

Lord Shrewsbury looks concerned. 'Could it be that when you push yourself too hard, you get ill?'

Pugin looks thoughtful. 'Well, I suppose it doesn't help. I think it's living by the river. It's not the healthiest of places. Lord Shrewsbury, you're very kind to take such a personal interest in my wellbeing.'

'Well, Pugin, Lady Shrewsbury and I are very fond of you.'

Pugin's wide mouth breaks into a full smile. There's a flicker of light in his grey eyes. 'Thank you, my Lord, and of course Louisa and I feel the same sentiments towards you and Lady Shrewsbury. Now, enough of my health. To business. I'm a little worried. I think I should have told Mr Barry we're meeting Prince Albert.'

Lord Shrewsbury frowns. 'Mr Barry isn't your lord and master, is he?'

'No, my Lord, but as you know, working for Parliament is fraught with politics. Mr Barry protects me from all of that. The last thing I want to do is to create any difficulties for him.'

'I understand that, of course, but I'm on the Royal Commission of Fine Arts and Prince Albert is the chairman. He's interested in your ideas and he has requested this meeting. He sees Mr Barry quite frequently; if he wanted him to attend he would have invited him. He is the husband of the sovereign. I really don't think that even Mr Barry could object to his request to meet you.'

Pugin looks reassured. 'Thank you Lord Shrewsbury. Do you know where our interview is to be held?'

'The Prince has set up an office, somewhere. Ah! Here's Webster for us.'

Webster is a tall, stooped, frail man, with frizzy white hair. He is wearing the coat tails and white bow tie that distinguishes him as an usher of the Palace of Westminster. Webster is as worn out as the building. Breathless, he holds onto the back of a chair for support. 'My Lord Shrewsbury,' he gasps, 'his Royal Highness, Prince Albert has requested your company in the Jewel Tower.'

'Thank you, Webster, I don't think I've ever been in the Jewel Tower.'

'It's quite a way, my Lord,' says Webster with a sharp intake of breath. 'Would you follow me, please?'

They follow the doddery Webster through a porch with an impressive vaulted stone ceiling. They enter into the dark, cavernous space of Westminster Hall. A glimmer of light comes from oil lamps, of the kind found in churches, which hang down from the magnificent hammer beam roof.

'This roof never ceases to impress me,' says Pugin looking upwards. 'It's the lack of any supporting columns that I find so remarkable.'

'It makes me feel as if I've entered into the ribs of a leviathan,' replies Lord Shrewsbury.'

Webster can't resist joining in. 'It's the largest medieval timber roof in Northern Europe, my Lord. It's not the original roof of course. This one was completed in 1401. It's relatively modern.'

'This roof structure should be the model for new railway stations,' says Pugin.

He has hit a raw nerve with Webster. 'Those railways are questionable things, sir!' They've already killed many and ruined the countryside.'

Lord Shrewsbury and Pugin exchange a furtive smile. 'Just a moment,' says Pugin turning on his heels. Lord Shrewsbury stops beside him but Webster keeps shuffling along. 'You see the great north window?

'Yes.'

'It has had clear glass since the Reformation. I'd very much like to put back a stained glass design.'

'That's a good idea. How's the work on stained glass progressing with John Hardman?'

'It's a complex process, it's going to take time and a lot more research to match the quality of the ancient craft, but we'll get there. It has to be manufactured from flint and many other surprising ingredients.'

'It sounds intriguing.'

'When we have it right, we'll do the windows at Alton Towers, and of course at Saint Giles.'

Lord Shrewsbury looks pleased. Pugin continues. 'Look at those angels up there, my Lord. Do you see them, holding up the beams?'

'I do, but come along Pugin! We can't keep the Prince waiting.'

They catch up with Webster. They assist him up the large flight of steps, and then it's through a door and they are back into the brightness. Webster leans against a wall and takes a moment to catch his breath. Lord Shrewsbury looks at his pocket watch. 'Is that the Jewel Tower over there, Webster?'

'Yes, my Lord.' He can't resist sharing another history lesson. 'It was built for King Edward III in 1365, to store his personal treasure.'

'I see, well, we'll make our own way over there now, thank you.'

Webster looks very relieved. 'Very good, my Lord.'

The large number of police officers is a clear sign that Prince Albert is present. A recent attempt on his life, whilst travelling in a carriage with Queen Victoria, has resulted in increased security.

A smartly dressed man in top hat and tails, aged thirty, the same age as Pugin, steps out from behind the police line. 'Good morning, my Lord Shrewsbury!'

'Oh, good morning, Mr Anson, allow me to introduce my friend to you. This is Augustus Pugin.'

'Ah, the architect, I'm delighted to meet you, sir. I'm George Anson, private secretary to Prince Albert. His Royal Highness is waiting for you.'

Mr Anson escorts them up a very narrow, spiral stone staircase. They enter into a first floor room, set within the massive walls of the medieval tower. The narrow windows are all open and the air is fresh. Starlings can be heard warbling in the autumnal gardens beside Westminster Abbey.

Prince Albert is dressed elegantly in a dark suit, navy blue waist jacket, and polished black hunting boots. He is tall, slim, handsome, and has stylish, long sideburns. He is not yet twenty-three. He leans across the conference table that is covered in drawings, and shakes hands with his guests. Lord Shrewsbury and Pugin bow their heads when they shake the Prince's hand.

The Prince speaks with a German accent. 'Mr Pugin, I've been looking forward to meeting you. I have a copy of your new book, *The True Principles of Pointed or Christian Architecture*, it's a most impressive guide.'

'Thank you, your Royal Highness.' Pugin looks into the Prince's intelligent, bright blue eyes. There are beaming smiles all around. The Prince is very chatty. 'I was in Birmingham recently, to see Mr Elkington's electroplating. It's really quite remarkable. He can turn anything into gold, or at least it looks like gold. I also saw your Saint Chad's. It's a very splendid building, for a moment I thought I was back in Germany.'

Prince Albert looks down at his feet, a little shyly. His wife, Queen Victoria, has warned him about being too enthusiastic.

'I heard about your visit to Birmingham, sir, didn't Mr Elkington turn a red rose into gold?'

The Prince abandons his royal reserve. 'He did! But let me tell you the most remarkable thing, Mr Pugin. We didn't see it until Mr Elkington dipped the rose into his concoction, but a spider had spun its web around the petals. This delicate web was also turned into the finest gold.'

'Astonishing!' gasps a wide-eyed Pugin.

'Indeed!'

The Prince turns to Lord Shrewsbury and he speaks in a more formal, business like tone. 'My Lord Shrewsbury, it's good to see you again.'

Lord Shrewsbury gives a second little bow and smiles. 'As ever, the pleasure is all mine, your Royal Highness.'

The Prince smiles, 'Let's sit down, gentlemen. Please, make yourselves comfortable.' Drinks are offered and declined. Prince Albert turns back to Lord Shrewsbury. 'I thought the last meeting of the Royal Commission was very productive.' He turns to Pugin. 'We agreed that the construction of the new Palace of Westminster should support British arts and crafts.'

'That's good to hear, sir. Are there any particular arts and crafts that you wish to support?'

The Prince looks thoughtful. 'Architectural features, such as stained glass, metalwork, carpentry, and interior furnishings of all kinds.' The Prince searches Pugin's face for a response.

Pugin nods approvingly. The Prince brushes his hand over the drawings in front of him. 'Now, I've been looking over Mr Barry's beautiful drawings. I'm sure it will be the finest parliament in the world.'

'It's actually Mr Pugin that produces the drawings, sir,' says Lord Shrewsbury.

'Oh, really, why doesn't he put his name on them?'

Lord Shrewsbury shrugs his shoulders. Prince Albert turns to Pugin, 'Is that right, Mr Pugin, do you do all of the drawings?'

Pugin is looking out of the window at a robin that has burst into song. He smiles, takes a deep breath, and turns back to the Prince. 'Er, yes sir, but I work under Mr Barry's direction. He's the principal architect for the project.'

The Prince clears his throat. 'Lord Shrewsbury has told me about the exciting work you're doing, building lots of churches, but I was also told that you used to work in the theatre, is that right, Mr Pugin?'

'Yes, sir, in Covent Garden, a long time ago.'

'Designing the, oh, what do you call it, on the stage, the...?'

'Sets, sir,' says George Anson.

'What has sex got to do with it, Mr Anson?' asks the Prince.

'*Sets*,' sir, repeats, Anson, with an emphasis on the *t*.

The Prince laughs, and the others laugh with him. 'Thank you George.' He turns back to Pugin. 'I must confess I am a fan of the theatre, and also of literature. I particularly enjoy the Waverley novels.'

'We have a common interest there, sir,' replies Pugin, keenly.

'Really? I'm also very interested in Gothic architecture, so there's another thing we have in common,' adds the Prince earnestly. He continues. 'I've been thinking, Mr Pugin, could the new artwork in the Palace of Westminster tell the story of Britain, the monarchs, the battles, the saints, the towns, the architecture?'

'Yes, it could, sir. That's an excellent idea.'

'And could Parliament be a stage that brings the

actors together every year?'

Pugin is not sure what the Prince means. He turns aside and he gives Lord Shrewsbury a questioning look. The Earl's face is a blank.

Pugin turns back to the Prince. 'The actors, sir?'

The Prince turns to George Anson with his own questioning look.'

'I think his Royal Highness means the actors of the State. The Queen, the Lords, the MPs.

'Oh, I see,' says Pugin.

The Prince continues. 'Yes, I was wondering if the Palace of Westminster could provide an annual spectacle. The British do love the theatre don't they?'

'Yes, sir, they do.'

The Prince continues. 'Well, I wonder if there might be a processional route, through the Palace of Westminster, once a year, something to connect the Sovereign, the Lords, the Commons, the Judiciary, and the people.'

Lord Shrewsbury interjects. 'Do you mean, sir, in similar fashion to ancient Rome, where they had processions through the triumphant archways?'

'There may be some similarity, but processions have been part of civilization ever since cities have existed. The Romans also had the forum didn't they, at the end of the processional route?'

'Charles Barry is working on Trafalgar Square at the moment,' adds Pugin.

'Indeed,' replies the Prince, 'I suspect he'll finish what Mr Nash could not, but perhaps Parliament could have a public square of its own, where the people can see the State in action. The trouble is it's always raining.'

'Perhaps it could be a covered space, integral to the building,' says Pugin.

'Yes, that's a good idea, and it could be full of beautiful British art. Did you read the article in *The*

Times recently, about Babylon? Apparently, there was a processional route, flanked by walls in blue glazed bricks, very impressive. I think Lord Shrewsbury is recreating the hanging gardens of Babylon at Alton Towers, isn't that right, my Lord?'

Lord Shrewsbury laughs, 'Yes, sir, although as you say, it's always raining, which is causing delays!'

Pugin continues. 'I missed that article, sir, but I'm very interested in the use of encaustic tiles.'

'Ah, yes! I've met Mr Minton of Stoke. I understand you're working together.'

'That's right, sir.' Pugin takes a moment to think. He taps the end of his nose with his finger. An idea is taking shape. 'I'll need to discuss this with Mr Barry, of course, but perhaps we could design a processional route through the Palace of Westminster, aligned with the Sovereign's throne, the chamber of the Lords and the chamber of the Commons, all displaying the best of British arts and crafts.'

'Excellent!' replies the Prince, 'We might have some German frescoes too.'

Lord Shrewsbury frowns.

'But what would the reason for the procession be?' asks the Prince.

Everyone is deep in thought for a moment. 'I have it!' exclaims the Prince. 'How about the Sovereign's State opening of Parliament?'

There are nods all around. The Prince continues. 'I think the Queen will approve of that. Perhaps the procession could be extended outside of Parliament too, so the people can witness the spectacle, as they did with the coronation.'

'Yes, sir, that's a good idea,' says Pugin. 'Perhaps the procession could begin at Buckingham Palace, with carriages and a military escort, and then Her Majesty could lead the procession, on foot, through the Palace of Westminster.'

'Why not on horseback?' asks the Prince.

'In the building?'

'It would be dramatic.'

'The horses might damage the artwork.'

'Of course,' replies the Prince. 'There is one thing that worries me,' he adds in a confidential tone.

'What's that, sir,' asks Pugin, leaning forward.

'Do you think the budget is sufficient to do the interiors properly?'

'I do not, sir.' Pugin seizes the opportunity to make a personal point. 'I'm only paid £2 a week. It barely covers the cost of my cabs. I have to pay from my own purse for much of the equipment.'

The Prince winces, but he doesn't want to get embroiled in the details of Pugin's expenses. He stands up, getting ready to conclude the interview. 'Do you know Mr John Crace?'

'Not personally, sir, but I know of his reputation,' replies Pugin, also rising to his feet. Lord Shrewsbury and George Anson are also standing now.

The Prince continues. 'He supplies furnishings, textiles and wallpapers, for the grandest houses. He's an excellent man. He came to see me recently. He's very knowledgeable about German frescoes. I wonder if he might be of assistance to you.'

'Oh, thank you sir,' replies Pugin, scratching his head. 'I will arrange to visit him.'

'He has a shop on Wigmore Street.'

'Ah, very good,' replies Pugin, amazed at the Prince's knowledge of detail.

'He's very interested in Gothic design too,' adds the Prince.

Pugin nods.

'The Queen and I take a great personal interest in the rebuilding of the Palace of Westminster, Mr Pugin. We're very pleased that you and Mr Barry are working on it. I know you will do an excellent job and finish it on time.'

Pugin detects an element of steel in the youthful Prince. 'We won't let you down, sir.'

Hands are shaken with bows, and then George Anson shows Lord Shrewsbury and Pugin out.

They stand for a moment on the street, in a reflective mood. The sun shines golden upon the glowing stones of Westminster Hall. The building is like an enormous chiselled jewel. Before they go their separate ways, Lord Shrewsbury and Pugin take a moment to admire it. 'You must ensure the new building respects it,' says Lord Shrewsbury, solemnly.

'It is a great responsibility, my Lord.'

Seven

Friday, 15th September 1843. The ticking clocks that
keep the pulse of Alton Towers announce midday with
a burst of musical chimes. Lord Shrewsbury sits at the
head of a highly polished ebony table in the well-
stocked library. The shelves are stacked full of gold and
brown leather bound tomes.

Lord Shrewsbury has turned fifty. His oval face is
fuller and his wrinkles are more pronounced. He is
concentrating hard on the notes in front of him. Sitting
beside him is Pugin. He and the Earl have become firm
friends since their first meeting at Oscott, over nine
years ago.

Sitting next to Pugin is Herbert Minton, who has also
turned fifty. He may be greying, but he is as stylish as
ever. He arrived earlier from Stoke on horseback. He
looks at his pocket watch because he needs to be away
for another appointment in Derby. Sitting on the
opposite side of the table to Pugin is John Hardman,
now thirty-one, the same age as Pugin. He came up
from Birmingham the previous day and stayed the night
at Alton Towers.

Sitting next to Hardman is John Crace, the debonair
furnisher from London, recommended to Pugin by
Prince Albert. This is his first visit to Alton Towers.
Lady Shrewsbury has received Crace very favourably.
She is keen to learn all about his prestigious clients,
especially her near neighbour, the Duke of Devonshire.

Sitting slightly awkwardly, out on a limb, is George
Myers, the master builder. He dislikes long meetings
and would much rather be outdoors, climbing the

scaffolding around a church steeple. His concentration is waning. He recalls that Pugin gave him a scrap of paper when they walked into the library, over two hours ago. He is now interested to discover what it might be. He covertly retrieves it from out of his pocket.

It is a drawing of a proposed new house, labelled, *The Grange, Ramsgate*. It is quickly scribbled with only a few lines, and yet it is a beautiful illustration. Pugin intends for Myers to build this new family home for him. Myers smiles approvingly, *Mr P draws like an angel*.

The proposed house is of a very unusual design. The main rooms are all off a reception hall. The servant's quarters and the children's rooms are not segregated from the main part of the house as usual. The plan is symbolic of how Pugin believes family life should be. Everything is more integrated. The most exceptional feature is a large, square tower, there is a note beside it: *For looking out to sea*.

Myers scratches his head. He has moved his household from Hull to London to be closer to Pugin, his main source of work. After all that upheaval, it now appears that Pugin is planning to move to Ramsgate. Myers glances out of the window, over the park, towards the brooding, wild moors. He is reminded of the vast open spaces of Yorkshire, which he misses.

These meetings are usually good-natured and not too long. They are held in a variety of places; railway stations, hotels, taverns, coffee houses, up and down the land. Lord Shrewsbury looks up from his notes. He speaks in a grave tone. 'Gentlemen, now, if you please, I turn to the final item on our agenda. In two months time we will have a royal visitor at Alton Towers, Henri de Bourbon, Count of Chambord, grandson of Charles X. He is the true heir to the throne of France.' The Earl turns to John Crace and notices he is looking confused. He provides some context. 'Mr Crace, we try to use

Alton Towers to promote cordial relations between the prominent families of Europe, Catholic and Protestant, as well as promoting the arts and industry.'

'That's very commendable, my Lord. Forgive me, but I read only a few days ago, the sons of Louis Philippe, King of the French, visited Queen Victoria, and it was reported that they were cordially received. '

'Yes, that's right, Mr Crace. I was with Prince Albert just last week, in Virginia Water, to celebrate his twenty-fourth birthday. He told me personally that the sons of Louis Philippe paid very gracious respects to the Queen from their father, the so-called King of the French, but I'm not sure I understand your point.'

Crace pensively bites his lower lip. 'I apologise, my Lord, I'm certainly no statesman, but didn't Louis Philippe banish Henri de Bourbon, the true heir, as you say, when he was a child?'

'What if he did, Mr Crace?

'Well, my Lord, I just wondered if it might result in a diplomatic difficulty if your Lordship were to accommodate him here. As I say, I'm no statesman, I was merely wondering.'

Lord Shrewsbury looks exasperated. 'Henri is free to visit whoever he wishes in England, and he may yet be the King of France, Mr Crace.'

'Very good, my Lord,' replies Crace meekly. 'If there's anything I can do to assist with the visit of the royal guest, I would count it a great honour.'

'Thank you, Mr Crace. Now, our architect has been giving the royal visit some thought. Mr Pugin?'

Pugin jolts with surprise at the mention of his name. He gets up from his chair and stretches. He begins to pace around the table. Lord Shrewsbury finds this rather disconcerting. Pugin is thinking. He rubs his chin with his right hand. At last he speaks. 'Since our meeting with Prince Albert last year, I've been thinking about the importance of processions.' He is becoming animated. 'My proposal is that we prepare a processional route for Henri, from his arrival point at the railway station, through the surrounding landscape, with a triumphant arrival at Alton Towers.'

Lord Shrewsbury raises an eyebrow. 'Will we have to do more building work? We've already got so much going on.'

Pugin is a little surprised by this negative comment from his patron, but he loses none of his ebullience. 'You may recall that my uncle, Louis Lafitte, was an artist at the French Court. He worked on the Arc de Triomphe. When I was a child he also worked with my father for the Prince Regent in London. To celebrate the defeat of Napoléon they designed light displays and enormous transparencies that covered Carlton House.'

Herbert Minton snorts, 'So, Pugin, Uncle Louis worked in Paris on the triumphant archway to celebrate Napoléon's victory, and then he worked in London for the Prince Regent on the celebrations for Napoléon's defeat. Have I got that right?'

'Yes, we're a very fickle family, Herbert.'

Lord Shrewsbury looks serious. He is staring at Pugin. 'What are *transparencies*?'

'Well, my Lord, they're painted onto enormous sheets of oiled paper and then they are hung from a scaffold attached to a building. They are backlit, which provides a very dramatic effect. If we apply this technique, we will not need to undertake more building works, although we will need to erect the scaffolding of course.'

'I like the sound of this, Mr Pugin,' says Lords Shrewsbury.

John Hardman interrupts. 'What did these transparencies display? I mean at Carlton House.'

'Images that represented the union of the Thames and the Seine, and such like.' Pugin turns back to Lord Shrewsbury to gauge his reaction.

'I like the idea, very much,' says the Earl with a satisfied nod. 'It needs to be of a dramatic scale. Remember, Henri might be King of France again.'

'*Again*, my Lord, you said *again*?' says Hardman. 'Has he been the King before?'

'Yes, of course he has, don't you recall? Henri was King of France for eight days, when he was nine years old. Then that rogue, Louis Philippe, expelled him. I first met Henri in Rome. He was a delightful boy. I could relate to his childhood.'

'How do you mean, my Lord?' enquires Herbert Minton.

'Both of us were banished from our homes when we were children. Both of us endured a nomadic adolescence. He lost his father before he was born, I lost...' The Earl straightens his back and he speaks more resolutely. 'I was particularly impressed with Henri's faith and his opposition to the anti-religious stance of Napoléon.' The Earl is tiring of his own voice. 'Do carry on, Mr Pugin.'

'Thank you, my Lord.' Pugin looks at each man in turn, as if assessing his virtues. 'To create a procession fit for a King of France, we're going to need the skills and dedication of everyone around this table.'

'Count me in, Pugin!' says Hardman with a nod.

'Me, too,' says Minton.

'And me,' adds Crace

They all turn to Myers who is gazing out of the window. He turns around and is surprised to find everyone is staring at him. He looks to Pugin for support, and gets a reassuring nod. Myers speaks hesitantly. 'Oh, eh, yes, me too.'

'Do you know what we're talking about?'

'No, but if it's for Mr P, it'll be all right.

Lord Shrewsbury looks pleased. 'Excellent, thank you gentlemen, now, I think we need a break. I'll call for some refreshments.'

Myers revives. 'A splendid idea, my Lord!'

After ringing a bell, Lord Shrewsbury rests his hands upon the back of his chair and leans forward. 'I think it's important to take a moment to reflect upon how much work Mr Pugin has done.'

'I've done nothing on my own, my Lord, we're a team, all of us here,' replies Pugin, modestly.

'Yes, of course, we're a team, but you are at the helm, Mr Pugin.'

The mood has become relaxed. The men are reclining in their chairs. Hardman's spectacles have slipped down his nose. He pushes them back in place. 'Thanks to Pugin, Birmingham is already half transformed. He's built Saint Chad's, there's a new house for the Bishop, the seminary at Oscott, the convent at Handsworth…'

'Indeed, John!' exclaims Lord Shrewsbury. He turns to Pugin, with a stern look. 'Pugin, you must take better care of your health, though. You were very ill again the last time I saw you.'

Hardman interjects, again. 'If I may say so, I think you should spend more time at home, with Louisa, let her look after you.'

Now Myers chips in. 'If you get ill again, Mr P, you could be doing us all out of business,' and then he adds, intently, 'I was quite shocked the last time I saw you.'

Pugin looks thoughtful. He was very ill a few months ago. Before he left for a European tour, his eyesight completely failed him, again. 'I'm touched by your concern, you're good friends, but don't worry. My trip to Antwerp and Cologne has done me the world of good. Crucially, I have returned with splendid new window designs for Saint Giles.'

'There's no doubt about it, you're making excellent progress with Saint Giles, replies Lord Shrewsbury.

'And with our other projects too, My Lord?' enquires Pugin. He and the Earl had an altercation yesterday about the final use of Alton Castle, and so he is fishing for support.

'Yes, the other projects are progressing, satisfactorily. As you know, I'm delighted with the refurbishments here at Alton Towers, and with Saint John's Hospital.' He turns to Crace, 'Saint John's is our humane alternative to the workhouse, Mr Crace. We're building it up by the castle.'

'Ah, yes, so I hear, my Lord. There's such a need.'

The Earl clears his throat. 'Of course, Mr Pugin, has completed lots of other projects too, and many more are in the pipeline.'

Hardman interrupts. 'There are dozens of them, across Britain, Ireland, even in Australia! There's also all of the work for Mr Barry of course, at the Palace of Westminster.'

'Yes, John, I hadn't forgotten about Mr Barry,' replies Lord Shrewsbury. He turns back to Pugin. 'This issue with your eyesight concerns us all. Please don't let Mr Barry push you too hard.' Pugin is conscious that several of his close friends have warned him about his professional relationship with Charles Barry.

At that moment the door to the library opens. There is a whirl of colour and laughter. Lady Shrewsbury enters with her beautiful niece, Mary Amherst. Two servants carry plates of sandwiches, cakes, and drinks. All the men rise to their feet.

Pugin is mesmerised by Mary Amherst. She was only a child when he first saw her, in her mother's house in Kenilworth. Now she is an exceptionally beautiful young woman. Her skin, her hair, and even her voice, remind him of his first wife, Anne.

Two months later...

It is a cold and clear November night, with a bright, half moon. The villagers of Alton, and the drinkers at the Talbot Inn, are all out on the highway, watching and waiting. All sorts of rumours have been spreading. Many think Queen Victoria and Prince Albert are coming to Alton Towers.

'Hush up, I can hear something!'

'Me too!'

They can hear the distant rumble of horse's hooves and carriage wheels. 'Look!' A galaxy of little twinkling lights can be seen down in the shadowy valley.

Henri de Bourbon is twenty-three years old and he is handsome. He is at the front of a long convoy. His entourage of nobility and attendants runs to hundreds. Henri appreciates attention to detail. The air is cold but he pops his head out of his carriage window. He likes all of the attractions designed by Pugin along the route. He smiles with satisfaction when he sees Alton Castle above the Churnet gorge. It is spectacularly illuminated with fire torches.

Henri's carriage passes through Alton and the villagers applaud, they know not whom. The long convoy winds its way up the steep hill, and through the pitch-blackness of Abbey Wood.

When Henri's carriage emerges from the trees, he sees Alton Towers, spectacularly illuminated and covered in transparencies. It is out of a fairy tale. The images include a vast Fleur-de-lys, the symbol of French royalty. BANG! There is an explosion and a bright flash in the sky. The park, the lake, the swans, are all suddenly visible – and then they are gone. The fireworks are impressive. Everything is timed to perfection.

Henri's carriage passes through an enormous triumphant archway, part of a temporary stage set created by Pugin. The carriage horses pull up beside the grand staircase at the entrance to Alton Towers.

The Earl and Countess of Shrewsbury are feeling a little nervous. They wait at the top of the steps, standing between the statues of hunting dogs.

Henri disembarks and his attendants fuss about him, ensuring his hair, hat, cravat, and coat are properly in place. He is dressed as an English gentleman in top hat and tails, and he carries a walking cane. As he ascends the steps his entourage rush out of their carriages and quickly form a line behind him.

Lady Shrewsbury wears a green silk dress and her dark hair is in ringlets interlaced with jewels. She would look at home in the court of Louis, the Sun King. Her face is flushed. As she gives a curtsy she looks Henri in the eye knowing if the French people could see him as she did they would surely crown him King. The Earl bows his head and shakes Henri's hand. Henri speaks first. 'My dear Lord and Lady Shrewsbury, it's been too long. His Holiness sends you both a blessing.'

The Earl's face is beaming. 'Thank you, your Grace. It's our great honour to welcome you to our home. How was your journey?'

'Oh, what a magnificent arrival, and fireworks! You have lifted my spirits.'

'I'm glad you liked them. We have to thank our architect, Mr Pugin, who has arranged everything.'

'Ah, yes, I know of him. His father was French.'

'Indeed.' Lord Shrewsbury is surprised by the extent of Pugin's reputation.

'Do come in your Grace,' says Lady Shrewsbury, gesturing with her hand towards the open door.

Edward, the blind harpist, is strumming away, but tonight he is part of a splendid orchestra. The Shrewsburys escort Henri through an interconnected sequence of rooms, each one grander than the next. Pugin has designed everything. Finally, they approach the banqueting hall. Pugin has transformed it into one of the grandest halls of England. Over one hundred dignitaries are standing in a line, waiting to greet Henri. Towards the end of it are Herbert Minton, John Crace,

George Myers, John Hardman, and Pugin. Even Pugin is dressed in a black morning suit. He looks very debonair.

A liveried attendant roars, 'All stand for Henri de Bourbon, Count of Chambord!'

The royal party enters. Hardman turns to Pugin and whispers out of the corner of his mouth. 'Do you think Henri is enjoying the show?'

Pugin whispers back. 'I hope so, but it's not Versailles is it?'

'It's not far off. We've done a good job in two months.'

Standing on the other side of Pugin is Kerril Amherst, the young man that Pugin met when he first visited Oscott College. He is a relation of Lord Shrewsbury. Kerril whispers his thoughts. 'Even a King of France could not fail to be impressed with what you've created, Mr Pugin.'

Standing next to Kerril, at the very end of the line, is his sister, Mary, twenty years old and radiantly beautiful. 'You'd better be quiet now, Kerril,' she whispers, 'the royal party's coming.' She wishes her corset wasn't quite so tight.

Henri and the Shrewsburys walk briskly past people, only stopping occasionally to exchange a few words. When Henri reaches Pugin, however, he halts and his face breaks into a friendly smile. 'Ah, it's Monsieur Pugin, isn't it?'

Pugin bows. 'Yes, your Grace. I'm very pleased to meet you, sir.'

'I understand you're responsible for our delightful journey from the railway station.'

'Well, actually, sir, all of these gentlemen were involved,' replies Pugin, gesturing to his team.'

'Ah, thank you, gentlemen.' Henri turns back to Pugin. 'The orchestra needs a conductor though, and so I thank you, Mr Pugin. The journey was music to my ears.' He leans forward and whispers, 'All the best artists are French.'

Henri moves on. Pugin furrows his brow as he wonders how to interpret that comment. Henri kisses the hand of Mary Amherst and leers at her cleavage. Mary gives a brief curtsy. Whilst Henri engages Mary in small talk, she keeps glancing sideways at Pugin. Lady Shrewsbury notices this and she is annoyed.

The following night hundreds of ladies are elegantly dressed in fashionable gowns and jewels, and the gentlemen are in white tie or military costume. The nobility and wealthiest merchants are gathered under a thousand flickering candles in the banqueting hall at Alton Towers. Lady Shrewsbury is determined that this ball, being held in honour of Henri de Bourbon, will outshine any of the glittering events held by the Devonshires of Chatsworth. She disapproves of the Duke of Devonshire's young mistress and refers to her as the floozy, and to the pair of them as the royal couple.

Pugin, Hardman, Crace, Minton, and Myers are all at the ball. The most beautiful woman is undoubtedly Mary Amherst. She is turning heads. The Shrewsburys are entrusted with Mary's care because her mother is unwell and remains in Kenilworth. Lady Shrewsbury has secured royal marriages for both of her daughters. Her priority is now to find a good match for Mary. She has arranged for the girl to dance with Henri, their royal guest.

The orchestra quickens the beat. Henri places his hands around Mary's waist. The dance begins. The hall is a sea of swirling silk. Lady Shrewsbury nods approvingly to her husband. She imagines being an aunt to the Queen of France, if only Henri would marry Mary.

'John, don't they make a beautiful couple?'

The Earl replies with a nod and a grunt. Lady Shrewsbury has to steady herself. She takes another glass of champagne and gulps at it. Lord Shrewsbury gives his wife a quizzical look before joining his guests.

The dance is coming to an end and Lady Shrewsbury has finished another glass of champagne. When she has resolved to make a match, she finds it hard to rest until it is accomplished. However, she has temporarily lost sight of Henri and Mary. Her eyes scan around the hall, searching for her quarry. It is difficult for her pick out faces.

Lord Shrewsbury has noticed the arrival of the Duke of Devonshire and his mistress. The Earl returns to his wife to inform her of their arrival. 'I have spotted the royal couple, darling.'

The Countess has a wild look in her eye. 'You've found them, are they still together?'

'Yes, of course, the old rascal has his hands full.'

'Don't be so vulgar, John,' replies the Countess lifting her hand to her brow. 'They are like us, when we first fell in love, everything was new. How soon can they be married?'

Lord Shrewsbury looks bemused. 'It's probably too late for marriage, Maria. I shudder to think what Bishop Walsh would say.'

'What do you mean?'

'Acting as if they're man and wife, in public, it's scandalous.'

Lady Shrewsbury looks aghast. 'What exactly are they doing?'

Lord Shrewsbury looks perplexed. 'Fornicating no doubt.'

'Oh, my, what will her mother say? I must find her.'

'Her mother?' replies Lord Shrewsbury with a raised eyebrow, 'what's she got to do with it?'

'Where are they?'

'I left them by the grand staircase.'

'Come along!'

Lady Shrewsbury ushers her husband across the hall as quickly as she can without losing any sense of decorum. She suddenly stops. 'Look!'

'What?'

'Mary is dancing with Pugin. Where is Henri?'

'I don't know.'

'I thought you said they were...'

'I was talking about the Duke of Devonshire.'

'Oh, you mean the Duke and his floozy?'

'Yes.'

A look of great relief flows over Lady Shrewsbury.

'You surely didn't think I was talking about Henri and Mary?'

'Of course I didn't, John.'

Since Pugin has become a household name, little groups of admirers gather around him. Women find him engaging. People are watching him now as he whirls Mary Amherst across the dance floor in a Waltz. He stares into Mary's eyes for too long. He feels as if he is looking into the eyes of Anne, his first love.

The dance finishes and Mary gasps for breath. 'Oh, Mr Pugin, my head is spinning. Would you take my arm?'

'Yes, of course I will, Mary. Are you feeling unwell?'

'I just need to sit down and have a rest, is there somewhere quiet we can go?'

'I'll take you to the garden room.'

Gwendalyn, Lady Shrewsbury's daughter, notices her mother looks distracted. 'Are you enjoying the ball, Mamma?'

'No, Gwendalyn, your cousin is embarrassing herself with Mr Pugin.'

Gwendalyn's eyes follow her mother's to where Pugin and Mary are walking out of the hall, arm in arm.

Lady Shrewsbury is furious. 'Mary is in our care.

Where's your father?'

'He's over there, Mamma, talking to the Prince. Shall I call him over?'

'No, no, don't disturb him. Look, there's John Hardman, bring him over to me.'

Just before Pugin walks out of the banqueting hall he turns back, suddenly aware that he might be under surveillance. He notices Lady Shrewsbury remonstrating with Hardman. Mary's delicate hand takes hold of his and she gently leads him away.

Eight

Saturday, 10th August 1844. The sky is speckled with high, white cloud, and it is hot. Pugin and John Hardman arrived together, half an hour ago, at Stafford railway station. Now they ride in Lord Shrewsbury's beautiful new carriage. It is painted black and has the letter 'T' written discreetly upon the doors in white. A team of four splendid chestnut horses pulls it. It is less flamboyant than the Earl's previous carriage, but people still stop and stare, and peep out of windows. The hood is up to protect the passengers from the fierce sun.

Pugin and Hardman are on their way to Alton Towers in preparation for a visit by the Duke of Cambridge, the seventh son of George III and an uncle to Queen Victoria.

'When was the last time you were at Alton Towers, John?' asks Pugin.

Hardman is hot and bothered. Since he turned thirty-two, his hair has receded. This annoys him as much as his fading eyesight. There is sweat on his brow and his round glasses have slipped down his nose. 'It was for the ball, it's the best part of a year ago now.'

'Ah, yes, people are still talking about that ball.'

Hardman looks agitated. He pulls at his beard, which goes from ear to ear, and frames his glowing face. It is the kind of beard worn by older, distinguished men.

'Are you all right, John?'

Hardman expels a shot of air through his nose, like an angry bull. He is annoyed about something. 'I needed the drawings for the windows in the House of

Lords and I couldn't get hold of you.'

Pugin sighs.

Hardman continues. 'You left me in a very difficult position with Mr Barry. He was quite unpleasant and understandably so. I don't want to be left in that position again.'

'I'm sorry, John. How many times do you want me to apologise?'

There is no answer from Hardman.

Pugin scratches his neck, 'Is anything else wrong?'

'I'm not sure if I should say this...'

'Go on, what's wrong?'

Hardman takes a deep breath. 'I don't think it's right that you left Louisa with six children at home in Chelsea, whilst you went off down the Rhine. She isn't at all well, you do know that don't you?'

Pugin looks anxious. Hardman continues. 'You told me you were travelling with Kerril Amherst, which seems rather odd, was it just the two of you?'

'We met up with his family in Cologne.'

'Ah, I think we're getting closer to the truth, now. Was Mary Amherst there?'

'Yes, she was, what of it?' Pugin wishes Hardman's blue eyes weren't quite so piercing. They look right through him.

'Mary is an exceptional young woman, but you are married to Louisa and you have six children. For goodness sake, she's over a decade younger than you.'

Pugin turns to Hardman with a look of indignation. 'What does that matter? I can talk to Mary as with nobody else, about faith, church, architecture... I thank God he has put us on the earth at the same time.'

'I think you're making a mistake.'

There is a long silence. Both men turn away from each other and stare out of their respective windows. The Staffordshire countryside has been parched brown by a week of hot weather.

At last, Hardman speaks again. 'You designed a beautiful gold chest for the remains of Saint Chad.'

'Why do you mention that?' replies Pugin, still looking out of his window.

'I've been reflecting upon the consecration of Saint Chad's cathedral.'

Pugin opens his mouth. He is about to say it isn't strictly speaking a cathedral, not yet, but Hardman continues before he can get a word out. 'It was a very moving procession with Bishop Walsh carrying the remains of Saint Chad from Oscott to the new cathedral. The procession started at Oscott, where you designed the interiors. Saint Chad's remains were carried in a chest designed by you. You orchestrated the whole procession. The Saint's remains were laid to rest in the cathedral designed by you...' Pugin tries to interrupt with a correction but Hardman will not be distracted. He continues. 'You even designed the vestments worn by the priests.'

'What are you getting at, John?'

'My father was standing by the doors of the cathedral when the procession arrived.' Hardman removes his spectacles and continues in a soft voice. 'It was so moving when those doors opened, the choir sang, the bells rang out, the city will never be the same again.'

'There was a sense of holiness wasn't there?'

'Yes, there was, and that's my point. When you extend God's kingdom, as you've done, it's inevitable the one you're taking ground from will attack you. You need to be on your guard.'

'Do you mean against the devil?'

'Yes.'

Pugin lowers his window, all the way down. The gentle breeze is refreshing. He turns back to Hardman. 'Mary Amherst is not sent by the devil, John.'

'No, she isn't, but perhaps you need ask where the source of your emotions is coming from.'

'You're making me feel uneasy.'

Hardman stares at him. 'Remember your calling, Pugin. It's a holy calling.'

'I'm not sure I'm up to it.'

'Well, he that's in you is greater than he that's in the world,' replies Hardman, referring to scripture.

'You're a good friend, John.'

Hardman smiles. 'Louisa's a good woman. Don't neglect her.'

'You're right.'

'Did I say my father is staying at Alton Towers?'

'No.'

'We'll see him there.'

'Splendid! I've used his house in Handsworth like a hotel. He's such a generous man.'

'Our family's partnership with you means the world to him. You're like one of the family. He prays for you, most days.'

Pugin looks Hardman in the eye. 'I need those prayers. So many of the buildings wouldn't have happened without him. Your family has been a blessing to me. I don't think you know what it's like, John, to lose your father, your mother, your wife, all within a year. I married Louisa a few weeks after my mother died. I didn't know what I was doing. She's a good wife and mother. It is a great relief she has come into the church of Christ, but…'

'But what?'

'I feel so alone.' Pugin lowers his head and sobs into his arm. Hardman puts his hand on his shoulder. He doesn't know what to say.

The chestnut horses trot through the park at Alton Towers. The weather is changing; clouds are blowing over. Pugin sees the mansion against a darkening sky. He feels a sense of dread. Panic is rising within him. He clutches the underside of his seat with both hands. 'Are you all right?' asks Hardman. Pugin glances at him with frightened eyes. He can feel the hairs on his arms tingling.

The carriage approaches the steps and they are surprised to see Lady Shrewsbury is standing alone, as if she is waiting for them. She is dressed very simply and her dark hair hangs loosely down her back. As soon as the carriage pulls up she rushes down the steps. Hardman clambers out of the carriage first. Lady Shrewsbury grabs his hands. Tears are flowing down her cheeks. 'Oh, John, something terrible has happened.'

'What is it, Maria? Tell me.'

'It's your father,' she cries. 'Oh, John, I'm so sorry. He was such a lovely man.'

Hardman gasps and raises a hand heavenwards, 'Oh, my God…' he places his clenched fist against his heart, 'Where is my papa?'

'His body is in the chapel…'

Pugin rests his large, strong hand upon Hardman's shoulder. Hardman turns to him, his face is beginning to crumble. 'We must bury him in Saint Chads…'

'Yes, John, we will, near to the Saint.'

The floodgates of Hardman's emotions burst open. He falls to his knees. He accidently knocks his spectacles off his face. Lady Shrewsbury picks the broken glasses up and then she sits down on the step, beside Hardman. She places her hand upon his shoulder and makes comforting sounds, like a mother to a sobbing child. Pugin squats down and he places an arm around Hardman's other shoulder. The driver of the carriage looks down from his seat, and sees the three of them, praying.

A week later Pugin is still at Alton Towers. At six o'clock in the morning, he crawls sleepily out of the enormous bed. Still in his nightshirt, he sits down upon the sumptuous Axminster carpet. A footman has already been in, to light the fire and fill a tub with hot water; all accomplished silently. Pugin wipes the sleep from his eyes and scratches his head. He has had a nightmare. His wife, Louisa, was dying in it. He takes off his nightshirt, washes, and gets dressed as quickly as possible. There is only one thing on his mind; he must get back to London.

Later, just after seven o'clock in the evening, Pugin pulls up in a Hansom cab outside his home in Chelsea. To his great alarm, Charlotte, the family's maid comes running out of the house, waving her hands in the air. 'Oh, sir!' tears are streaming down her face, 'we sent a messenger for you. Mrs Pugin is in bed, mighty ill. The doctor says she hasn't got long! He's up there with her now.'

'Where are the children, Charlotte?'

'Ann Greaves from next door took them in yesterday. Their nanny is with them too, sir.'

Pugin drops his bag on the floor and rushes up to the bedroom. Louisa is lying on top of the sheets. Her long, black hair is wildly strewn across the pillow. Her face is lily white. The young doctor by her side stops taking her pulse and he gently places her arm back on the bed. Pugin is horrified to see his wife so lifeless. The doctor rises to his feet. Pugin has never seen him before. He looks grave and he shakes his head sternly. His Scottish brogue is as clear as a Highland stream. 'I'm very sorry, Mr Pugin, she hasn't got long now.'

Louisa remains unconscious for several days. Pugin does not leave her bedside. At half past two o'clock in the morning, Thursday, 22 August 1844, Louisa dies.

Nine

Wednesday, 9th October 1844. The weather is autumnal, sunny, and fresh. The salty smell of seaweed fills the air. The sky is chalky blue. The echoing, shrill meow of sea gulls fills the town and reminds old sailors of life on the sea. The big clock on the pier strikes four o'clock.

Pugin is walking slowly along the wide, stone pavement on Marine Parade, hand in hand with his ten-year-old son, Teddy. Marine Parade is the most fashionable street in Brighton. It is the place to be seen. Everywhere is full of colour and bustle.

Apart from being small and skinny, Teddy is a miniature version of his father. He even wears an identical sailor's jacket. Their day began with an early departure from Ramsgate in the bumpy horse drawn stagecoach to London. From London, it was a two-hour journey by train to Brighton. They have seen some beautiful countryside, and yet the grandeur of the downs has not impressed them greatly on this occasion. The boy misses his mother.

Father and son walk along with their heads hung low. They are oblivious to the wealthy families passing by in their Landau carriages. The carriage hoods are down so the ladies can be seen and admired. People are everywhere, on foot, on horseback, and riding upon bicycles.

'Just a tick, Teddy,' says Pugin gently to his son. He retrieves a notepad from the large pocket in his jacket and flicks through the pages. He looks up at a gleaming white rendered Regency house. 'Oh this is it, do you want to ring the bell?'

'Yes, Papa,' says Edward, flatly, and without any of his usual enthusiasm. They climb the steps and wait under the portico. From their vantage point they look out over the choppy sea. On the far horizon the milky sky gives way to impressive cloud formations.

Much closer, a group of fishermen haul their boat down the steep, shingle beach. The mercurial sea is eager to whisk them away. It swirls ominously between the groins. A group of boys has gathered to see the boat off. One of the fishermen beckons to them. Just before the boat hits the water, one of the boys jumps aboard. Pugin smiles. He looks down at Teddy and ruffles the boy's hair. 'That little boy's going to have an adventure,' he says with a nod towards the boat. Teddy presses himself against his father. Pugin's smile drops. He notices the boy is shivering but it is not cold. Since the death of his mother, Teddy follows him everywhere.

'Everything is going to be all right, Teddy.'

Both of them suddenly jump as a loud voice comes out of thin air. 'I hope you're training that boy to be your apprentice!' The words come from a large, jolly, red-faced man, with slightly sagging jowls. The face is partly obscured behind cigar smoke. It is Charles Barry, speaking through the open side of the bay window.

'Oh, Mr Barry!' replies Pugin, 'yes, be assured, sir, the lessons have already begun. He is quite accomplished at drawing.'

'Glad to hear it!' growls Barry, 'I've done the same with my boys. Doris, the maid is just coming. I can't walk.'

The front door suddenly opens and standing before them is a tired looking middle-aged woman, dressed in a maid's uniform with a white apron. She speaks in a cockney accent. 'Mr Pugin is it, sir?'

'Yes, that's right, Doris. Pleased to meet you.'

'Very good, sir, Mr Barry says to show you into the

drawing room. This way please, sir.' Her dull eyes don't register the existence of Teddy until they enter the drawing room. Then she notices Teddy's large brown eyes staring up at her. They smile at each other, briefly, and then she leaves the room.

The drawing room is literally a drawing room, an architect's office. Drawings and plans cover the patterned carpet. Filing cabinets stand against the walls. Wherever there is free wall space, Charles Barry has hung his paintings.

Barry stands larger than life in a black suit, white shirt, and black cravat. He is leaning against his drawing board, which is positioned beside an elegant, speckled marble fireplace. A small fire burns in the hearth and a large cigar burns in the corner of Barry's mouth. The smell of smoke fills the room. With the aid of a crutch Barry hobbles over to Pugin and they shake hands. 'Thank you so much for coming down, Pugin, it's good to see you,' says Barry, speaking out of the corner of his mouth. 'Is this young Edward?'

'Yes, this is Teddy.'

'My, how he's grown.'

'He's still very upset by our bereavement,' whispers Pugin.

Barry nods sympathetically and removes his cigar. 'I'm afraid Sarah and the children are up in London, it's just Alfred and me down here. Here's just finished up at King's College. He should be here shortly. I'm sure he'll show Edward the beach.'

Teddy flashes a stern look at his father. Pugin smiles reassuringly at the boy, and then he turns to Barry. 'We were sorry to hear about your leg, a train wasn't it?'

'Yes, it was a bloody train! I suppose I have only myself to blame. I tried to board when it was pulling off. I fell over, got my leg caught in the gap.'

Pugin winces.

'I'm fortunate I didn't lose it, or get myself killed.'

'Is it getting better?'

'Yes, but very slowly. As I said in my letter, I've had to stay on down here to aid my recovery. I'm missing London, dreadfully. I haven't been to a scientific lecture for months.'

'A *Christmas Carol* opens tonight,' chips in Teddy.

'Really? Oh, I should very much like to see that, young man, anything by Mr Dickens. Now, do take a seat gentlemen.' Barry ushers them towards the comfortable chairs, beside the bay window. There is a splendid view of the sea. 'I'll sit on the settee, if I may,' says Barry, 'It will allow me to put my leg up.'

'I do like your paintings. Are they your own work?'

'Thank you, most of them are. They're reminders of my Grand Tour. I was very fortunate to take a few years off for travelling, when I was a young man. You can see I went to Greece, Egypt, the Holy Land, and of course to Italy, the home of the Renaissance. You've toured Italy haven't you, Pugin?'

'No, but I've been to Northern Europe.'

'What? You've never been to Italy?'

Pugin shifts uncomfortably in his chair. 'No, sir.'

Barry frowns. Suddenly, Alfred, his son, bursts into the room. He is a large, intimidating figure, much like his father, but not yet eighteen. 'Pleased to meet you again, Mr Pugin,' he booms. He gives a little bow and shakes Pugin's hand.

'Good to see you too, my boy, you've grown,' replies Pugin, 'allow me to introduce my son, this is Teddy.'

Charles Barry interjects, 'Albert, be a good chap and show Edward the beach, would you please?'

'Of course, Papa.'

Teddy looks up at Pugin with a pleading look.

'Oh, I think Teddy will be all right here with me,' says Pugin, putting a hand on the boy's shoulder.

Charles Barry looks down at Teddy and his voice rises to a roar. 'What? Don't you want to see the boats young man?' He turns back to Pugin and adds covertly; 'We do need to get through a lot of business.'

'I'll go and see the boats, Papa,' says Teddy dutifully, in a high-pitched voice.

'There's a good little man,' says Barry and he points towards the door with his crutch. Alfred takes his cue to leave, and he takes Teddy with him.

Barry continues. 'There is good news, Pugin.'

'Oh, what is it?'

A budget has been agreed. It's enough, at a pinch, to decorate the interiors of the Palace of Westminster, properly in the Gothic style.'

'That's excellent news.'

'It's a large project, Pugin. Can I rely upon you to produce *all* of the details?

'I have to be honest with you, Mr Barry, I already have a full programme of work. I'm also finishing off the Grange, it's our new family house in Ramsgate. Alas, my health has not been good. The fever returned to me recently.'

At the mention of fever Barry shuffles along the settee, further away.

'What do your doctors say?'

'They say I need a holiday.'

'Well, as I said in my letter, this Brighton sea air will do you good.'

'Indeed.'

'Show me an architect that doesn't need a holiday. Do you know what the answer is?'

Pugin looks pensive. 'Well, I suppose I might have to resign from this commission.'

'No! You need to get an apprentice. I was in quite the same predicament as you, making myself ill with overwork, but then I got a couple of apprentices trained up. Get some help in, Mr Pugin, that's the answer!'

'Oh, I'm not sure about that, Mr Barry. I've never had an apprentice, perhaps when Edward is fifteen, he can work with me full time, and then I could resume my work with you.'

'That's too long to wait. Get a good apprentice now; he will increase your capacity for work. I suggest you learn the art of delegation. Do you recall in the book of Exodus, Moses' father-in-law, Jethro, advised him to appoint trustworthy men as his deputies, so he wouldn't wear himself out?'

Pugin nods. 'I will give the matter proper consideration. Thank you for your advice, Mr Barry,' says Pugin, earnestly.

Barry hasn't finished yet. 'And sometimes you just need to say *no* to distractions. It seems that every duke in the land wants me to design a country house for him at the moment. I'm turning them all down!'

'Because of your leg?'

'No, sir! The Palace of Westminster takes precedence. It is for the good of the nation. We have to do it. But I would only want you to work according to your conscience. I would not wish to intrude upon your leisure time, or put your health at risk.'

'Well, when you put it like that...'

'Nobody but you, Mr Pugin, has the knowledge of Gothic design that's required to produce the detailed work for the Palace of Westminster.'

Pugin is looking more interested. 'Is the budget sufficient to pay our fees?'

'We will be paid, don't worry about that.' Barry laughs, but then his countenance changes. He looks severe. 'There is one problem.'

'Oh, what's that?'

'The ridiculous committee has said we've got to work with that damnable heating engineer, Doctor Reid. He'd use up the whole budget twice over on ventilation if I'd let him. I'm going to have to be very strict with that man.'

'I'd rather not get involved with Doctor Reid, or the

committees. I'll just do the drawings for you. I would be grateful though, if my employment could be on a contractual basis.'

'A contract?'

'Yes, most of my clients are insisting on them these days.'

'As are mine. It's a sign of the times. I suppose it's a sensible precaution when working with politicians. You will have your contract then, and I will protect you from Doctor Reid, the committees, the MP's, the Lords, and...' he turns away and looks out of the window, '...and from Prince Albert.'

'Prince Albert?'

'Yes, he's a meddler.' From the look on Pugin's face Barry realises he probably shouldn't have said that. He adds, 'He's a fine young Prince of course, I say all of this in the strictest confidence.'

Pugin nods and changes the subject. 'You must come over and see the Grange, Mr Barry. I mean when your leg is better, of course. It's my attempt at a Gothic house of a domestic scale.'

Barry is intrigued. 'What do you mean by *domestic*?'

'Well, it's of a scale that would suit a professional man, who lives in one of the new suburbs and goes to work in town on the train.'

'There's nothing I would like more,' replies Barry annoyed he hasn't come up with the idea himself. 'Has your builder, oh... what's his name?'

'George Myers.'

'That's the fellow. Has he been involved?'

'Yes, he's built it for me.'

'And the rest of your famous team?

Pugin laughs. 'Yes, they've all had a role to play. Mr Myers has built it. Mr Crace has provided furnishings, Mr Minton the tiles...'

'And Mr Hardman?'

'Mr Hardman has done just about everything else.'

Barry smiles and nods. 'I'm sure Ramsgate is a fine town, but won't you miss London?'

'No, we couldn't stay in London. It was unbearable for us after the death of my wife, Louisa.'

Barry nods sympathetically. 'Well, you're a good father, but of course in our line of work, you do have to be frequently away.'

'The children have an excellent new governess, Miss Keats.'

'Good. In the fullness of time, perhaps you will marry again, you're still a young man.'

Pugin would like to mention his attachment to Mary Amherst, but he hesitates. Since the death of Louisa, he has been wracked by guilt about the way he neglected her. He has been to confession numerous times, but has found greatest solace in his correspondence with Mary Amherst. Their letters have become increasingly affectionate. 'I have met somebody,' he bursts out, surprised by the sound of his own voice. He continues more cautiously. 'She is younger than myself, but she is a great comfort to me. Her letters have helped me through my bereavement.'

Barry appears to be shocked, but he quickly covers it up. He doesn't want to get too embroiled in Pugin's private life. 'Well, it has been good to catch up on family news. Now, we have two days together to get some work done, shall we make a start?'

Pugin is still thinking about Mary Amherst. He looks dreamily out of the window. 'We are soon to be married.'

Friday, 29 November 1844. A wintry gale blows the remaining leaves off ancient oak trees, to the delight of a little girl wrapped in a winter coat, who runs after them, down Fieldgate Lane. Her smiling parents watch on.

Fieldgate House is the smart three-storey residence of Mrs Amherst. On the opposite side of the lane, rising above the hedgerow, is the reddish brown fastness of Kenilworth Castle.

Mrs Amherst is in residence with her adult children, Kerril and Mary. On the driveway, grooms and footmen attend to the carriage and horses belonging to a distinguished visitor.

Kerril and his sister Mary stand beside the bay window. Mary looks out longingly over the Warwickshire countryside, towards the remains of the Forest of Arden. She is desperate to be out of doors. On the other side of the drawing room, Mrs Amherst and Lady Shrewsbury sit together upon a large settee, sipping tea. Landscape paintings by Italian and Dutch artists decorate the walls.

Lady Shrewsbury is a dazzling figure in a crimson silk dress and with ribbons in her hair. Her enormous skirt leaves little room on the settee for Mrs Amherst, who by contrast, is attired very simply in a black dress, of the kind she has worn since becoming a widow. Her hair is tightly pulled back and a large crucifix hangs around her neck. She wears the expression of a pilgrim, who still has many miles to travel. She is no stranger to pain, having lost not only her husband, but also, many years ago, a child to cholera.

'Is it really so long since I was last in this delightful house?' asks Lady Shrewsbury.

The tone of Mrs Amherst's voice is rather cold. 'Yes, it is, Maria, but your girls have stayed with us many times, when you've been on your foreign excursions.' Mrs Amherst discerns Lady Shrewsbury's uneasiness, and so she adopts a kindlier manner. 'They're very dear girls, and they're always most welcome here, as you and John are.' She turns to her children, 'Isn't that right?'

Kerril and Mary nod dutifully.

Lady Shrewsbury smiles and returns the pleasantries. 'The girls have happy memories of playing with their cousins, and you my dear, are such an example to us all, with all the charity work you do.'

Kerril is looking bored. 'Was there a particular matter that brought you to see us, Aunt Maria?'

'Kerril!' exclaims Mrs Amherst, shocked by her son's bluntness.

'Well, actually, yes, Kerril, it isn't just a social visit, there's the matter concerning Mary, which we need to discuss, as a family. Uncle John would have come too, but he has to be in Rome.'

Mrs Amherst raises a hand to her brow. 'So, you know, Maria, that Mr Pugin, has proposed marriage to Mary.'

'Yes, dear, that's why I've come.'

Mrs Amherst has not informed her children about the correspondence that has passed between her and the Shrewsburys concerning Pugin's proposal. Both Kerril and Mary are shocked by how much Lady Shrewsbury knows.

'May I ask if you've you come to your conclusion?' asks Lady Shrewsbury, directly.

Mrs Amherst takes a deep breath. 'It's clearly not an acceptable proposal, he has no social standing, and anyway, Mary is too young to marry.'

'I totally agree, my dear. John and I are not at all sympathetic to his proposal.'

Kerril is never one to raise his voice, but now he speaks in a tone that betrays his emotions. 'Well, personally, I'd be delighted to have him as my brother in law. He's a fine teacher and I found him to be excellent company on our travels together. He's also a great asset to the church.'

Lady Shrewsbury puts her cup and saucer down, calmly. She looks up at Kerril. 'Mr Pugin is also my friend, Kerril,' now she turns to Mary, 'but, it's simply out of the question, Mary, you cannot marry him. You cannot marry without your mother's consent anyway, that is the law.'

'It isn't long before I'm twenty-one,' sobs Mary. Kerril places an arm around his sister's shoulder.

'Would you really dishonour my wishes, Mary?' asks Mrs Amherst, aghast.

'I want your blessing Mamma, but I love him.'

'You will not marry that man!' replies her mother, sternly. The debate between mother and daughter has been going on for several days. Mrs Amherst has had enough of it. Lady Shrewsbury forces a sympathetic smile. 'He is so much older than you, Mary. He's not a gentleman. He already has six children from two wives. He has, peculiar ways.'

'Oh, really!' says Kerril, exasperated.

'Don't excite yourself, dear,' pleads Mrs Amherst. She is very protective of her son. She kept him back from Eaton when he was a boy because of his poor health.

Kerril continues. 'He's building the new Palace of Westminster, for goodness sake, isn't that respectability enough?'

'I understand that Mr Charles Barry is the principal architect for the new Palace of Westminster,' replies Lady Shrewsbury rising to her full height, 'and from what I discern, he's doing everything possible to ensure that Mr Pugin remains in obscurity.'

'What does Lord Shrewsbury have to say about Pugin's marriage proposal?'

'Your Uncle John is very fond of Mr Pugin, as am I, but I don't believe he would ever employ him again if he married Mary. Your mother and I know what is best, Kerril. It would be a terrible mistake for Mary to marry him. He doesn't have a regular income. She can do so much better.'

Lady Shrewsbury turns back to Mrs Amherst.

'Remember, dear, Henri de Bourbon has expressed an interest in our Mary. He might still be King of France, let's not forget that.'

Mary sobs out loud. 'If I can't marry Augustus Pugin I will follow my sister into the convent!'

Ten

Monday, 23rd December 1844. It is a few minutes before seven o'clock in the evening. It is cold and dark outside. Amongst the travellers huddled together for warmth in the stagecoach is John Powell, aged seventeen. Mrs Bing, a garrulous grandmother, sits' opposite Powell. A tartan blanket covers her knees. 'Oh! I shall be glad to get off this bumpy coach. Do you see those lights, young man, just coming into view, in the distance?'

'Oh, yes, I see them, Mrs Bing,' replies Powell, with a polite smile.

'That's Canterbury. Ramsgate isn't far away now.'

A sudden gust of wind splatters icy rain against the carriage windows. All of the travellers groan. 'At least it's not snow,' says Mrs Bing, 'although a drop of snow on Christmas morning wouldn't go amiss.'

It has been a long day for Powell. He will be relieved to arrive in Ramsgate. It was at the suggestion of his uncle, John Hardman, that he wrote to Pugin to ask if he could serve as his apprentice. Uncle John told him not to get his hopes up. Pugin may be happy to spend several hours at a stretch with Lord Shrewsbury, Hardman, Myers, Minton, and Crace, but he has always resisted having an apprentice. However, he has agreed to take Powell on for a trial period because of the demands of Charles Barry.

Powell was a boy of ten when he first set eyes upon Pugin in Paradise Street, Birmingham, back in 1837, when Pugin made his first covert inspection of the

Hardman manufactory. Powell was in his Uncle John's carriage, which passed Pugin on the street. The eccentric young Pugin, dressed in sailor's garb, made Powell laugh so much. Pugin became a frequent visitor at Powell's grandfather's house in Handsworth. They all went to Mass together. It is still a big step though, for Powell to work for Pugin and to live in his house. He has never lived away from home before.

When Powell first arrived in the chaos of London, en route to Ramsgate, he already felt homesick. He spent a few hours looking around Saint Paul's Cathedral, which impressed him, and then he walked beside the lively wharfs that line the river, before boarding the stagecoach to Ramsgate.

Powell stares out of the carriage window into the blackness. The road is skirting around a hill. The flickering lights of Canterbury are clearly visible. He feels quite excited.

'Would you like another sweet, dear?'

'Yes please, thank you, Mrs Bing.'

With his enormous brown eyes, long flowing black hair, and boyish face, women easily warm to Powell. He has grown his sideburns and fashioned them into what he considers to be the look of a bohemian artist, but he is also a devout young man.

Mrs Bing asks a question. 'What is it you'll be doing in Ramsgate, my dear?'

'I'll be an apprentice to Mr Pugin, the famous architect.'

Mrs Bing's eyes open wide and dart around the carriage, in a somewhat agitated manner. Powell senses that something is not quite right. After gathering her thoughts, Mrs Bing decides to remain silent about the dispute between her husband and Pugin. She realises that getting to know Powell a little better might provide some useful information. Pugin has reduced the size of the chapel at the Grange because Mr Bing owns the neighbouring land and has come up with no end of objections. Mr Bing is a friend of the architect Matthew Habershon and both of them object to there being a new Catholic church in Ramsgate. Mr Bing and Pugin have resolved to build right up to their boundaries.

The stagecoach arrives in Ramsgate. It is pouring with rain and the wind is getting stronger. Powell graciously declines the offer of dinner from Mrs Bing, who is becoming quite insistent. She is wrapped up in an enormous cape and peeps out from under her bonnet. Her nose has gone very red. 'But the weather is so inclement, do come in for a little while, to warm yourself, and you can meet Mr Bing. Come along, my dear.'

'Thank you, ma'am, but I really must get off and meet with my employer.'

'Well, they say he's a funny fellow, so you'd better be on guard. He seems to be building a whole town up there at West Cliff.' Mrs Bing scurries off towards her house. Powell lifts the collar on his raincoat against the weather and he starts walking. He recalls the warning of his uncle about Pugin's state of mind. He is under instruction to report any strange behaviour back to him. Powell is a little worried now about what kind of man Pugin may have become.

A gale is blowing in from the English Channel. The rain smacks at Powell's face. He keeps walking. He is relieved to be stretching his legs and to be breathing fresh, sea air. He feels a wonderful sense of freedom. He follows the route meticulously given by Mrs Bing. The map and instructions provided by Pugin have been forgotten and remain in Powells bedroom in Birmingham.

At last, Powell sees a Gothic house, with light brown brick walls, stone mullion windows, and an impressive tower. He recognises the hand of Pugin. This is the

Grange. Beside it is a sturdy church, finished in knapped flint. It is all still a building site. There is scaffolding around the Grange's tower and a large tarpaulin, like the sail from a ship, flaps violently over the top of it. A sudden gust of wind blows the tarpaulin off the scaffolding. It lands seventy feet away in a field. The interior of the tower is now dangerously exposed. Powell rushes up to the Grange, searching for the front door. At ground level the house is windowless and resembles a fortress. This is intentional, to repel anti-Catholic troublemakers. The rain lashes at Powell's eyes. He finds the entrance, hidden at the side of the building. He thumps the knocker against the solid door.

A baby can be heard screaming from within the house and then the voice of Pugin. 'Who on earth's knocking like that?'

'It's Powell, sir! The 'paulin's blown off your tower!'

The maid's voice is heard on the other side of the door. 'The door is locked. I can't find the key.'

'Where's Teddy? Has the boy gone off with the key?' asks Pugin.

The maid again, 'Ah, no, wait, I have it around my neck!'

Now great bolts can be heard sliding back. The door opens. Pugin is a powerful figure dressed in black. The storm is reflected in his grey eyes. 'Ah, it's Powell! Welcome my boy!'

'Mr Pugin, sir, the storm's blown your 'paulin off the tower.'

'What?' Pugin's face is suddenly panic-stricken.

Before Powell is allowed to enter the house he must help in rescuing the tarpaulin.

He joins with Pugin, Teddy, and Mr Mayman, the carpenter, in hauling the large, heavy, canvas, back up the scaffolding and over the tower. There are flashes of lighting. The rumbles of thunder are so close Powell can feel them vibrating in his body. He does not have a great head for heights and the tower is very high. The wooden scaffolding and the ladders are slippery and wet. The canvas is heavy. Powell feels his head spinning. Mr Mayman sees he is struggling. 'Don't look down!' he yells but the wind snatches his words away.

Powell concentrates hard. He tells himself he mustn't fail this first test. Pugin gets his corner of the tarpaulin fixed in place. He moves around the scaffolding and helps Teddy. Mr Mayman assists Powell in getting his corner tied down. At last the canvas is back in its proper position. The gaping hole is covered and the tower is safe.

Once inside the Grange, Powell removes his dripping raincoat and hangs it in the scullery to dry. He stands in the kitchen for a moment and looks around. He has never been in a kitchen in which so much careful design attention has been lavished. It is clear to him that Pugin has designed everything, including the furniture.

A buxom lady, almost as wide as she is tall, clutching a rolling pin, bustles down the corridor and enters the kitchen. 'Good evening, are you Mr Powell?'

'Yes, ma'am, may I ask who you are?'

'Who am I?' she repeats the question and concentrates hard on the answer. 'Oh, I'm Charlotte, sir. I'm the maid, the cook's help, the nurse, the housekeeper, and anything else that needs doing,' she chuckles to herself. 'So, you're to be Mr Pugin's apprentice, is that it?'

'Yes, ma'am.'

Charlotte continues. 'Well, that's an honour, sir, he's a great man, our Mr Pugin,' and then she adds with feeling, 'he's a very great man!' She looks Powell up and down. 'He's never had an apprentice before, you know? You must be very special, sir. You're certainly a very polite young man.' She raises her jowls with a big smile. 'You can call me Charlotte.'

'Thank you, ma'am, I mean Charlotte.'

Powell finds Charlotte to be a curious creature. He suspects he can get some useful information out of her. 'Tell me, Charlotte, is it a happy household. Is Mr Pugin strict?'

'Happy? Strict?' Charlotte fold hers arms over her enormous bosom. She is wearing a look of indignation. 'Look about you, sir. What do you see?'

'What do I see?' says Powell scratching his head.

'Yes, sir, what do you see?'

Powell plays along. 'Well, there's a sturdy looking dresser over there, a dining table, benches, all crafted in the Gothic style, no doubt by Mr Pugin.'

'And above you, sir?'

Powell lifts his head. 'Above me I see the ceiling rises into the roof space. In between the roof trusses the plaster is painted dark blue and it's studded with golden stars. It's all very beautiful.'

'All this for that ungrateful cook! If he treats her like this, I'm sure he'll treasure you, sir, his one and only apprentice. I sometimes wonder if he ever notices me, but he's a very busy man, to be sure.'

Powell feels reassured.

'Oh, here's the young master,' says Charlotte.

Teddy is standing in the doorway, smiling. He rolls his eyes at Charlotte.

'He is quite the little man,' she adds, busying herself with pots and pans.

'Shall I show you up to your room, Mr Powell?'

'That's very kind of you, Teddy. I'll just get my bag.'

'Supper will be in fifteen minutes, gentlemen!'

'Thank you, Charlotte, I'm famished.'

'Oh, I do like a young man with an appetite,' says Charlotte as she whacks a ball of pastry with her rolling pin.

They walk down a long, narrow corridor paved with blue and brown terracotta tiles; it connects with the main reception hall. 'Just a moment, Teddy,' says Powell. He wants to take this in. The square shaped reception hall rises to the full height of the second storey. The floor is covered in exquisite tiles made by Minton. Above their heads is a galleried landing and a ceiling painted red between timber beams. A great Gothic chandelier hangs down with oil lamps emitting a soft, pulsing, glow. The wallpaper above the highly polished timber panelling is red, gold, and green. It incorporates the heraldic martlet bird, from Pugin's treasured family coats of arms.

Teddy smiles, 'Are you ready?'

Powell breathes deeply. 'This is so impressive, do lead on, Teddy.'

They continue up the stairs, past a great stone mullion window that looks onto the stormy, black night. The rain is thrashing against the glass. Powell feels cast adrift by the storm, but the vessel he finds himself in is safe and warm. He is intrigued by it. His fingers slide along the smooth, handrail. The balustrade beneath it is of an intricate design and it has an invigorating woody scent. He has never seen the like of it before. He guesses it must be French.

They continue along the landing, onto which the family bedrooms connect. The crimson coloured carpet feels thick beneath Powell's feet. At the end of the landing they turn a corner and enter the tower. Now they climb a narrow staircase. Half way up the tower, they come to a half landing with a doorway. Teddy stops and opens the door. 'This is your room. It's a bit small, but wait until you see the view in the morning.'

Powell pops his head in. A small fire crackles in the hearth. 'Oh, it's perfect, and fresh flowers too. Thank you, Teddy.'

Powell dries off. He kneels down upon a rug covering the dark floorboards, and he says a prayer of thanks for his safe journey. He rises to his feet, braces himself, and prepares to join the rest of the household in the dining room.

A lively fire dances in a beautiful white stone fireplace. The wallpaper in the dining room is red and patterned similar to that in the reception hall. The ceiling, between timber beams, is a stunning ultramarine blue, studded with golden crosses. Powell stands in the doorway. His heart is beating quickly. Most of the household seated around the table are strangers to him. 'Come and sit down next to me, my boy,' says Pugin who is sitting at the head of the table. His round face is glowing in the firelight. 'Miss Greaves has prepared a hearty stew for us,' he adds.

Powell takes a seat and Pugin pours him a glass of water. 'Is your room to your liking?'

'It's very pleasant, thank you, sir,' replies Powell, knocking the glass of water over with his elbow. The glass goes flying and lands with a smash. The children burst out laughing. Pugin, who has only just got dry after rescuing the tarpaulin, is covered in water again. He douses himself with a napkin. 'Don't worry my boy, it's quite all right. It was my fault. I shouldn't have left the glass there.'

Miss Keats, the children's governess, gets on her hands and knees and picks up the broken pieces of glass. Powell's face is bright red. 'I'm very sorry.'

'It is no trouble at all,' replies Miss Keats, equally flushed.

'Here, let me help you,' says Miss Greaves.

'I can manage, thank you,' snaps Miss Keats.

Miss Greaves looks slightly put out. Both women are young, single, and competitive for Pugin's attention. Most of their antics go over his head. Now Pugin turns to Powell. 'Miss Greaves is very charitable. She looks after us all.'

'Oh, it's no charity, Mr Pugin,' replies Miss Greaves, followed by a sharp look down at Miss Keats who is still on her knees.

Powell looks confused. 'Is Miss Greaves the housekeeper?'

Pugin shudders. 'No, no... Miss Greaves is a good family friend. She was our next door neighbour in Chelsea.'

Miss Greaves smiles warmly. Miss Keats gives her a frosty look from the floor, and adds, 'Why don't you serve the stew now, Miss Greaves?'

Pugin turns back to Powell. He speaks in a confidential tone. 'Miss Greaves was a good friend to my wife, Louisa. The children love her dearly. She very kindly agreed to come and look after them.'

Miss Greaves places a bowl of stew in front of Powell. Pugin repositions the bowl, which is Minton, away from the edge of the table. He gives Powell a wink as he does this. Powell is assessing Miss Greaves. He considers her to be feisty and not unattractive, with long, light brown hair. Pugin adds in a whisper, 'She isn't a Catholic yet but she does join in with our services.'

Everyone is ready to eat. 'Where's Father John?' inquires Pugin.

Miss Keats opens her mouth to speak, but she is too slow. Miss Greaves gets her words out first. 'Father John is down at the seaman's mission.'

Mayman quietly enters the room and takes a seat next to Miss Keats. 'Three lost at sea,' he says with a grim face.

'We must pray for them,' says Pugin. He turns to Powell. This gentleman here is Mr Mayman, our master carpenter, you'll be working closely with him.'

As they say grace, Powell's eyes scan around the

table. The family consists of Pugin and his six children. They are all handsome. The children sit ranked by age. The eldest, Anne, is twelve, then Teddy, Agnes, Cuthbert, and Catherine. Sitting upon Anne's lap is Mary, who is eighteen months old. Miss Greaves is the most commanding woman in the household, and she sits next to Pugin. Miss Keats, the children's governess, sits next to her, and then Mayman. The children occupy all of the other seats.

As he eats his supper, Powell is aware that Pugin is chatting to him, but he finds it hard to concentrate because the food is his priority. Pugin continues. 'Bells ring to announce the offices of the day. The first one, at six o'clock, is time to rise, at seven, breakfast, at eight, morning prayers, at one o'clock, lunch time, at eight, night prayers, at nine, supper, and finally at ten o'clock, lights out. That's when the greater silence begins. The front door is locked.'

Powell gulps. 'Would I be permitted to go into town, sir, at the weekend, and perhaps return a little after ten?'

Pugin turns to Miss Greaves with a puzzled look. Her face is equally perplexed. Pugin turns back to Powell. 'When the door is locked we will all be in our beds.' Pugin is trying to work out why Powell might want to be out of the house at such a late hour. He decides to ask a few probing questions. 'Do you hope to have an interest in a young lady, perhaps?'

'No, sir.'

Pugin's eldest daughter, Anne, blushes and lowers her head. She pretends the baby needs some attention.

'Mr Powell might like star gazing,' interjects Miss Greaves, with a maternal smile.

'Oh, is that it?'

'No, sir.'

'Do you have any hobbies?'

'No, sir.'

'But you'd like to go sailing with me wouldn't you?'

Powell is no fan of the sea. 'I expect my time will be committed to our work together,' he replies.

Powell wakes up in the middle of the night feeling very anxious. He stands upon a spacious, carpeted landing, looking over a precipitous drop on the other side of the balustrade. He does not know where he is. His head is spinning. As a child, he was a frequent sleepwalker, but it is a rare occurrence for him now. This is an inopportune time for it to happen again. He no longer feels the raw, animal terror he did as a child when he awoke in a strange place, but it is still very unnerving. He can hear a man sobbing. Powell breathes deeply and places both hands upon the balustrade. He falls down to his knees. He tries to rationalise the situation. He tries to recall where he fell asleep.

Pugin is crying over a letter he has received from Mary Amherst, the beautiful young woman he has fallen deeply in love with. He has waited until this late hour to open it. He recently wrote to Mary's mother, Mrs Amherst of Kenilworth, asking for her daughter's hand in marriage. The answer has now come, not from Mrs Amherst, but from Mary herself. She writes that she will never see him again.

Letters have been going back and forth between Pugin and Kerril, Mary's brother. Kerril has informed Pugin about the great rows that have occurred between Mary and their mother. But there was no warning about Mary's catastrophic decision. Pugin sobs. 'Oh, Mary! Mary! I'm lost without you, I'm so alone...'

Powell remembers where he is. He rises to his feet and walks down the landing. His ankle suddenly gives way and he falls down with a thud. A door opens beside him. Pugin is looming over him with a candle and a brass poker.

'Is that you Powell? What on earth are you doing

down there? I thought you were a burglar.'

Powell staggers to his feet. 'I'm sorry, Mr Pugin, sir. I sometimes walk in my sleep.'

Pugin puts the poker down and raises a hand to his forehead. He closes his eyes and shakes his head. He speaks without opening his eyes.

'Are you hurt?'

'No, sir.'

'Good. Well, off you go to bed now, Powell. I'm afraid I've just had some rather bad news.'

At six o'clock the following morning, Powell is awoken by the violent sound of Teddy ringing a bell outside his door. Teddy runs on; Powell immediately falls asleep again. He sleeps through the seven o'clock bell. At eight o'clock, still in bed, Powell is again awoken, this time by Teddy ringing the bell that announces morning prayers. He struggles out of bed, pulls back the curtains and is pleased to see the sun shining upon fallow Kentish fields. Now he pulls the curtains back on the window on the adjacent wall. 'Good gracious!' He has a view of the sea and the clear, blue horizon. Invigorated, he washes, dresses, and makes his way to the chapel.

Powell stops for a moment beside the balustrade, where the landing forms a gallery above the stairs. He recalls the previous night. He feels embarrassed. *Sleep walking and oversleeping. What a start!* He continues down the stairs. This is the first time he has seen the house in the light of day. The hallway is radiant with light streaming in from the interconnecting rooms, and directly from the big mullioned window beside the stairs. This window also provides a pleasant view over a courtyard garden. Everything is gleaming and smells new. It is like being in a beautiful, medieval, dream world. Footsteps are heard and then Pugin appears. His round face lights up with a smile. 'I've saved you some breakfast, but come and join us in the chapel first.'

Powell follows Pugin into the small family chapel. It is full of bright, colourful light.

Monday, 3rd February 1845. It has just turned eight o'clock in the morning. Outside it is chilly and bright. The Grange is a hive of activity. Powell is still struggling to settle in. He longs to see his family, friends, and the familiar sights of home. When he isn't working, he spends most of his time in his room, but there is no time for introspection today. Powell finishes his breakfast, quickly.

Pugin is dashing around the house in a state of anxiety. His face appears at the kitchen door. 'The House of Lords is our only concern now, Powell. Mr Barry will be here at any moment. It's best for you not to talk to him, unless he asks you a direct question. I will introduce you, of course. After all, he suggested I take on an apprentice.'

There is a loud knock upon the front door. Pugin jumps. 'Here he is! Do wipe the porridge off your face, Powell. Charlotte! Charlotte! Charlotte!'

'Here I am, sir! What is it?'

'I will receive Mr Barry in the drawing room.'

Charlotte's face is flushed. She raises her hand to her glistening brow.

'Are you all right Charlotte?'

'Oh, I've got a bad head, sir. It's the strain of them six little darlings 'an all the chores, I'm rushed off me feet today, sir.'

'Do put your feet up then for a moment, Charlotte. I'll let Mr Barry in myself.'

'Oh, you're a proper saint, sir! I'll be all right in ten minutes, sir.'

Pugin unbolts the front door and opens it. Charles Barry is leaning against a crutch. He looks pale. He removes his top hat. His enormous face is suddenly distorted by a forced smile containing a mouthful of discoloured teeth. He bows his head. 'It is simply splendid to see you again, Pugin!'

The pleasantries about health and the journey are cordially conducted in the drawing room. 'When is the big day?' asks Barry. 'Sarah and I do hope to be invited.'

Pugin's face is a blank. 'Big day?'

'I'm referring to your wedding day,' replies Barry, cautiously.

'Ah, I'm afraid it's not to be. Mary's mother is... violently unwell. It has had to be... postponed.'

'Oh, I'm very sorry to hear that,' exclaims Barry, with some discomfort. He is unsure of how to proceed with the conversation. After a moment's silence he says, 'Wives can be such a distraction.'

'It's not good for the man to be alone,' replies Pugin with a far away look.

Barry grunts. He turns to business. 'Now, I have everything set up ready for you at Westminster. The craftsmen are waiting for you to train them up, and then they'll get to work.'

'Very good,' replies Pugin. 'I'd like to show you the workshop I've created. It's my own little manufactory in my garden, all dedicated to the Palace of Westminster.'

'Oh, very well,' replies Barry, slightly irritated.

Barry hobbles after Pugin, into the reception hall and down the corridor. Pugin recalls that Powell is still in the kitchen. 'Oh, as I said in my letter, I've taken your advice and appointed an apprentice. Young Powell has been here two months already.'

'Ah, excellent! It's good to know you've increased your capacity, Mr Pugin. If we don't complete the House of Lords on time, they will dismiss us, or at least slash the budget for the rest of the Palace of Westminster. I should like to meet this fortunate fellow.

How's he getting on?'

Pugin scratches his head. 'He sleep-walks, which scares me half to death, and he's dreadfully homesick for Birmingham, but he's a fine fellow and a talented artist.'

'I'll see if he'll join us. Powell! Powell!' There is no response. Pugin turns to Barry and whispers. 'These young men do need an awful lot of training though, don't they?'

Powell strides out of the kitchen and joins them in the hallway. His gangly frame stands beside Pugin. Barry shakes his hand. 'I'm delighted to meet you, sir. I know your uncle, John Hardman, quite well.'

'Yes, I know, sir, I'm pleased to meet you, sir.'

'Follow me please, gentleman,' says Pugin. 'We're going to show Mr Barry the workshop, Powell.' They walk through the kitchen and step out into the bright sunshine. Pugin has already appointed a gang of men, including a couple from Lincoln Cathedral, who are busy working under the supervision of Mr Mayman, the master carpenter.

'Attention, men!' says Mayman to the workers. They stand upright and form a line. None of them are wearing anything on their heads, so they mime the action of doffing their caps.

'Here it is,' announces Pugin, proudly. 'In this workshop we'll have the casts and models made, for all of the carvings to go into the House of Lords.'

Barry ushers Pugin aside. 'Do you really need to make all these models, Pugin?'

'It's the only way to ensure we do a first rate job, Mr Barry.'

'But how much will they cost?'

'I have an estimate, it's close to £200.'

Barry splutters. He catches his breath. 'But, there's no budget for models, you do know that don't you, sir?'

'But we must get the right result. I'll incur the cost

myself.' Pugin has just committed himself to an expense which is half his annual salary from Parliament.'

'Very good!' exclaims Barry. A bit of colour has come back into his cheeks. 'Now, we have three days together to get the detailed drawings done for the House of Lords. It's good of you to give me free board and lodgings. I'd be so grateful for a quiet room. I haven't slept properly for days.'

Pugin scratches his head. 'Charlotte has the guest bedroom ready for you.'

'Thank you. I say, can we trouble Charlotte for some refreshments?'

Tuesday, 14th October 1845. It is half past two o'clock in the afternoon. The drawing room clock chimes the half hour. Miss Greaves' world is falling apart. She is sitting on the red settee, trying not to cry. Her father, Charles Greaves, a successful boat builder, is a kind, wiry little man. He sits beside her. Pugin sits opposite, leaning forward, looking desperate. John Hardman stands beside the window, looking out over the grey sea, which is covered by low cloud.

Charles Greaves tries to comfort his daughter. 'You see, my dear, Ann, when Mr Pugin proposed to you, and you accepted, he thought his engagement to Miss Mary Amherst was off, because she no longer loved him; but now she has written to him to say that her affections are unchanged. Now she is of age they can be married, even if her mother, Mrs Amherst, maintains her objection.'

Miss Greaves places her hand over her mouth to contain a sob. Her father continues. 'Mr Pugin has agreed to pay us compensation for this great disappointment. I believe we must accept the situation as it is.'

Ann Greaves breathes deeply; she is determined not

to break down. 'When did you discuss all of this with Mr Pugin, Papa?'

'Last week, he came to visit me in Chelsea, with his colleague here, Mr Hardman. Wouldn't you like to come back home with me now, my love?'

'But what about the children? I've been a mother to them, I can't just leave them.'

'They'll have a new nurse and you can still visit,' replies her father. 'Isn't that right, Mr Pugin?'

'Yes, of course,' whispers Pugin, close to tears.

'Well, if Mr Pugin is to be married to another, of course I can't stay here.' She looks up at Pugin.

'I'm sorry, Ann. You're so dignified and full of Christian virtue. I don't know how I would have got through this last year without you. I'm just so sorry. I hope there will be no bitterness between us.'

Ann replies, falteringly. 'There will be no bitterness... my conversion to Catholicism wasn't just so we could be together. My faith will pull me through... but for now... I'm quite broken-hearted...'

Her father places a hand upon her shoulder. 'Pack your things, Ann, we can go home now.'

Eleven

Friday, 3rd of April 1846. It has just turned half past seven o'clock in the evening. It has been a pleasant, spring day in Staffordshire, but now the sun has set and it is getting chilly. Pugin has been working late at Saint Giles Church in Cheadle. He pulls his collar up and sits back. A horse and trap from the Shrewsbury's stable is taking him back to Alton Towers. He is staying there for a few nights whilst he oversees the building works.

The wheels clatter down the shadowy, country lane and Pugin's head nods to the rhythm of the horse's clippity-clop. Moths flutter around the carriage lamp. The pressure from the work at the Palace of Westminster has been relentless, and so Pugin is glad to get away for a few days. However, when he arrived in Staffordshire, not everything was as he wished to find it. Without telling Pugin, Lord Shrewsbury has had some of the stained glass windows at Saint Giles altered, to let more light in. Pugin has now given fresh instructions to John Hardman to restore the integrity of his original design.

Night has descended. The horse continues up through the blackness of Abbey Wood. The only sound is horseshoes on the road. Suddenly, there is a bloodcurdling scream. Pugin jumps. It is only a fox. They emerge from the wood. The dark silhouette of Alton Towers is seen against the silky sky. A few lights are twinkling in the Shrewsburys' apartments. Lord Shrewsbury is away on business in Rome, which is probably just as well, as it has prevented an altercation over the windows. Lady Shrewsbury is in residence.

Pugin steps down from the trap and he turns to the driver, 'Good night.'

'Good night sir, wind's getting up, winter's not finished with us yet.'

Pugin nods. 'You're right.' He then ascends the steps leading up to the entrance. He stands for a moment, between the stone Talbot dogs, and looks over the park. All is still and silent. A scattering of stars shine above the snow-covered moors. Pugin shivers with the cold. He dislikes staying at Alton Towers when Lord Shrewsbury is away. It feels eerie. He comforts himself with the thought that a fire will have been lit in his bedroom. He decides to retire early.

Something has happened. In the middle of the night a sense of dread, like a shadow, descends upon Pugin. He is in his bed, frozen with fear. The wind is blowing up the Churnet Gorge making strange, howling noises. Pugin is convinced a pack of wolves has got into the building. He can hear them scratching at his door. The bell in the tower above him begins to clang. Pugin tries to move but he cannot, he is unsure if he is awake or in the middle of another nightmare. Several hours pass and then exhaustion finally takes him into a fitful sleep. The side effects of the mercury are increasingly terrifying.

The following morning, Pugin is awake at six o'clock, but he feels as if he could sleep through the whole day. He drags his aching body out of bed and sees a note has been placed under his door. Lady Shrewsbury is requesting the pleasure of his company for breakfast. Pugin washes and dresses and then he makes his way down to the breakfast room.

Lady Shrewsbury is bright and breezy and elegantly dressed. They exchange greetings and Pugin gives a servant his order for bacon and eggs. Now Lady Shrewsbury turns to Pugin, with a look of great concern. 'Are you very upset about Mary Amherst going into the convent?'

'I beg your pardon, my Lady'

'Are you upset that Mary has entered the convent?'

Pugin feels groggy and he looks confused. 'Mary is with the Sisters of Mercy in Nottingham, on a retreat. It's only for one week.'

'Oh, is that what you've been told?'

Pugin looks more serious now. 'Yes, why, have you been told something different?'

Lady Shrewsbury puts her cup of coffee down. 'Oh, dear.'

'What is it?'

'Mary has taken religious orders. She has become a nun. I have received a letter from her mother. Bishop Walsh has also confirmed it.'

'What?' Pugin rips the napkin from his collar. 'They must have forced her. I must go at once!' He pushes back his chair and it falls over. A footman rushes over to pick it up. Pugin makes his way to the door, and then he turns back. 'May I take your horse and trap to the railway station?'

Lady Shrewsbury remains in complete control of her emotions. 'Why? You are not going to Nottingham are you? I don't think that's a good idea, Augustus. They will not let you see her.'

Pugin is out of the room. He races up the stairs to collect his belongings.

Several hours later, Pugin is knocking loudly upon the front door of the convent of the Sisters of Mercy in Nottingham. The door remains closed to him, hour after hour. A Hansom cab pulls up. A grey haired cleric pops his head out of the window. 'Brother Pugin, please get in!'

The sight of the man calms Pugin down. 'Is that you, Bishop Walsh?'

'Yes, I have come to collect you, come on, get in…'

'I can't your Grace, I'm here to collect my fiancée, Mary Amherst.'

'Do get in, I need to talk to you.'

Reluctantly, Pugin enters the cab and it pulls off. 'Where are we going?'

'Back to the railway station.'

Pugin goes to open the door so he can jump out.

'Wait! Wait! You're being too emotional, Augustus.'

'Forgive me, your Grace, but you don't know the agony I'm feeling.'

'My son, you know that I supported your proposal of marriage to Mary, although many others did not, but she has now responded to the call of God upon her life. We must respect her decision.'

Pugin wipes the tears from his eyes. 'Oh, Bishop, if you value my life, you will not let this happen. This is her mother's doing. She is twisting things against Mary's will, she will do anything to prevent our marriage.'

Bishop Walsh places his hand upon Pugin's shoulder. 'This is Mary's own choice, Augustus. She has found peace. It's not her mother's doing.'

'It would be easier if she stabbed me in the heart. I have lost too much. My career is over. My life is over. I shall leave England. I will not return.'

'And what about your beautiful children?'

Pugin sniffs and wipes his eyes on his sleeve. 'I must get away.'

'You will get over this, in time, you must forgive Mary, do not grow bitter over this, Augustus. Don't let this be your downfall.'

Monday, 31st August 1846. It is a quarter to ten o'clock in the morning. It is rare for Charles Barry to be attending a service in a Catholic church, but this is no ordinary church. Over a thousand flickering candles reveal it to be alive with colour. This is the consecration service for Saint Giles, Cheadle. Everyone is talking about it. Royalty, aristocrats, art critics, and bishops from around the world are in attendance. Catholics and Protestants mix together and everyone wants to see Pugin.

John Newman from Oscott arrives in the church. He is the most famous of the recent converts to Catholicism from Anglicanism. An usher directs him to sit down next to Lord Shrewsbury. The two men shake hands. Newman smiles. 'I'm quite overwhelmed by the vibrancy of this building, my Lord. In fact, it's the finest parish church I've ever seen.'

Lord Shrewsbury is now in his mid-fifties. His face is beaming. 'That's praise indeed, from one as well travelled as yourself. How are you finding life at Oscott?'

'Splendid. I must thank you, Lord Shrewsbury, you and Augustus Pugin have played a vital role in opening the doors for people of faith to convert to Catholicism.'

'I know it hasn't been an easy journey for you.'

'Indeed. I have lost some friends, and some of my family will no longer speak to me, but things are much easier than they were in the past.' He looks amused. 'These days it's almost fashionable to be a Catholic convert.'

Lord Shrewsbury smiles and then he spots Pugin. 'Ah, here's the architect.'

Pugin has just returned from a summer of travelling in northern Europe. He has a freckled face from being out of doors, but he looks tense. He is still in a fragile state of mind. Now in his mid thirties, some of his black hair has turned grey. He remains preoccupied by thoughts of Mary Amherst. He yearns to receive a communication from her. He has sent her hundreds of letters, but there hasn't been a single reply since she took Holy Orders.

Whilst Pugin has been away, Powell has been left in charge of business at the Grange. Left unsupervised, his correspondence to Charles Barry, all written in Pugin's name, has become rather presumptuous and even rude. Barry has been confused by these letters, and on occasions, enraged. Pugin's son, Teddy, has been supporting Powell with the drawing work. Miss Keats, the children's governess, found the responsibility of so many children too great, especially after Miss Greaves departed, and she too has left. A more brittle, older governess, Miss Holmes is now taking care of the children. Pugin's youngest daughter, Anne, has grown in confidence. Spurred on by Powell, she is in the process of testing poor Miss Holmes.

Newman shuffles up along the church pew and he beckons for Pugin to sit beside him, which he does. 'I'm so impressed with this church, Mr Pugin. I feel I have seen heaven's gate!'

'Thank you, sir, this building is my one consolation.'

'How do you mean?'

'Well, clients tend to ruin things, but Lord Shrewsbury is a delight, of course.'

He nods at Lord Shrewsbury and smiles. Lord Shrewsbury returns the smile. 'It is so good to see you, Mr Pugin, we have much to talk about.'

'Indeed, my Lord.' Pugin turns around and greets his colleagues. He nods at Charles Barry and at George Myers who is already deeply affected by the singing and the smell of incense. Beside Myers is John Crace and next to him, Herbert Minton. Crace leans forward and whispers to Pugin. 'Where have you been?'

'Let's talk afterwards,' replies Pugin.

Crace nods in reply and turns to Minton. 'All of your hard work with encaustic tiles has paid off. The pavement is magnificent.'

Lord Shrewsbury, who is sitting in front of them,

turns to face them. He intends to shush them as the service is about to begin, but instead he also compliments Minton. 'The tiles are the best I've ever seen. Well done, again, Minton.'

The service begins. A priest swings a single chain thurible, full of incense. There is a procession through the church with clerics in colourful vestments and bejewelled mitres. There is some sense of theatre, which Pugin adores. The choir is heavenly; it lifts the congregation to a higher plane. Myers weeps. Barry is curious to observe how many times the people around him make the sign of the cross. The rituals are curious to him. The confirmed Catholics take communion. Pugin drinks deep from a silver chalice. The red wine is magnificent and it warms him inside.

A rousing sermon is given by the fiery Father Gillis, with many gasps, responses, and amens from the congregation at appropriate times. After the service, all of the architectural details in the church are closely inspected. Lively conversation fills the place. No one wants to leave. There is a tantalising mix of people and conversation. A Catholic Bishop from Australia chats to a potter from Stoke, whilst the Duke of Devonshire tells a young female artist about his appreciation of life drawing. Journalists from across Europe form a little queue beside Pugin and Lord Shrewsbury. His Lordship is getting quite carried away. 'I can tell you the building has cost me in excess of £30,000.'

'How much?'

'£30,000!'

'That is a staggering amount for a parish church.'

A journalist from Paris pushes himself in front of Pugin. 'How long has it taken to build, Monsieur?'

'It's been just over five years, not too long really.'

'Have your French roots influenced your work, Monsieur?'

Pugin frowns and then his round face breaks into a

smile. 'Well, at Saint Chapelle, I never saw images so exquisitely painted. They inspired me for what you see here.'

'Ah, oui, the eyes of the world were upon Saint Chapelle in Paris, but now they are upon Saint Giles in Cheadle. 'Ow does this make you feel?'

Pugin chuckles. 'Formidable!'

Pugin's spirit has been lifted. He feels more like his old self. He engages with the crowd and tells a few jokes. He even helps the ushers to ferry people towards their carriages. Lord Shrewsbury has invited everyone back to Alton Towers for a great banquet.

The following day Pugin returns to the Grange, feeling very unwell.

Monday, 2nd November 1846. It is nine o'clock in the morning. A fire is roaring in the hearth of Pugin's bedroom at the Grange. He is in bed, very ill indeed, he can hardly move. The doctor is standing beside him. He is an elderly man with thinning grey hair, and a long, grey beard. He wears a curious expression as he stares into Pugin's swollen, bloodshot eyes. Three days ago Pugin's eyesight completely failed, again. It has been a terrifying ordeal for him. His vision has now partially returned, but he is still very weak.

John Hardman has been at the Grange for the last two nights. He is helping Powell with the backlog of work. The two of them now stand together, outside Pugin's bedroom, while the doctor conducts his examination. Hardman whispers to his nephew. 'I heard him crying last night, did you hear him?'

Powell looks grave. 'He cries most nights, Uncle John. He keeps calling for Mary Amherst. The poor gaffer thinks she's going to come back to him.'

'Are you coping all right, Powell?'

'Yes, I'll stick by him, Uncle John.'

'I wonder what's wrong with him.'

'Well, what ever it is, Mr Barry doesn't help.'

'You mean with all of his revisions?'

'Yes. The gaffer took a turn for the worse when Mr Barry rejected the benches we'd made for the House of Lords. The gaffer had a terrible go at me, and then he collapsed. Me and Teddy had to carry him to bed.'

'Thank goodness you were with him. You don't let his tantrums get to you, do you?'

'No, it's Mr Barry's temper I fear most. He came around here a few days ago, he was so red in the face, steam coming out of his ears; furious he was. Just because some of his amended drawing hadn't been done; revision number forty-six if you please.'

'Mr Pugin told him to his face he was thinking about resigning.'

'Really? He hasn't stood up to him before. How did Barry respond to that?'

'I never saw anyone change their manners so quickly. He became very gentle, said he'd move his household to Ramsgate, to make things easier for Mr Pugin. Thing is, he's renting a house now with his whole family, within sight of the Grange, worse luck.'

'Shush, the doctor's coming.'

The door opens and the doctor stands before them, looking grim.

'How is he, doctor?' asks Hardman.

'He's very weak, indeed, sir,' responds the doctor. 'I've given him another dose of mercury to reduce the swelling in his joints. I'm extremely concerned about him. Please do send for me if there is a turn for the worse.'

'Will he... live?' gasps Hardman; behind his spectacles his piercing blue eyes are fixed upon the doctor.

'I don't know, sir,' replies the doctor, shaking his head.

Powell wipes away a tear.

'What the bloody hell is going on out there?' roars Pugin from within. He raises his head off his pillow, and then he collapses.

Miss Holmes, the governess, steps out from the nursery, and shows the doctor out. Hardman takes Powell aside. 'I must go too now I'm afraid, Powell. I've got to get back to Birmingham. The next shipment of glass is due out for the House of Lords.'

'I'll come to the station with you, Uncle John'

'No, no, you stay here, Powell, you've got enough on your plate.'

Hardman walks through the chill morning air to Ramsgate's new railway station. Waiting on the platform he can see his breath in the air. He sits on a cold metal bench. His breathing is unsteady, he wonders if Pugin is dying.

Over the following week the Grange is strangely quiet, but the pressure from the Palace of Westminster continues, relentlessly. Powell does most of the running around whilst Pugin feebly gives instructions from his bed. He checks every drawing and detail, before allowing Powell to issue it. One morning he beckons with his hand for Powell to come closer. 'What is it, gaffer?' whispers Powell.

Pugin winces. 'Don't call me that.'

Powell recalls he is not to call Pugin, *gaffer* and so he corrects himself. 'Sorry, Mr Pugin.'

'Powell, do you think we'll meet the deadline to complete the chamber of the House of Lords.'

Powell looks anxious, as if his life depends upon giving the right answer. 'Do you want me to be honest?'

'Of course.'

'The opening ceremony is less than six months away. I don't think we've got half a chance, Mr Pugin. Do you?'

Pugin speaks with his eyes closed. 'The House of Lords is going to be the most splendid part of the Palace of Westminster. It's going to be at the heart of everything.'

'How do you mean?'

'At the State opening of Parliament, it's the chamber where the Sovereign, the Peers, the Judiciary, and the Members of Parliament will all be gathered together.'

'Blimey, the heat is on.'

Pugin sighs. 'You may well say that, Powell. Queen Victoria, Prince Albert, Mr Barry, and all the rest of them expect us to meet this deadline.'

'It's Mr Barry's fault, sir, it's his demand for revisions, but what's to be done?'

Pugin throws his legs out of the bed. 'Give me your hand, Powell.'

'What are you doing?'

'I'm getting out of bed.'

'Why?'

'We've got work to do!'

Twelve

Monday, 29 March 1847. It is a quarter past ten o'clock in the morning. Pugin has recovered his health and is in good spirits. He is walking through the building site that is the Palace of Westminster, swinging his arms as he goes. He has been working all weekend. He has convinced himself that Mary Amherst is in the past. He has moved on.

Pugin arrives in the middle of the chamber of the new House of Lords. Over a hundred workmen are busy fixing, banging, drilling and sawing. The scene is one of a great commotion. Many of the men doff their caps when they recognise Pugin.

Herbert Minton is dressed as immaculately as ever, with his double cravats. He is on his knees polishing tiles with his men. John Crace is up a ladder, hanging curtains. John Harman has his sleeves rolled up; he is up in the gallery fixing a metal balustrade. George Myers has been called in by Pugin to fix the great golden canopy over the Sovereign's throne. Myers is being very particular about which workmen are allowed to even touch it. Lord Shrewsbury is in the chamber, in his capacity as a member of the Royal Commission of Fine Arts, advising on the positioning of the new paintings.

The rotund figure of Charles Barry enters the chamber. He is accompanied by the taller, grander figure of Sir Augustus Clifford, who has the honour of being Black Rod. His retinue of ushers and under-ushers follow in his wake. Sir Augustus is dressed in a dashing, black uniform. He is sixty but remains very agile. He is quite capable of arresting any errant Lord and has the commanding voice of a naval captain. Now he roars. 'Silence!'

About half the workmen stop what they are doing. 'Silence!' he repeats. Everyone is now standing to attention. 'Her Majesty will be here in less than half an hour. Please lay down your tools, as tidily as you can. Then I want you to form two orderly lines at the back of the chamber. Those of highest rank should be at the front. Do not speak to Her Majesty or Prince Albert unless you are spoken to. You will address the Queen as your Majesty, and thereafter as ma'am, to rhyme with jam. You will address Prince Albert as your Royal Highness, and thereafter as sir. Are there any questions?' The men all look rather worried, but there are no questions.

Sir Augustus turns aside to Charles Barry. 'I will introduce Her Majesty and Prince Albert to you when they enter the chamber. You should take a few minutes to walk them through, explain how progress is going and such like, and then I will take them out the other side.'

Barry bites his lower lip. He nods keenly and his jowls shake. Stopping the building works for a royal visit is the last thing he needs. He is seriously worried that the completion deadline will not be met, the opening ceremony will have to be postponed, and his reputation will be tarnished. His head is spinning with contingency plans. The Queen has requested the visit to see how work is progressing. Of course, it is really Prince Albert who has orchestrated everything. He wants to spur the workers on, so they will do the impossible, and meet the completion date of 15th April 1847. That is when the opening ceremony is due to be held. It is just over two weeks away.

The Queen and Prince Albert are now both in their late twenties. They are an attractive couple and generally popular with the public. They enter the chamber. There is no fanfare. This is a private visit and ceremony is kept to a minimum. The Prime Minister, Lord John Russell, accompanies them. Queen Victoria is much shorter than Prince Albert. She has a good figure and a pleasant face, with round cheeks and a small mouth with full lips. Her lustrous, brown hair is worn up. She is a woman, very at ease with herself. She takes in the splendour of the chamber. Her eyes rest upon the throne under the richly decorated, golden canopy. 'Oh, Albert, look.'

Sir Augustus stands solemnly behind the Queen. As Black Rod he is the Queen's official guide within the Palace of Westminster. He coughs to gain her attention. 'Just a moment please, Sir Augustus,' says a tired looking Prince Albert. He whispers to the Queen, some details about the design of the throne. She nods and smiles at her husband and then she turns to Black Rod. 'Do carry on, Sir Augustus.'

'Thank you, ma'am. May I introduce the architect to you, Mr Barry?'

'Good morning, Mr Barry,' says Queen Victoria.

'Good morning, your Majesty, it is a great honour to see you, ma'am.'

'The chamber is looking magnificent, we are very impressed, but will it be finished on time?' she asks doubtfully.

'Oh, yes, your Majesty, I think I can assure you of that.' There is sweat on his brow.

Prince Albert steps forward and shakes Barry's hand. 'I am pleased to see you again, Mr Barry. There is still a lot to be done. Where is Mr Pugin, we had expected to see him here?'

'Ah, yes, my... draughtsman is in the line with the workmen... there he is at the back, sir.'

Prince Albert frowns. 'Well, we must see him before we leave. Would you like to walk us through the chamber, Mr Barry?'

'Yes, sir, it would be my pleasure.'

They walk slowly through the House of Lords chamber. There are thousands of individual items of artwork already in place, and many more are still to arrive. Most of the benches are in, but the red leather is still to be stuffed. Queen Victoria admires the woodcarvings and the magnificent stained glass windows. When they arrive at the throne the Queen places her hand to her chest. She seems to be quite overcome.

Prince Albert smiles at her warmly and he whispers, 'Let's have a word with Mr Pugin, he's designed this for you.' Queen Victoria turns away from the throne and she spots a familiar face. 'Look Albert, there's Lord Shrewsbury, I must speak to him first.'

Lord Shrewsbury realises he has been spotted and he offers the Queen a little bow. The Queen smiles and she makes her way over to him. The men all bow their heads. The Queen knows Lord Shrewsbury, personally. 'It is good to see you, my Lord. We are very impressed with the new paintings.'

'I'm pleased you like them, your Majesty. Prince Albert has guided us along the way, most skilfully.'

'We look forward to seeing you at Osborne, soon I hope.'

Queen Victoria moves on and she stops in front of John Crace. 'Good morning, may I ask what your occupation is?'

'Furnishings, your Majesty,' replies Crace, a little disappointed at not being recognised. He adds; 'I have had the honour of upholstering your throne, ma'am.'

The Queen places her hand against her chest, again. 'Really? Thank you. It is splendid. I look forward to sitting upon it,' she says with a wry smile.

Prince Albert gently pushes some men aside and ushers Pugin to step forward. 'This is Mr Pugin, my dear, he has designed the whole of this magnificent interior.'

The Queen smiles and her whole face lights up. 'Ah, Mr Pugin, I'm pleased to meet you. We are very impressed with all of your hard work.'

Pugin's grey eyes sparkle and his face breaks into a radiant smile. 'Thank you, your Majesty. We're fortunate to have a good team of craftsmen here.'

'I understand you've met Prince Albert before.'

'Yes, ma'am, I've had the pleasure of meeting his Royal Highness.'

'It is good to see you again, Mr Pugin,' interjects Prince Albert, as he shakes Pugin's hand. He continues. 'We look forward to seeing you at the opening,' and then he adds in a hushed voice, 'but will it be done on time?'

'Please be assured, it will, sir.'

Prince Albert does not look convinced. 'There is also something else I would like to talk to you about... I will be in touch.'

The Queen moves down the line, smiling at terrified faces. She stops beside a young man with ginger hair, who appears to be more relaxed. 'Good morning. Are you enjoying your work here?'

'Yes, thank you, your Majesty.'

'Do you live far away?'

'Lambeth, ma'am. Forgive me, ma'am, but I have a family in Ireland. A million are dead from starvation. Could you please have a word with your Prime Minister about...' Before he can finish, a scowling Sir Augustus is ushering the Queen away. The royal party is leaving. The Queen is flustered. She turns to Lord John Russell. 'That young man has just made a valid point, Prime Minister. I have said we must do more to assist Ireland.'

Lord John Russell is in his mid-fifties. He has intense

brown eyes, a large nose, and slightly unkempt black hair. 'We have made funds available on loan for relief of the poor in Ireland, ma'am. There are wealthy people in Ireland; they need to be encouraged to pay into the Poor Law rate.'

'We'll discuss this again at our next audience.'

Charles Barry walks over to Pugin. 'Can I have a quick word with you please, Mr Pugin?' he asks.

'Pugin nervously rubs the back of his neck. 'Yes, of course Mr Barry.'

Barry takes Pugin aside. 'Mr Pugin, you're working so hard, and I'm grateful. When I was a young man, I was fortunate to take the Grand Tour, I went to Italy…'

'Yes, sir, you have told me, when I visited you in Brighton, I saw your paintings.'

'Quite so, quite so, now, I want you to take a little holiday, I recommend a tour of Italy, as soon as possible. Don't worry about taking the time off. I will cover for you here. Think of this as a gift, from me to you.'

Pugin looks confused. 'But I have such a backlog of work, there are all my other projects, churches, houses, schools… I don't think I could take a tour, Mr Barry, but it's very kind of you to suggest it.'

Barry continues, unabashed. 'Now, I have taken the liberty of mentioning your holiday to Lord Shrewsbury. He's also very keen for you to visit Italy, and perhaps you can stay with his relations in Rome.'

'I really don't think I could…'

'Barry interjects, slightly agitated. 'Mr Hardman approves of you taking a holiday too. He and your apprentice, Mr Powell, can manage your affairs in your absence. I know you don't care for tiresome ceremonies, so don't feel you have to attend the opening of the House of Lords. I will cope with everything here.'

Pugin scratches his head. 'Well, I have been meaning

to go to Italy for some time…'

'Excellent! That's settled then.' Barry makes a quick exit and returns to his palatial office. There are press releases to be written about the grand opening and he has decided to write them himself.

Thirteen

Wednesday, 21st April 1847. It is a few minutes before half past nine o'clock in the morning, The sky is a clear blue and the air is unseasonably cold. Pugin looks a little lost as he waits at the coach station beside the River Seine, close to Notre Dame. He rubs his arms with his hands for warmth. He is waiting to board the diligence, a French stagecoach, to Avignon. A few passengers are huddled around a fire in a metal bin. The kindling emits a pleasant scent of pinewood.

The bourgeois Parisians stroll by on the riverside promenade. Pugin notices they are dressed less flamboyantly, but perhaps more stylishly than in London. On the other side of the road, he observes the busy scene of people walking and riding along the cobbled street that leads to Notre Dame. Most people have their winter coats on, and those that haven't are feeling the cold. Pugin flinches when he sees how the young people leave it to the last possible moment before they get out of the way of the horse drawn carriages.

Pugin catches a glimpse of a picture on the front page of a discarded Paris newspaper. He picks it up and sits on a wall beside the embankment. The picture is of the Palace of Westminster. His lips move as he translates the article.

On Wednesday, 15th April 1847, the chamber of the House of Lords was the first part of the new Palace of Westminster to be officially opened by Queen Victoria.

He reads on and learns how the opening ceremony

was a lavish occasion. Prince Albert is singled out for praise and so is the architect, Monsieur Charles Barry. Most of the contractors are mentioned, including Herbert Minton, John Crace, John Hardman, George Myers, and the list goes on. There is, however, no mention of Augustus Pugin.

Unbeknown to Pugin, newspapers around the world have been full of articles that celebrate Britain's new House of Lords. It is widely accepted to be one of the finest buildings in the world. Charles Barry's name is everywhere. He has become a national hero. Pugin's name is not mentioned in any of the newspaper reports.

Pugin had packed his bags, kissed his children goodbye, and departed for Calais, the day before the opening ceremony. Nearly thirteen years earlier, on a ferry back to England, Arthur, the student of antiquities, exposed Pugin's ignorance of Italy, the Renaissance, and Classical design. Now, at the persuasive nudging of Charles Barry, he has been provided with the opportunity to address this omission in his education.

Pugin lifts his collar against the cold north wind. He crosses the street so he can get a better view of Notre Dame. Ravaged during the Revolution, it has somehow survived. Pugin tilts his head. The flying buttresses appear to be interceding between heaven and earth. The cathedral reminds Pugin of William the Conqueror's Abbaye aux Hommes, in Caen, but it is more feminine, more French.

A bell rings out beside the stagecoach; it is ready to leave. Pugin rushes back over the street and joins the passengers. In a slightly confused state of mind, he passes his luggage to the driver and climbs aboard. The diligence is considerably larger than an English stagecoach, but it is overcrowded and stuffy. Pugin is fortunate to get a seat by the window.

It is quite a sight to watch the diligence pull off. There are eight people within it, three outside upfront, and six upon the roof, where the luggage is also piled high. A team of four strong horses pull this clattering heap along. It looks as if it could topple over at any minute.

Pugin reflects that the suspension is not as good as with an English stagecoach. He pulls back the curtain and observes as fine white, limestone terraces pass by at seven miles per hour. The terraces have a pleasing rhythm of windows, doors, balconies... he has nodded off.

When Pugin opens his eyes again, the diligence is rattling down a bumpy rural lane. It will take four days to get to Avignon.

The fireball sun descends on the horizon and Avignon comes into sight. The towers of the Palais des Papes, France's largest Gothic fortress, rise above the town walls. All is bathed in crimson light. Pugin sighs. He has never been this far away from home before. He is utterly exhausted, dishevelled, and in need of a bath.

The diligence pulls up beside a churchyard, full of shadows. The air is warm, fragrant, and full of the sound of chirping cicadas. Pugin collects his luggage, and walks off, upon unsteady legs. He finds a hostelry with blue shutters and a blue front door.

After a fitful sleep, Pugin is up early. Sitting out on a garden terrace, he enjoys a good breakfast and strong coffee served by a beautiful, dark woman. He then goes to visit the Palais des Papes, home of the popes in the fourteenth century.

Over the next four days Pugin undertakes a tour of Provence, mostly in a hired hay cart, pulled by a mule that only the cantankerous old farmer can control. He sees herds of wild, white horses galloping through the Camargue. They are splendid, but the brackish landscape is barren and the sun is too hot for him. He studies the Roman ruins at Arles. He is impressed with the well-preserved aqueducts. He stays in a friendly farmhouse in Aix-en-Provence. When the farmer pours him a glass of wine, he drinks deeply, and for several seconds hears angels singing.

The light of Provence, and the translucent blue commonly used for doors and window shutters, make a great impression upon Pugin. This blue reminds him of Titian's ultramarine, revealed to him by Lord Shrewsbury at Alton Towers. He wishes John Hardman could see this luminous, living blue, in the creamy, southern light. The knowledge of such colour is invaluable to the manufacturer of stained glass.

The beauty of the olive skinned French women in Provence has not gone unnoticed by Pugin. However, his increasingly dishevelled appearance means they do not pay him much attention. In fact, no one takes much notice of him, and he enjoys the anonymity. In London or Ramsgate, people recognise him, and they like to share their thoughts. It can be annoying.

Pugin also finds himself thinking a lot about Helen Lumsdaine, the twenty-one year old daughter of an Anglican clergyman, and the niece of his next-door neighbour. She has been in residence next door to the Grange for several months, and has spent a considerable amount of time playing with Pugin's children.

Back on board the diligence, Pugin travels from Aix-en-Provence towards Marseilles. The carriage rattles through a vast, sweet scented juniper forest, the resting place of a few grey wolves that have wandered south from the Alps. The forest provides a pleasant shade from the fierce sun. The trees eventually thin out and the diligence continues through a stunning open landscape, filled with the scent of thyme. The bush-covered hills remind Pugin of English heathland. The horses struggle up a steep hill and then the glittering

Mediterranean Sea fills the horizon. Pugin is excited.

As they descend the hill, the sea constantly reappears around every bend. Then the port of Marseilles is seen, shimmering white under the bright blue sky.

The diligence pulls up close to the docks in Marseilles. Pugin collects his bag from the carriage roof and gets his bearings. The sun is still hot and blindingly bright. With his bag thrown over his shoulder, he walks purposefully along the narrow, golden streets, headed for the sea front. People are bustling about everywhere.

A refreshing, sea breeze blows over Pugin's face. Beside him, the water is lapping against the harbour wall. With a sense of abandon, he sits down on the ground and removes his stockings. He dips his calloused feet into the cold sea. It feels wonderful. Pugin stays like that, with his feet dangling in the water. His eyes scan beyond the harbour walls. The exotic, aquamarine colour captivates him. He allows his eyes to rest upon the forest of ship's masts. There are dozens of them in this busy port. Now Pugin lifts his feet out of the water and places them upon the warm stone. His skin dries quickly. He decides to explore.

The port is full of people, sailors, merchants, prostitutes, and the smell of spices. Pugin has spotted a number of black skinned men. They sit together in huddles, chatting, playing dice and cards. They are from North Africa, the crew of merchant sailing ships, enjoying shore leave. Pugin has seen black people before on a number of occasions in London. He once attended a dinner party at the Shrewsburys London house, where the guest of honour was Madame Christophe, Queen of Haiti. Following the suicide of her husband she took up residence in London and lived there in considerable style before retiring to Pisa in Italy. But Pugin has never seen so many black men gathered together. They wear colourful tunics and turbans. The bright sun makes their clothing appear all the more vivid.

Pugin strolls along the seafront, towards the hotel where he has a reservation. He now feels lonely amongst the hustle of the port. He sits in the shade for a while, surrounded by the familiar sound of chirping of sparrows. His thoughts drift homeward. He imagines how the larks must be singing above the cornfields around the Grange. He wonders what his daughter, Anne, is doing. He reassures himself that she will be taking good care of her brothers and sisters. He also realises she will probably be making life difficult for Miss Holmes, their governess.

Pugin gets his notebook out of his sailor's jacket pocket. He writes a letter to Anne. After a few minutes he finishes the letter by asking Anne to give her brothers and sisters a kiss from him; he adds they can have whatever pudding they wish, whenever they want. He sends her all his love.

He puts the notepad down and shakes his head. He is surprised to feel a rising anger at the thought of being separated from his children. He wonders if he was too passive in accepting the advice of Charles Barry. *Why not go home, right now?* He wags a finger in the air and speaks out loud. 'Don't forget you have an audience with Pope Pius IX!' A black sailor passes by. He smiles at Pugin sympathetically, as one might to a harmless vagrant. Pugin nods at him and then he looks out to sea. He remembers why he agreed to the trip, he has never been to Italy before. He wants to press on, to meet the Pope, and to see the architecture and the paintings.'

Pugin arrives at his hotel. It is an elegant, golden stone villa, with tall casement windows overlooking the azure sea. Given Pugin's unkempt appearance, the refined middle-aged landlady initially gives him a frosty reception. However, when he is established as being the famous architect, the landlady becomes more gracious. She accepts him as being an eccentric Englishman. She is also keen to practise her English. 'Ah, one moment please, Monsieur Pugin! You 'av a letter, one moment!'

Pugin is handed a scented letter in a pink envelope. He opens it. It is from Helen Lumsdaine, his next-door neighbour's niece. He is delighted. He takes a few steps away and reads it, privately, beside the window that overlooks the sea. It is a chatty, affectionate letter.

Pugin sleeps in a comfortable bed, in a beautiful room with a sea view. When he awakes in the morning, the sun is streaming in through a gap in the curtains. The combination of the villa, the letter from Helen, and a good sleep, has revitalised him. He feels the urge to continue his journey.

It is a sunny morning. Pugin eats his breakfast of croissants, jam and honey, on the garden terrace. There is a spectacular view of the coast. As he sips his hot coffee he watches the progress of four sailing ships. All sails are up, and they have caught the morning breeze. A larger vessel, with a tall smoking funnel is approaching the port. In a few hours Pugin will be on that steamer, heading for Rome.

fourteen

Pugin's appearance has been transformed. He is clean-shaven, his hair is cut short, he is wearing morning dress, and polished black boots. Prince Doria, the young and dashing husband of Mary, Lord Shrewsbury's daughter, has provided the expensive clothes. He and Pugin chat easily together as they stroll amongst lemon trees in the luxuriant gardens of Villa Doria, the home of the Prince and Princess.

The villa, built of white stone, is perched upon a hill, surrounded by pinewoods, in the heart of Rome. The terraced gardens are dotted with ancient Roman ruins. The men stop for a moment and enjoy the panorama. 'That really is a breath-taking view of Rome,' says Pugin.

The Prince is pleased that Pugin is impressed. He turns around and looks up at his seventeenth century Baroque palace. It shimmers against the cobalt sky. He speaks in perfect English. 'Does my family's ancestral home meet with your approval, Mr Pugin? I'm sorry it's not in the Gothic style.'

Pugin turns around. It is hard not to be impressed. The villa contains over a thousand rooms and priceless treasures including many paintings by Raphael. The Prince's family is one of the wealthiest in Italy and they have many residences, but this is one of their favourites.

'I haven't seen the like of it before, your Grace. I'm sure it must be one of the finest palaces in Europe, but ...'

'But what?'

Pugin scratches his head. 'I don't understand though, why a room should be dedicated to Jupiter.'

The Prince's face is now masked by a frown.

Pugin doesn't want to upset him. 'The gardens are also remarkable,' he adds with a reassuring smile.

'It was originally the home of Pope Innocent X,' says the Prince with some pride.

'Incredible,' replies Pugin, solemnly. 'I feel so honoured to be staying here with you and Mary. It's a haven of peace. You're both so very kind.'

'Well, we're delighted to have you here as our guest,' replies the Prince, graciously. 'It's the least we could do. We're so pleased with the apartments you've designed for us at Alton Towers. It makes visiting Mary's parents so pleasurable.'

Pugin nods and smiles, he likes it when a client is pleased with his work.

The Prince continues. 'We don't have too much time before your audience with the Holy Father. I must show you some of the ancient sights. Shall we proceed?'

'Of course…'

Prince Doria turns to Pugin with a proud expression. 'It's nearly two thousand years old, and it's still in use!'

The two men are standing together looking up at the magnificent concrete dome of the Pantheon, with its central circle open to the clear sky. They have the building almost to themselves. Pugin's neck is beginning to ache. 'Who built it?' he asks.

'It was commissioned by Marcus Agrippa.'

Pugin looks mildly impressed. 'For what purpose?'

The Prince pauses; he seems to be a little embarrassed. 'To honour the Roman gods, but we can still admire the architecture, can't we?'

Pugin tries to be positive. 'At least it's sheltering us from the hot sun. It's refreshingly cool in here.'

Somewhat deflated the Prince turns to face the exit.

'Come along, Mr Pugin. You don't want to be late for your audience.'

Pugin has to stride purposefully to keep up with the Prince as they walk up the hill towards the Vatican. He breathlessly asks a question he meant to ask earlier. 'Is there anything I should avoid saying to the Holy Father?'

Prince Doria isn't the slightest bit out of breath. 'I wouldn't mention Henry VIII of England, Emperor Napoleon of France, or that upstart Garibaldi,' replies Prince Doria, laughing. He stands still for a moment and straightens his face. 'Seriously, though, there's an air of tension in the Papal State at the moment.'

'Why's that?' gasps Pugin.

'Nationalism is growing. Many Italians want a unified country. There's talk of revolution and expelling the Austrians in the north. Assassinations have become common.'

'I feel a little nervous about meeting the Holy Father.'

'Oh, don't worry, Mr Pugin, an audience with the Pope lasts for about two minutes. I'll have to leave you now, or I'll be late for my business meeting. There's the entrance, do you see the large gates, up there?'

'Yes, I see.'

'I'm afraid you'll have to get past all of those street traders. Will you be all right?'

'Yes, of course, thank you for the fascinating tour, your Grace.'

'I will see you tonight for dinner. We have arranged for a number of interesting artists to meet you. Give my greetings to the Holy Father.'

Pugin takes a moment to observe a colossal statue of a horse, and then he elbows his way through the ranks of noisy street traders. He keeps his head down and clutches his bag close to his chest.

Pugin arrives at the gates of the Vatican. He presents copious amounts of paperwork to an official and then negotiates his way through a huddle of clerics. At last he is allowed to pass under the fortified walls. His heartbeat quickens. He is directed to the edge of an expansive courtyard, where he is told to wait for Monsignor Anthony O'Brian.

There are ranks of Swiss Guard soldiers, marching back and forth, dressed in ceremonial blue and yellow-striped uniforms, together with black helmets topped with crimson ostrich feathers. Each guard has a javelin in his hand. Pugin feels more anxious about his impending audience with the Pope.

A cleric dressed in a black cassock approaches. He is very animated. 'Mr Pugin?'

'Yes.'

'Ah, It's an honour to meet you, sir. I'm Father Anthony, from Reading, Berkshire. I've been assigned as your guide.' They shake hands.

'Thank you, Father Anthony, I hadn't expected to see so many of the Swiss Guard on duty, are there always this many?'

'A Head of State has just had an audience with the Pope, I forget who. We have an hour or so before your audience, would you like to see the gardens?'

'Yes, thank you, Father, that would be pleasant, although I've walked quite far already. Would it be possible to see inside the Apostolic Palace?' Pugin is keen to see the interiors that are normally hidden from public view.

Father Anthony is slightly taken aback by Pugin's candour. He looks down at the ground and squeezes the tip of his nose between his finger and thumb, as if this will help him to find the answer. It seems to work. 'Yes, that's a good idea, would you like to follow me?'

Father Anthony guides Pugin around the edge of the vast courtyard, and they enter the Pope's immaculate, verdant gardens. A bright green parakeet screeches over their heads. After a very brief stroll, Father Anthony says, 'Right, we'll get into the Apostolic Palace through here.' He whisks Pugin through offices, libraries, and painting galleries displaying masterpieces. Pugin openly criticises what he doesn't like, much to Father Anthony's astonishment. After walking down endless corridors they arrive at the Sistine Chapel. Father Anthony speaks in a whisper. 'Mr Pugin, this is a sacred place, do take your time.'

Father Anthony and Pugin are the only people in the chapel. Pugin stares in silence at Michelangelo's remarkable ceiling for several minutes. He observes the finger of God and the finger of Adam reaching for each other. His eyes scan across hundreds of figures; he wonders about their nudity. He kneels down in front of the altar and prays for his children, for his departed parents, for his first love, Anne, for his second wife, Louisa, for Aunt Selina, and finally he prays for the church, and he asks that his audience with the Pope will go well.

Father Anthony gently taps Pugin on his shoulder. 'It's time to go for your audience now.'

They walk into an ornate, Baroque style anteroom. There are two Swiss Guards on duty, one either side of the doorway. 'I will leave you here, Mr Pugin. It's been an honour to meet you. God bless you.'

'Thank you, Father Anthony.'

Apart from the Swiss Guards, Pugin is now alone. He sits down upon a finely carved bench. The room is decorated with Renaissance paintings; most of them depict Rome. There are display cabinets full of ornaments. Pugin's eyes rest upon an attractive enamelled vase; it could be by Minton. When he sees what is depicted upon it, he has to rub his eyes. He says out loud, 'It's Oscott College!' Pugin stands, open-mouthed, but before he can say another word, a stern looking cleric enters. He is wearing a crimson vestment and he is ushering Pugin to follow him. The cleric whispers a few instructions before gently pushing Pugin into the presence of Pope Pius IX.

A soft light enters the room from high windows, revealing tiny specks of dust floating in the air. It is almost silent, but a dove is cooing by an open window. The city is a distant whisper. The Pope is sitting upon a golden throne, smiling serenely with an outstretched hand. He is a large man with a strong looking face. He has white hair under a round, white cap and is dressed in white vestments. Two monsignors in crimson vestments sit either side of the throne. Swiss Guardsmen are dotted around the room. Pugin approaches. He makes the sign of the cross, falls to his knees, and kisses the Pope's ring; all as instructed.

The Pope begins to speak in Italian. He has a musical voice. Pugin cannot understand a word that is being said, but it sounds beautiful, and so he smiles approvingly. After a moment one of the monsignors in crimson vestments gets up and whispers something into the Pope's ear. The Pope stops speaking and his face lights up with understanding. He rises to his feet and looks down at Pugin. He chuckles. 'Ah, God bless you, my son.' he speaks in good English, but slowly, and with a strong Italian accent. He continues. 'Augustus Pugin, I am very pleased to meet you.' Even the monsignors are now smiling. Pugin gets up off his knees. The Pope continues. 'I hear from Bishop Walsh, and Lord Shrewsbury, that you have been building beautiful churches in Great Britain. The Pope smiles again and then he adds; 'In Gothic architecture, is that right?'

'Yes, Holy Father, I believe it's an authentic, Christian style of architecture. I have a gift for you, Holy Father, may I present it to you?'

'Yes, of course, my son, how kind of you.'

Pugin presents the Pope with a specially bound copy of his book, *Contrasts*. The Pope takes the book with a smile. 'Thank you, my son.' He gently turns a few pages, as if handling a priceless artefact. He is intrigued. 'The Emperor Constantine built the first Christian church here, around the tomb of Saint Peter, three hundred years after Christ, but the present Basilica is mainly the work of Michelangelo. Do you not approve of its style, my son?'

'Do you want me to be honest, Holy Father?'

'Of course.'

'I have come with an open mind, to learn about Classical architecture, but all the buildings I see speak to me of worshipping idols. I would recommend building in the Gothic style, Holy Father.'

The Pope remains thoughtful. 'John Newman is staying here at the moment, preparing for his ordination, do you know each other?'

The monsignor to the right of the Pope leans forward a fraction, anxious to hear what the Holy Father is going to say about Newman.

'Yes, Holy Father,' replies Pugin, wondering where the conversation may be going.

There is a moment's silence. The monsignor touches the lobe of his ear. He knows that John Newman, and the new Catholic bishops in England, will be expected to take over many of the political functions performed by the laity, such as Lord Shrewsbury and his architect.

The Pope changes tack. 'Have you seen the Sistine Chapel?'

'Yes, Holy Father.'

'What do you think of it?'

'Magnificent.'

'Ah, so have we done something right, Augustus?'

'Yes, Holy Father, but there is so much nudity.'

The monsignor snorts.

The Pope looks perplexed. 'Tell me, Augustus, how

do you feel England is faring under Queen Victoria?'

Pugin looks thoughtful. 'Well, Holy Father, the country does feel different.'

The Pope gesticulates with his hands. 'How so?'

'It seems to be a younger country, and yet it's perhaps more solemn.'

'Solemn?' The Pope appears to be surprised by the answer. 'Let us be grateful to God for Catholic Emancipation,' he says earnestly and then he adds, Sir Robert Peel saw the light.'

'Like Saint Paul,' adds Pugin.

The Pope smiles and hands his copy of *Contrasts* to the ear-stroking monsignor. The Pope continues. 'Lord Shrewsbury has done great work for the church and so have you, my son.' He gives a nod to the other monsignor who now approaches with a cushion with a medal resting upon it. The Pope says a blessing over the medal and the then he presents it to Pugin.

'Thank you, Holy Father.'

'Augustus, you may not find the style of architecture you are looking for here in Rome. My advice is to go north, to Assisi. Discover the land that inspired Saint Francis. Visit the simple, country churches, perhaps only then go to Florence and Venice.'

The audience is over.

Pugin follows the Pope's advice. The next day he sets off on a tour of northern Italy. What he encounters is a revelation to him. He is pleasantly surprised when he sets his eyes upon Assisi. It is a shimmering citadel perched upon the side of an Umbrian hill, under the caressing sun. Pugin spends several days in the town, walking, drawing, praying, and eating good food. He falls in love with the surrounding hills covered in cypress forests and olive groves dating back to antiquity.

The sense of holiness in the simple thirteenth century

chapel Porziuncola, in which Saint Francis prayed, moves Pugin to tears. He is deeply affected by the life of Saint Francis, the wealthy young man who gave up everything to pursue a life of faith, prayer, and service. Pugin considers the Baroque shell that encases the chapel to be an affront.

After Assisi, he travels to Verona, where he learns more about architectural composition through sketching the town's interconnected streets and squares. It is the ancient buildings and lively public squares that impress him, rather than the Renaissance grandeur.

Then to Florence, capital of Tuscany. The Gothic buildings and the town planning of the Medici dynasty remind him of Oxford. The quality of the stonework in the Duomo is the best he has ever seen. The pushy goldsmiths in the neighbouring streets remind him of the craftsmen of Birmingham.

Pugin sketches and writes down his thoughts. When he has a new idea for the design of wallpaper at the Palace of Westminster, he wastes no time in posting off his drawings to John Crace in London. When he has new ideas about stained glass windows, the drawings are posted to John Hardman in Birmingham. Pugin is also writing down his thoughts about love and faith, and these are being sent to Helen Lumsdaine.

Pugin is the only passenger in a gondola, progressing slowly through the shimmering, green waters of the Grand Canal. There are many other vessels. Pugin is in a thoughtful mood. All of his preconceptions have been blown away on this tour. It has been a revelation to discover that Italy is full of Gothic buildings.

He leans forward in the gondola and stares at a beautiful church. Franciscan monks, the order created by Saint Francis, have built it. Pugin is astounded to see they have developed a different kind of Gothic idiom. He has never seen the like before. It is a very simple church, built in red brick rather than stone. Pugin notes that the only ornamentation is around the entrance, where it can be seen and touched. He also admires how they have incorporated Byzantine influences. He gets his sketchbook out, and with a few strokes he captures the pointed arches, oriental motifs, and zigzag brickwork. It is all strangely exotic, and yet it works beautifully.

The swarthy, young gondolier is looking at Pugin, expectantly. He cannot resist saying something. He is clearly well educated. 'Do you mind me talking, sir?'

Pugin is taken by surprise. 'No, of course not, you speak good English,' he replies, looking up from his sketchpad.

'I see you are drawing, do you want me to stop the gondola?'

'No, carry on, I have it now.'

'Ah, you draw quickly. The church, it's nice, eh?'

'Yes, I like the red bricks'

'Buildings in the lagoon don't have... oh, what do you call them? Foundations. They are supported on, trees.'

Pugin smiles. 'We call them piles.'

'Ah, *piles.*'

Pugin nods his head. 'Brick is much lighter than stone, of course.'

'Yes, of course, there is a very fine palace coming up, on the right, the wealthy merchants tried to match the Doges.'

Pugin smiles. 'When was the Doges palace built?'

The gondolier leans against his pole and shrugs apologetically. 'I don't remember, exactly. It's over four hundred years old. Are you English or American?'

'English. You seem to know a lot about buildings.'

'I'm saving up to study. Are you an architect, sir?

Pugin smiles. 'Yes.'

The gondolier raises his eyebrows. 'Do you like

Venice?'

'Yes, I do, very much, it's charming.'

'The Gothic has lasted for a long time here in Venice, sir.'

Pugin puts his sketchbook down. 'You're right. Why didn't the Classical design take over?'

'Venice has no Roman remains. We're a trading port. We look to the east. We Venetians like beauty, colour, and the sea.'

fifteen

Friday, 18th June 1847. It is one o'clock in the afternoon. It is sunny and bright in Ramsgate, but dark clouds are moving in from the east, over the English Channel. Pugin is back at the Grange, leaning against his drawing board in the studio, singing loudly in his baritone voice. The windows are open. Outside, above the barley, the larks join in with the singing.

Pugin disembarked in Ramsgate three days ago, returning from Italy via Germany. He briefly returned to the Grange to see his children. On arrival, he was very shocked to see that old Mr Bing, the builder, is erecting a terrace of houses right next to the Grange. Mr Bing has also marked out other plots for development.

Pugin was distressed but he didn't have time for a row. After seeing the children, he left almost immediately for London. He needed to check on progress at the Palace of Westminster. There he met with Lord Shrewsbury, who wanted to hear every word spoken by Pope Pius IX.

Powell is on the other side of the studio, trying to work, but it is impossible. He puts his pen down, sighs, and looks out of the window. He cannot concentrate with Pugin singing so loudly. He has become very fond of his gaffer, as he still calls him. He has been at Pugin's side through sickness and health for nearly three years, but living and working in the same house as him is challenging.

When Pugin was travelling in Italy, Powell had a great deal of work to do, but he revelled in having the studio to himself. Since Pugin's return, Powell realises he wants more freedom. The regimented life at the Grange is demanding and it can also be boring for a young, single man. Powell has grown his black hair longer and he now has a dainty waxed moustache. He is twenty and he wants to have some fun. He wants to make friends and meet young ladies.

Powell can see that his gaffer is in a good mood. When Pugin stops singing, Powell makes his move. 'Mr Pugin, sir.'

'Yes, my boy, what is it?' Pugin knows something is up because Powell's voice is slightly hesitant.

'May I ask you a question?'

'Of course you may,' replies Pugin, smiling warmly.

'Would it be acceptable to you, sir, if I were to take lodgings in the town?'

Pugin's smile drops. 'Why would you want to do that?'

'I was just thinking that it might be good for me to be closer to the town.'

'Closer to the town?'

'Yes, and perhaps if I was to work from some lodgings, just for one day a week, it would give you more space here.'

'Give me more *space*? Nonsense, no, I don't need more space. I don't think that would be at all appropriate, Powell. The success of the House of Lords means we have so many orders coming in, our designs are going into the shops. We have a public following. I have created this studio for us. I would miss you and the children would miss you, dreadfully. Mr Mayman and the workmen would miss you...'

Powell's lower lip is beginning to quiver.

Pugin continues. 'Ramsgate has become quite dangerous you know?' He stops his diatribe and thinks for a moment. He has an idea. 'Perhaps we could get a couple of the young men, your old friends from the

Birmingham manufactory, to be based here. We could do with the extra hands and at least you'd have some company of your own age.'

Powell nods his head. He seems quite interested in this suggestion. The doorbell suddenly rings. Pugin remembers why he is happy. Helen Lumsdaine is coming for lunch.

Helen looks beautiful in her flowery summer dress and matching bonnet. She is twenty-one years old.

'Helen, Oh! My dear!'

'Mr Pugin! I have so much to tell you!' She removes her bonnet and her golden curls flow down over her shoulders.

They greet with a kiss on both cheeks. The children appear from nowhere and gather around Helen. Pugin allows them a few minutes to exchange their stories and then he ushers Helen into the drawing room, alone. He kisses her on the lips. She raises her hand to her heart. 'I've decided to become a Catholic!'

Pugin clutches her arm. 'What, just now?'

'No, silly, I've been thinking about it while you've been in Italy. Your letters and books have helped me to reach my decision.'

'Oh, Helen, this is wonderful news.' He embraces her.

Helen breaks free and stamps her foot. 'Of course, mamma and papa don't know yet.' She pulls a little girl's grimace. Then her face breaks into a radiant smile. 'When I'm a Catholic, we can be together.'

Pugin clasps his hands as if in prayer and mouths the words, *thank you*.

On the other side of the drawing room door, Anne, the eldest child, and Powell, are eavesdropping. A voice screeches down from galleried landing. 'What are you doing down there?' It is Miss Holmes, the governess. Anne turns to Powell. 'Miss Lumsdaine is too young to marry my Papa.'

Tuesday, 30th November 1847. Pugin is sitting in the busy dining area at the rear of Aitchison's Grocer's Shop on Queen Street, in Edinburgh's New Town. The area is a masterpiece of Georgian urban planning. Pugin looks up from his coffee and stares out of the shop window. The trees in the gardens on the other side of the street retain a few golden leaves. He glances at his pocket watch and fidgets nervously. There is still no sign of her.

Suddenly, Pugin is on his feet, standing to attention. He waves his hand in the air. Helen has entered the shop, wearing a red coat and bonnet. Helen spots Pugin and she runs towards him. She looks beautiful. They embrace in the middle of the shop. Customers stop what they are doing. An elderly gentleman clears his throat. 'I say!' A regal looking lady gasps and she speaks in an Edinburgh brogue. 'Well, really, young people today!' She flashes a look of disgust at Mr Aitchison, the proprietor, as if he might be running a brothel, and then she bustles out of the shop.

Mr Aitchison wipes his hands on his striped apron and he folds his arms over his enormous stomach. He is trying to make his doughy face look fierce. He needs the indomitable Mrs Aitchison to be there, but she is visiting her mother. Pugin and Helen are oblivious to all of this. They are already sitting down, staring into each other's eyes.

Helen speaks first. 'Will you forgive me for my letter, my dearest?'

'When you said you never wanted to see me again, I thought my life was over. When you returned all the books I gave you, I felt so alone, but now you're with me, all is forgiven.'

'I'll never do that to you again. It was my mamma and papa. We had such a terrible row, but I'm of age. I can make my own decisions.'

Pugin holds both of Helen's hands in his. 'Helen, will you marry me?'

Helen gasps and looks down at the table. Then she looks into Pugin's sparkling grey eyes. 'Yes, I will marry you.'

Pugin is beaming. 'You are all I want, Helen. We will be happy together.' He wipes a tear from his eye.

'We must keep it a secret though.'

'Of course, I know your parents will do anything to stop us marrying.'

'They want to stop me from becoming a Catholic, too.'

'You'll have to be very brave, my darling.'

'I know, pray for me Augustus, to have courage.'

'Of course, I will. You must come to the Grange as soon as possible. The children love to see you. We could get married in our chapel, at the Grange, in secret.'

Helen laughs. 'I will be down as soon as I can. In the meantime, you have your children and your work. In your letter you mentioned designing soft furnishings with Mr Crace, even carpets, whatever next? You're so clever, Augustus.'

Pugin smiles, he doesn't want to talk about his work. He just wants to look into her emerald eyes. 'When shall we get married?' he whispers.

'After next Easter. Goodness gracious me, it will soon be 1848! Doesn't that sound exciting?'

'We're nearly half way through the century.'

'I wonder what 1848 has in store for us.'

'Only good things, I'll make sure the Grange is a beautiful home for you.'

Mr Aitchison is still staring at them. He recognises Helen now. His wife is a friend of her mother.

Saturday, 1ˢᵗ January 1848. It is twenty minutes to ten o'clock in the morning. Pugin is sitting at his desk, feeling content as he looks out over the grey English Channel. He reflects it has been a very happy Christmas at the Grange. The house has been full of children, guests, glowing hearths, and good cheer, but now he is keen for everything to be back to normal. Not only does he have a lot of work to do, he also has his wedding to plan.

The following months prove to be a difficult time for many people living in Great Britain. The economy is in recession following the collapse of overpriced railway bonds. The poor are going hungry. There are revolutions across Europe. Many ex-kings, including Louis-Philippe of France, get washed up on England's shores. Members of Parliament are constantly grumbling about the funds needed for the on-going building works at the Palace of Westminster. Charles Barry instructs Pugin to dismiss some of the men, which he does, reluctantly.

Pugin remains surprisingly jovial through all of this turmoil; life is ticking along pleasantly for him. His fiancé, Helen Lumsdaine, and preparations for their wedding, are a distraction from Charles Barry and the Palace of Westminster. Pugin's seemingly never-ending work for Lord Shrewsbury at Alton Towers is keeping him financially afloat.

Tuesday, 18th April 1848, a quarter past one in the afternoon; the week before Easter. Pugin is back in Mr Aitchison's shop, on Queen Street, in Edinburgh's New Town. He is sitting alone, in the dining area at the back of the store, finishing his last mouthful of delicious soup. Mr Aitchison is eyeing him suspiciously.

Pugin stares out of the window at the sunny gardens on the other side of the street. They are lush in their spring foliage. He is thinking about Helen and their wedding, which is only a few weeks away. He wonders how John Crace is getting on with Helen's dress, how

Hardman is progressing with her jewellery, and how Myers is getting on with the finishing touches to the Grange.

Pugin checks his pocket watch. It is time for him to make his way to the church. Helen is to be received into the Catholic Church today. Pugin has also been invited to attend the family reception afterwards. He feels very nervous about meeting Helen's staunchly Anglican family.

The following day Pugin steps off the train at Ramsgate railway station feeling downhearted. His spirit lifts a little when he sees Powell is there to meet him. The two men shake hands. 'Hello, Powell, are you here for me?'

'Yes, gaffer, I was in town and I saw the steam. I thought I'd check to see if you were on the train.'

'Is everything all right? Did the moulds get off to Birmingham?'

'Yes, Mr Pugin, they went off without any problems. Shall I carry your case?'

'Oh, thank you, Powell.'

'Has Miss Lumsdaine been received into the church? Did the service go well?'

Pugin rubs his chin. 'The service was very moving, Powell. Naturally, I'm overjoyed Helen has become a Catholic, but...'

'Is there something wrong?'

'Well, it was just the reception afterwards, come along, shall we walk home?'

They walk out of the station and head down the road towards the Grange and the sea. Powell is curious. 'So, what happened at the reception, Mr Pugin?'

Pugin stops walking and rubs his chin again. 'It was very strange, Powell. Nobody would talk to me. It was very awkward.'

'What, you mean they sent you to Coventry?'

'Yes, that's it. I've never met such rude people.'

Every day over the next two weeks Pugin sends Helen a letter. He receives no reply. He can feel it in the pit of his stomach, something is wrong. It is making him feel sick. He is worried about Helen. After two weeks, he decides to visit Mr Benson, his neighbour, who is Helen's uncle.

Pugin knocks on Mr Benson's door, loudly. A maid answers the door and shows him into the parlour. Mr Benson is a gentleman with rosy Kentish cheeks and bushy side burns. When he sees Pugin, his face drops. There is a troubled expression behind his whiskers. 'It's you is it, Mr Pugin?

'What's wrong, Mr Benson? What is it? Has anything happened to Helen, is she sick?'

'I have a letter for you, Mr Pugin.'

'A letter, you say? How long have you had it? Why didn't you give it to me?'

'Steady on now, steady on...' Mr Benson fetches the letter from a sideboard. He holds it with an outstretched arm, hesitantly, as if it might bite him. He presents it to Pugin, who rips it open. Pugin's lips move silently around the words of a single sentence. He reads it again with incredulity.

I will never, under any circumstances, unite myself in marriage with you, or see you, or receive any letter or communication from you again.

Pugin feels his legs are giving way beneath him. He collapses in a heap on the floor.

Tuesday, 20th June 1848. It is half past nine o'clock at night. The sun has set over the Kent countryside, leaving a burnt orange streak above the blue hills. Pugin is slumped over his drawing board in the studio at the Grange. He is reflecting upon the fact that he feels lonely. He has lost his mother, his father, Aunt Selina,

177

his first wife - Anne, his second wife - Louisa, Mary Amherst is in the convent, and now his fiancé, Helen, has left him.

Pugin spends much of the following week in his bed, feeling utterly dejected. He rants incessantly to Powell, and to anyone else that will listen, about the infelicitous behaviour of the Lumsdaine family. He decides to publish a pamphlet, to be sent to the wedding invitees, describing how Miss Lumsdaine has betrayed him.

Powell secretly gives John Crace a copy of this pamphlet, before it is published. Crace writes to Pugin the following day, making it very clear that such behaviour is unworthy of him. He also shows the pamphlet to George Myers.

Wednesday, 28th June 1848. It is a quarter past one o'clock in the afternoon. Myers is so concerned about the pamphlet, and about Pugin taking to his bed, that he has boarded the train from London to Ramsgate. It is all steam and whistles as the train pulls into Ramsgate railway station. Myers disembarks and he huffs and puffs under his own steam, all the way to the Grange. He leans against the front door with one hand, breathing heavily.

Miss Holmes, the governess, opens the door. 'Oh, good afternoon, Mr Myers, I don't think we're expecting you, are we? Mr Pugin is not receiving...'

Myers gently pushes Miss Holmes out of the way, 'Good afternoon to you ma'am.'

Powell is in the hallway. 'Can I help you, Mr Myers?'

Myers raises his hand in a stop sign. 'No thank you, young man.' He walks past Powell and climbs the stairs. Miss Holmes and Powell look at each other in disbelief. Myers knocks on Pugin's bedroom door, and enters. 'Sorry to burst in Mr P! How are we today?'

Pugin looks up with a start. He is lying on his bed in

his nightshirt, under the crucifix that is attached to the wall. He is composing another letter about Helen's betrayal. Even in his beleaguered state, Pugin has continued working. Papers and drawings cover his bed and the surrounding carpet. Stubble has grown on his face and he has shadows under his eyes. He puts his pen down. Myers stands for a moment with his hands on his hips, looking around the gracious room. The colours are blue and yellow. He snatches a glimpse out of the window at the stunning green sea under the blue sky. Having built the Grange, he is quite familiar with all of its rooms, but buildings take on a new life when they are occupied. He nods approvingly at his workmanship, and turns back to Pugin. 'Things are going awry at Saint George's without you being there, Mr P.'

'Oh...'

'It's our biggest church, the biggest Catholic church in London, so we should get it right. It's already been ten years in the making, Mr P, so let's finish it well. Mr Knill, on the committee wants a progress meeting with you and me, tomorrow. I think it's time to get back to work now.'

Pugin sits up and scratches the back of his head. His hair has been falling out since the catastrophe with Helen. He turns to Myers. 'Of course, I'll attend the meeting with Mr Knill. Let me get dressed now. I'll be down in a moment.'

'Right you are, Mr P.'

'Oh, George.'

'Yes?'

'Thank you, for coming over, I'm most grateful.'

Myers gives Pugin a wink and he leaves the room.

The following day Pugin and George Myers are sitting in a Hansom cab, driving through a district south of the River Thames, east of Lambeth. The driver pulls up beside Walworth House. It is a grand pile but needs a lick of paint. Pugin pays the cabby. Myers walks up the steps and rings the doorbell. A maid opens the door but she is quickly ushered out of the way by an attractive young lady, who looks as if she could have stepped out of a painting by Rossetti.

'Good afternoon, sir,' she says to Myers whilst staring at Pugin who is still chatting to the cabby.

When Pugin turns around he is immediately struck by the appearance of this young woman. He takes a moment to study her noble face. She has large, gentle brown eyes. He can see she is quite tall and has a good figure. Her complexion, like his, is quite dark. Myers notices the two of them are staring at each other. He speaks up. 'Hello, miss. I'm Mr Myers and this is Mr Pugin. Are you John Knill's daughter?'

'No, Mr Myers, I'm Jane, his niece,' she replies, and turns back to Pugin. Her smile is growing. Myers is speaking but Pugin can hardly hear him. His voice and the sounds of the street are falling into the distant background. Pugin's heartbeat is quickening, like a drum in his ears. He is mesmerised by the way that Jane's full lips are holding her smile. Her brown eyes are fixed on his grey eyes. Pupils are dilating. Now she is working her lips, words are gushing out, crashing down upon his ears like a breaking wave. Amongst the roaring, spray and froth, it is difficult for Pugin to discern their meaning. He knows they are important. His eyes narrow and he concentrates hard. Jane smiles again. Pugin feels he is coming up for air. He can breathe again. He looks down at the pavement for a second.

Jane discerns what Myers is saying. She takes a deep breath and turns to him. 'My mother and I have lived here with my uncle since Papa passed on. We are a large and happy family.'

'Oh, I'm sorry to hear that, my child. I mean about the death of your papa, not about you being a happy family,' replies Myers.

Jane is looking at Pugin again. She giggles and turns back to Myers. 'Thank you, sir.' She turns back to Pugin. He has had a good night's sleep and he has tidied himself up, so he looks quite dashing. Jane gives him another big smile. His heartbeat quickens. Now her lips are moving again. 'Are you the architect, sir?'

His throat is dry. 'Yes, miss, I'm Pugin.'

A man roars from deep within the house. 'Is that Pugin?'

Jane pops her head through the open doorway. 'Yes, uncle! I'm bringing him up to you!'

Pugin takes a step forward. He coughs. Now Jane takes a step forward and she is beside him. She whispers conspiratorially into his ear. 'Have you got a cough, sir?'

'No, miss.'

'I'm afraid he's a little grumpy today.'

Pugin can feel her breath. She is standing too close to him. His head is spinning. 'Who?' he asks, surprised by the high pitch of his own voice.

Jane looks curious, 'Why, my uncle, of course.'

Pugin pulls himself together. 'We'll cheer him up for you.'

Myers sighs. He can see what is happening.

Jane shows Pugin and Myers into the drawing room at the front of the house, at first floor level. Mr Knill, Jane's uncle, is a commanding figure. He stands in the middle of the room with his hands on his hips, staring at Pugin. He looks like a yeoman farmer. He prods Pugin with his large finger. 'Are you well, sir?'

'Quite recovered, thank you, Mr Knill.'

'The fourth day of July, Mr Pugin, that is going to be the grand opening for Saint George's is it not?'

'Indeed it is, Mr Knill. Please do not worry, sir. I will ensure everything is ready.'

Mr Knill nods his head and smiles with relief. He

pats Pugin hard on his shoulder, as a farmer might pat a young bull. Pugin has to hold onto the back of a chair to keep his feet. Jane catches Pugin's eye and they both start to giggle. Knill and Myers watch on, bemused. Jane is nearly twenty-three, thirteen years younger than Pugin.

Thursday, 10th August 1848. Pugin and Jane are the first couple to be married in Saint George's, Southwark. Jane looks resplendent in the dress made by John Crace and the jewellery made by Hardman, all to Pugin's designs. Jane has been told about Helen Lumsdaine, and she knows the dress and jewellery were initially intended for her.

The Shrewsburys have sent Edward, their blind harpist down. He is strumming away at the front of the church. Late arrivals are being ushered to their seats.

The Mintons, Craces, and Hardmans are all sitting on adjoining pews on the groom's side of the church. Herbert Minton leans forward, smiling, and he taps John Hardman on the shoulder. Hardman turns around and pushes Minton's excessive double cravats out of the way. Minton continues. 'Isn't this wonderful, John? I'm so pleased Pugin has found happiness at last.'

Hardman frowns. 'Yes, of course, but remember he only met Jane six weeks ago.'

Minton shrugs this off. 'They're a perfect match. Nothing will go wrong this time.'

Hardman whispers back. 'You're an old romantic. At least she's a Catholic, her whole family converted some years ago.'

'And do her family approve of our Mr P?'

Hardman nods, 'I believe so.'

'Where's George Myers? He only lives around the corner.'

'It's not like him to be late. I suppose the less distance you have to come the less time you give yourself to get ready. Ah, here he is, look. With his brood following like ducklings.'

Myers and his family have walked the short distance from their smart new home at Laurie Terrace. Myers gives a nod towards Hardman and Minton and then he squeezes himself into a pew towards the back of the church.

A peal of bells rings out jubilantly to celebrate the marriage of Augustus and Jane. On the street, in front of the church, children throw petals into the air, covering the newlyweds as they walk towards their sleek, black cabriolet carriage, pulled by two white horses.

Augustus and Jane chat as their carriage pulls off. They are headed to Walworth House, the home of Jane's uncle, Mr Knill, for their wedding breakfast.

'Oh, Mrs Pugin, we'll go on such adventures, together.'

'I can't wait for our honeymoon, Augustus. Five whole weeks together, such bliss!'

'Are you really happy to do a tour of the cathedrals, Mrs Pugin?'

'Of course, Mr Pugin!'

'We must pursue other pleasures too, Mrs Pugin. I've never asked you, do you like the opera?'

'Oh, Mr Pugin, I've never been to the opera.'

'Really? I can't believe I didn't know that. I will take you to Covent Garden.'

'That would be delightful!'

Jane's face suddenly drops. 'What's that commotion over there?'

'Don't look, darling, it's Bedlam. Look the other way, my sweet.'

Jane and Pugin do not look the other way. They see an unruly crowd pulling faces and throwing stones at the shaven-headed inmates who have been let out into the exercise yard. This mocking of the insane is a daily routine at Bedlam.

Sixteen

Tuesday, 29th August 1849. The sun is high over the Grange. Jane Pugin is sitting on a chair on the lawn at the front of the house, doing embroidery. A green parasol shields her from the sun. She has positioned herself to await her husband's return. Pugin has been in Ireland for several weeks, managing numerous building projects.

Jane rises to her feet and stretches her arms. She is heavily pregnant with Pugin's seventh child. She half closes her eyes and stares down the empty lane, a bend prevents her from seeing very far, but dust is rising. Soon there is the familiar sound of a pony trotting and a black Hansom cab comes into view. Jane keeps staring.

Charlotte, the family's middle-aged maid, drags her wide frame out of the kitchen. She wants to make sure Jane is comfortable. Charlotte stops for a moment, breathes in the fresh air, and wipes her calloused hands upon her apron. She has been baking and her hair is streaked with flour. Her eyes are bright. She looks up and smiles at the fields and the sea. She spots her mistress. 'Is everything all right, ma'am, would you like a cup of tea?'

'Oh, Charlotte!' replies Jane, 'tell the children a cab is coming. It might be their papa.'

'Very good ma'am! Anne is getting the little darlings dressed up.' Charlotte lifts her skirt above her ankles and waddles as fast as she can back towards the house. She is muttering to herself. 'His nibs is a great man, and no mistake, the little ones will be so pleased.'

'Is there a fire ma'am?'

Charlotte turns around and gasps open mouthed, when she sees the tanned and wizened face of Mr Mayman, the carpenter. Charlotte's eyelashes are fluttering. 'Oh, Mr Mayman, it's you!'

Mayman folds his arms and flashes a look at Charlotte's ankles.

Charlotte giggles. She is still holding her skirt up. 'Mr Mayman! You're shocking, sir! The master's approaching!'

Mayman's smile drops. 'What, is Mr Pugin back?'

'Yes, he's back from Ireland! Goodness knows what palaces and cathedrals he's been building for 'em.'

'I'll get the men ready. Good day to you ma'am.'

'And to you, Mr Mayman,' replies Charlotte with a wistful look.'

The cab pulls up. The door opens. Pugin steps out. He rushes over to Jane and gently embraces her. He greets his unborn child by kissing Jane's belly. The cabby deposits the luggage beside them and Pugin pays him the fare. Then Pugin sits on the chair and pulls Jane onto his knees. 'I've missed you so much.'

'Careful! I've missed you more.'

'Where are the children?'

'Anne is getting them dressed up for you. They'll be out in a minute.'

'Have they been well behaved?'

'Not all of them.'

Pugin pulls a face. 'Is it still Agnes?'

'All six children are very dear to me, Augustus, but, yes, Agnes has been difficult.'

'Things will be easier when she goes to school.'

'There's a house full in there, you know? It's not just the children'

'Oh, who else is in there?'

'Where shall I start? We've had several old sailors asking for alms. They say you always give them food and clothes.'

'Yes, darling, you know that's why the clothes trunk is in the hallway.'

Jane continues. 'There's Miss Greaves, apparently she's your old neighbour from Chelsea.'

Pugin cringes. 'Oh, dash it!' 'I'm sorry, she sent me a letter, I must have forgotten to give it to you. She was the children's nurse. She still likes to visit them.'

Jane looks concerned. 'So I gather,' she lowers her voice to a whisper, 'but how long will she stay?'

'She only ever stays a couple of nights, darling.'

'And Powell's mother is also in residence. Why is she here?'

'I told you in my letter from Ireland, dearest, didn't you read it? John Hardman thought she could help you get to grips with the household, especially as you haven't been very well. It's also nice for Powell to see his mamma.'

'Mmmm.'

'Isn't she a help?'

'Just seeing you is my greatest help, but we're hardly ever together.'

'Oh, come now, Jane, we had five weeks on our honeymoon, visiting all of the cathedrals.'

'That was last year.'

'I have to work, darling, to keep the roof over our heads.'

'I know, it's just that…'

'What is it?'

'I miss you.'

'I miss you, too, very much. I can't stand to be away from you and the children.'

Jane raises her eyebrows. 'I've just remembered something important. Do get up.'

They are both standing now. 'What is it?'

'Powell has something to tell you about the land. Mr Habershon has purchased the fields next door.'

'What? Matthew Habershon, that scrawny old architect?'

'Powell said Mr Habershon has put in plans with Mr Bing to build a terrace of houses, right up to our boundary, over there, next to Saint Augustine's. Powell thinks he wants to block access to the church, but why would he do that?'

Pugin's eyes tighten to narrow slits. 'He doesn't like Catholics. That old rascal's been after me for years. He's like the devil incarnate. I'll have to fight this!'

'Oh, don't speak like that, Augustus. Powell has got all of the details for you. Do speak to him, darling. Perhaps you should do so straight away.'

'Yes, I will, after I've kissed the children.'

There is a sudden commotion. The children come running out from around the corner. 'Look! Here they are!'

Anne, Pugin's eldest daughter, has got the children dressed up in their Sunday best to greet their father. She marches them out in a military line. After Anne there is Teddy, Agnes, Cuthbert, Catherine, and Mary. The line breaks as soon as the children see their papa. There are howls of joy. Pugin flings his arms around each of them in turn. After he has given each one a hug and a kiss he turns to Anne. 'How beautiful and grown up you are.' Now he turns to Teddy. 'Would you find Powell for me please, my boy, and tell him to come to my study, straight away.

'Yes, Papa.'

Pugin kisses Jane again. 'I'll see you as soon as I've spoken to Powell.'

Pugin makes his way into his study, which is full of the medieval carvings he has collected on his travels. A decorative wooden box sits on the edge of his desk. He opens it. It contains the death mask of Anne, his first wife and the mother of his first child. He gives a half

188

smile and closes it again.

Powell is standing outside the door.

'Come in!'

Before Powell enters he yelps. Anne has crept up behind him and she is tickling his ribs. 'Go away. I'm going in to see your father.'

'Are you going to ask him?'

'Yes.'

'Really?'

'Yes.'

'Give me a kiss.'

'No, go away.'

Pugin can hear something is going on. 'Come in, Powell!'

Powell enters. He is still blushing. 'Hello gaffer! How was your trip?'

'Ah, Powell, my boy, it's very good to see you.' They shake hands. 'I understand you have something important to tell me.'

'Oh, so you know do you?

'Yes, I've been told.'

'Did Anne tell you?'

'Anne? No, Jane told me.'

'Really?'

'Yes, really, well, spit it out then.'

'Oh, right, well, ah, you know that it is not good for man to be alone.'

Pugin furrows his brow, 'Yes.'

'And without love, we are nothing, isn't that right?'

'Do get to the point, Powell.'

'Well, I don't want to be, isolated, sir.'

'*Isolated?* We have to protect our views and the dignity of the church, don't we?'

'Of course, sir, that is why I want to do everything properly.'

'All right, what are the options?'

'Options? There is only one option, sir.'

'What's that?'

'A partnership, a holy union.'

'With Matthew Habershon? Are you out of your mind?'

Powell looks baffled. 'I don't want to marry Matthew Habershon.'

'What on earth are you talking about, Powell?'

'May I ask for Anne's hand in marriage, sir?'

Before Pugin can open his mouth, there is an almighty explosion.

'My God! What on earth was that?'

'Oh, no, the kiln!' cries Powell.

'What have you been doing with the kiln?'

Powell is already half way out of the door. As he rushes to the workshop he is praying there will not be too much damage. Pugin catches up with him. Powell is on his knees with his head in his hands. Pugin looks around the workshop, mouth agape. It is a scene of utter devastation. The kiln has split in two. White plaster covers the floor, walls, drawing boards, and hundreds of valuable mouldings. In fact, every surface is covered in it.

'Powell! What on earth have you done?'

'I was doing an experiment,' whimpers Powell.

'An experiment?'

'Please don't get angry.'

'But you've destroyed the workshop, what was the experiment?'

'Rather than making the casing for the mouldings in Birmingham, I thought we could have a go at making them here. I thought it would be quicker and cheaper.'

'*Quicker* and *cheaper*, have you gone mad?' Pugin runs his finger along the wall. The plaster has already set, hard. He scrapes at it with his fingernail. It will not budge. He can feel his blood pressure rising. 'You will be the utter ruination of me, Powell, the utter ruination!'

Seventeen

Friday, January 11th 1850. It is a quarter to four o'clock in the afternoon. Queen Victoria has been on the throne for nearly thirteen years and she has been married to Prince Albert, who is now officially called the Prince Consort, for ten years. The royal couple have both turned thirty. Discerning members of the Court, and fashionable society, have developed a taste for heritage and for the style of Pugin, but there is a new mood in the air. The old half-century is done. There is a desire for change.

The driver shakes the reigns and the horse quickens to a trot. Herbert Minton rubs his hands together for warmth. He is as richly decorated as one of his ornaments back in Stoke-on-Trent. He is dressed in a dark blue, silk waistcoat interwoven with a pink pattern. Around his neck are two cream coloured cravats. He pulls the collar up on his thick, black overcoat. Even within the carriage, his breath is visible in the cold air.

'Did you sell many Christmas cards this year, Henry?'

'Oh, yes, that enterprise is going very well, thank you,' replies Henry Cole. He is the well-known editor of the *Journal of Design*. He is in his early forties and his appearance is a little untidy. He wears a wrinkled, black business suit, and a thick grey overcoat.

'We had a thousand cards from you this year.'

Cole smiles and he scratches the back of his rather unkempt, long hair. 'I hope you find they're an effective way of engaging with your clients, they do spread good will.'

Minton pulls back the curtain so he can get a better look out of the cab window. They are descending down Madeira Walk, a steep cutting, with a rough stone faced wall to one side, and the flat, green sea to the other. 'We're nearly there now. It's hard to believe it, but Ramsgate's a jolly place in the summer, especially for the London day-trippers.'

Cole pulls back the curtain on his side of the cab. He frowns. 'It's not as genteel as I thought.'

'What were you expecting?'

'Oh, I don't know, something more like the Riviera.'

Minton laughs. 'Why did you think it would be like that?'

'Well, the great architect lives here doesn't he?'

'Oh, there's nothing genteel about Pugin.' Minton looks out of the window again. 'They're knocking up these guesthouses quickly, there's more of them every time I visit.'

Cole looks anxious. 'I don't know why, but I feel quite nervous about meeting him, now.'

'You've met him before haven't you?'

'Yes, but this is different, going into his house.'

'Oh, relax, Henry, you're in for a treat. Pugin is excellent company. Oh, by the way, he humbly apologised for cancelling on the previous occasions. It was due to his poor health.'

'I hope he's better.'

'I'm afraid he's often not very well, we'll have to be gentle with him.' Minton continues. 'The Grange is really quite special. I'm sure he'll give you a tour. The design of everything has come out of his head.'

'Perhaps it's being inside Pugin's head that is making me feel nervous. Is his family crest really on everything?'

Minton frowns. 'Not on *everything*. Actually, I think the two of you have a lot in common.'

'In what way?'

'How shall I put it? You shape public opinion.'

Cole seems to like that. He is smiling.

Minton continues. 'Pugin has mentioned you a few times, he likes your journal'

'Really?'

'Yes. He knows you respect him, even though you don't like his Catholicism. He respects you too.'

'That's good to hear. You're sure he's happy for me to accompany you on this visit?'

'Yes, of course, his reply to my last letter said you'd be most welcome for afternoon tea.'

'How long are you staying for?'

'A couple of nights, we've got a lot of business to get through.'

'Is it all to do with the Palace of Westminster?'

'Other projects too, but the top priority is to get the chamber of the House of Commons finished. Charles Barry changes his mind about the details every day. I find him difficult but I can't imagine what effect he has on Pugin.'

Cole is rubbing his hands together. 'Is it true that Barry won't speak to the ventilation engineer any more? Is that what's causing the delays?'

'That's right. Barry is taking legal action against him. I hope he doesn't do the same with us.'

Cole is pensive. There is one thing above all others that he wants to achieve on this visit. He cuts to the chase. 'So, Minton, do you think Pugin will agree to design a stand at the Great Exhibition?'

Minton does not respond. He is deep in thought.

Cole continues. 'It's an opportunity for him to present his ideas to the world.'

'I know, but try not to overwhelm him, Henry. Remember, he's been very ill. Look, here's the Grange now, do you see the tower through the trees?'

The Grange is brooding in the chill, north wind. It is

wearing the dark, English Channel as a shawl over its shoulders.

'Ah, it looks impressive, in a domestic kind of way,' replies Cole. 'I say, that terrace of houses has been built awfully close.'

'Matthew Habershon built them. He's a neighbour.'

'Good grief, I wouldn't want him as my neighbour.'

Charlotte, the maid, opens the front door to Herbert Minton and Henry Cole.

'Good afternoon, gentlemen, Mr Pugin is expecting you. May I take your overcoats?' she asks, discreetly wiping the flour off her hands. Minton and Cole pile their coats and hats onto Charlotte's outstretched arms. Like a beast of burden, she is now hidden beneath their garments.

The eyes of Henry Cole are darting around the reception hall. He is drinking in the colours and the architectural detailing.

Unable to see where she is going, Charlotte walks into a doorframe, but she is well padded and unhurt.

'My dear, lady, let me help you with those coats,' intercedes Minton.

'Oh, you're a kind soul, sir.'

Minton removes the coats and hats from Charlotte's outstretched arm, revealing her flushed face. 'Oh, there you are, Mr Minton!' Her smile suddenly drops and she furrows her brow. 'Oh, sir, isn't it dreadful, all the children starving to death in Ireland?'

Minton is taken aback by her candour. 'Yes, the potato blight is indeed dreadful.'

Charlotte continues, in a whisper. 'Mr Pugin says the gentry's horses are well fed over there. He says it's scandalous, sir, *scandalous!* Millions dead or they've fled for America. You'll not catch me in one of those ships, pack them in like slaves they do, sir.' She looks at the coats. 'Just put them down on the clothes chest for now, Mr Minton.'

Charlotte takes a deep breath and she shows them into the drawing room. The crackling fire, the warm colours, and the stained glass windows, are all comforting and homely. Charlotte puffs up the cushions on the red settee. 'Do take a seat, gentlemen.' With a kind smile, she stuffs a cushion behind the back of Minton as he sits down. 'Mr Pugin's so busy rebuilding Parliament, God bless him, but as I say, he is expecting you.'

After a couple of minutes of listening to Charlotte's anecdotes about the greatness of Pugin, Minton and Cole are relieved when the man himself enters. Pugin is dressed in his untidy black smock and he looks pale.

'That will be all, thank you, Charlotte.'

Charlotte blushes and gives a little curtsy, 'Very good, sir.' Before she leaves the room she reaches out to touch Pugin's arm, but pulls herself back.

Pugin turns to Minton. He greets him effusively. 'Happy New Year to you, my friend. How are you, my dear fellow?'

'All the better for seeing you, Pugin. You've lost a lot of weight, sir. You're not fully recovered are you?'

'I'm a lot better than I was. Now, doesn't 1850 sound impressive?'

'It certainly does, it certainly does.'

'Before I forget, thank you for our splendid Christmas card.'

Pugin turns to Henry Cole. They shake hands. 'I'm delighted to meet you again, Mr Cole, a Happy New Year to you.'

'And a Happy New Year to you too, sir. I'm very impressed with your splendid house.'

'Would you like a tour, perhaps after our tea?'

'I would like that very much, indeed.'

'Very well, please do sit down gentlemen.'

There is a knock on the door. 'Come in,' yells Pugin.

Charlotte pops her head through the door and stares in, wide-eyed. 'I have the tea, sir!'

'Ah, very good, do bring it in, Charlotte.'

Charlotte bends down and picks the tray off a side table. She has difficulty straightening up.'

'Are you all right, my dear lady?' asks Minton rising to his feet; he takes the tray from her.

'Oh, it's just my back, sir. It'll come right in a minute.'

The doorbell rings. The voice of Miss Holmes, the governess, is heard from the hallway. 'I have it!'

Charlotte is clutching her back. 'If only someone would massage it for me.' Minton and Cole exchange a worried look. 'Here let me have a go,' says Pugin and he massages Charlotte's shoulders for a few seconds. 'That's better already,' says Charlotte, straightening up. 'I swear you do have healing hands, Mr Pugin!'

Pugin looks slightly embarrassed, 'That'll be all then, thank you, Charlotte. I will serve the tea. As Charlotte leaves the room, Miss Holmes is talking to an old sailor at the front door.

The three men sit together drinking tea from exquisite Minton china. Minton himself sits on the edge of his armchair. He sips his tea and crosses his legs. Cole appears to be quite relaxed. He looks at Minton. 'Should I tell Mr Pugin about Paris now, Herbert?'

'Yes, of course, Henry.'

'Paris, Mr Cole?' asks Pugin, leaning forward. 'What do you need to tell me about Paris?'

'Well, sir, you probably know that Herbert and I attended the Paris Exhibition last year.'

'Ah, yes, I would have gone myself, if it wasn't for the Palace of Westminster. How was it?'

'It was very impressive, but we believe we can go a step further, with an international exhibition, in London.'

'Oh, you said *we*, who's *we*?'

'Well, a few members of the Society of Arts had a meeting with Prince Albert at Buckingham Palace, just before Christmas. The Prince is keen to host a festival such as the world has never seen. So, *we* is Prince Albert and the Society of Arts, but a Royal Commission is also planned.'

Pugin nods sagely, 'I see.'

Minton places his cup and saucer down. 'Henry is being rather modest, Pugin. He is the one that's going to be directing this new exhibition. It's all going to happen very quickly.'

'Oh, right.'

Henry Cole interrupts. 'Prince Albert said he'd mentioned it to you, Mr Pugin.'

'Yes, he did mention something to me, very briefly, when we met in the House of Lords. His idea was to celebrate British manufacturing and to integrate design and industry. I think he referred to it as the Great Exhibition.'

'That's it. We'd like you to design one of the stands, Mr Pugin, in fact we'd like you to design the main stand.'

'Me? But, Mr Cole, I'm not an industrialist.'

'Oh, I disagree. You design the total environment, you make it and you sell it in the shops, things that people want, that's all very impressive, sir.'

'Forgive me, Mr Cole, but I didn't think my Christian designs were to your taste.'

'I recognise quality when I see it, Mr Pugin. You craft things, beautifully, whether it's a paperweight or a cathedral.'

'Thank you.'

'I hear your son, Edward, is working with you now.'

'Yes, Teddy's part of the team, he's close to sixteen now.'

'And you have a young apprentice, John Hardman's nephew isn't it?'

'Yes, Powell, he's doing tolerably well. He's a good lad.'

Cole smiles. 'And how is the House of Commons progressing?'

'Oh, it's all consuming,' he turns to Minton and frowns. Minton pulls a face back at him.

Cole interjects, 'It'll all be finished soon won't it?'

'By the grace of God the Commons will soon be finished, but the Palace of Westminster is more than the Commons, the project will go on, and on.'

'But, surely you'll need a fresh challenge. Will you at least consider designing the main stand for the Great Exhibition?'

Pugin scratches his head. 'I'll certainly think about it.'

Cole is disappointed with Pugin's reticence. 'I think it'll be a great opportunity for you, Mr Pugin.'

Minton raises his hand to stop Cole from going on. He knows the best way to get Pugin on board. 'If you were going to design a stand, Pugin, how would you do it?'

'Well, I'd present all of our work in an integrated way. Your tiles, Hardman's metal work and glass, Crace's furnishings, and Myers' carpentry and stone masonry.'

Minton responds with another question. 'When you say you'd present it in an integrated way, how would you do that?'

'Well, perhaps I'd recreate a medieval court, to show how we can make everything today just as well as our forebears did, but more efficiently and at a fraction of the cost.'

Cole claps his hands. 'That's exactly what we want.'

Pugin appears to be coming around to the idea. 'Would we have to submit our designs for approval?'

'Yes, but it'd just be rubber stamping, by a board of leading figures.'

Pugin senses that Cole is withholding something. He pushes further. 'Who is the chairman of the board?'

'The chairman?'

'Yes, the chairman.'

'It's Charles Barry.'

Pugin rolls his eyes. The idea of submitting more drawings to Charles Barry is the last thing he needs. 'Well, as I say, Mr Cole. I'll think about it.'

'I will ensure you have the prime site.'

Pugin nods but he isn't going to commit himself. He rises to his feet. 'Now, would you like to have a tour of the Grange, Mr Cole? I suggest we start next door with our church, Saint Augustine's. It's very nearly finished.'

Cole and Minton are on their feet. They all step out into the hallway. Pugin continues to address Cole. 'My faith underpins everything I do, Mr Cole.'

'Everything?'

'Yes, everything. Now, you'll need to put your coats on'

Minton is standing next to the clothes chest, looking perplexed. Cole's grey coat is where he left it, but his own black overcoat has gone. He turns around and sees the gaunt figure of Miss Holmes standing beside him, with her hand to her mouth. She looks mortified. 'Oh, sir, was that your black overcoat?'

'Yes.'

'There's been a terrible mistake, sir. I've given it to Bobby, the old sailor,' she turns to Pugin, with panic in her eyes.

'Stay calm, Miss Holmes, we can get it back off Bobby,' replies Pugin. He turns to Minton. 'Bobby sleeps at the back of the church.'

'Never mind, Bobby can keep the coat, really, let him keep it,' says Minton, genially.

Monday, 21st October 1850. It is nearly one o'clock in the afternoon. The sun sparkles upon the open casement window. The only sound is the rustling of autumn leaves. Jane Pugin stands in front of a full-length bedroom mirror, dressed in a stunning pale lilac gown. Pugin pads along the landing carpet and he enters the bedroom. He walks up behind Jane, holds her waist and kisses her neck. 'You look absolutely beautiful, my darling. How are you feeling?'

'I'm fine, Augustus. I'm really looking forward to today. Let me go now. How are you feeling?'

'I've had another cold bath. I've taken my medicine. I just hope the sweating will stop.'

'You must stop working so hard. You worked seventeen hours yesterday. The doctors told you to rest.'

'I'll die if I rest.'

'Don't talk like that please, Augustus. There are several ironed shirts in the wardrobe, in case you need to change. How's your throat?'

'Sore. I just hope I don't cry. Anne may be eighteen but she's still my little baby.'

Jane turns around and strokes his face. 'I know she's your baby. You're going to be fine. We're all going to be all right.'

He kisses her on the lips. 'You've been a wonderful stepmother, Jane. You know Anne loves you, don't you?'

Jane smiles and moves away so she can put on her jewellery. 'Yes, I do know that. I love her too. I love all of the children, hard work though they are. I even love Powell, in a way.'

'Powell has got to buck his ideas up. Have you heard what he's done now?'

'No, what?'

'I wasn't going to tell you.'

'Go, on, it's best I know everything.'

'Well, when we go into Saint Augustine's, be prepared for a shock.'

'Come on, tell me.'

'He's made a mix up with fabric orders. The golden silk fabric that was supposed to be used for the altar canopy has instead been used for Powell's cushions at 3 Southwood Terrace. The fabric for his cushions, with those garish flowers, has been used for the altar canopy."

'Oh, no, really?

'Yes.'

'So, Powell's cushion fabric is actually now in the church?'

'Yes, great reams of it. I was absolutely furious.'

Jane starts laughing, she bends over, she can't stop. She catches her breath. 'Oh, it'll be all right, it'll be pretty. Poor Powell! He's had a lot on his mind.' Jane stands up straight and places her hands on her hips. 'He was so upset when that no popery graffiti was daubed on their new house. It really was shocking.'

'Yes, I know, poor Powell. He only has his mamma and John Hardman attending today. No other family is coming.'

'Mrs Powell is a very loyal mother.'

'Oh, that reminds me, I think Father John has been drinking.'

'What? Again?'

'You can smell it on his breath. I think he takes the communion wine to steady his nerves. This is our first wedding in Saint Augustine's. I wanted it to be perfect for Anne.

'Don't worry, Augustus, dear. Anne and Powell are going to have a wonderful day, even if Father John is overly merry.'

Eighty miles away in Kensington, a servant opens the garden doors in the dining room at Holland House. A roar of laughter travels over the manicured lawns and reaches the delicate ears of Lady Holland and her guest, Lady Frances, the wife of the Prime Minister.

Lady Holland frowns. 'Shall we go for a walk in the woods, dear?'

They walk off together, arm in arm, in their wide-brimmed hats, decorated with flowers.

Inside the dining room the men are finishing off their dessert, apple pie and custard. Most of them are members of the Great Exhibition Royal Commission. Sitting next to Lord Holland is Lord John Russell, the Prime Minister. Beside him are Lord Shrewsbury and Henry Cole. There are nineteen men in total gathered for this business lunch. At the other end of the table sits Charles Barry. He is drinking his third glass of wine. Sitting next to him is the architect, Matthew Habershon. A waiter goes to top up Barry's glass but he raises a hand to stop him. 'No more for me, thank you. I have to go back to work, later on.'

Habershon nods with approval. 'I commend you for your discipline, Charles, and congratulations on being awarded the gold medal from the Institute. I understand Prince Albert is delighted with the House of Lords. The Palace of Westminster is coming along splendidly.'

Barry draws on his cigar and slowly exhales. 'That's very kind of you, Matthew. Thank you. We mustn't forget all of the contractors too. They have all worked very hard, apart from that bloody ventilation engineer. Of course, there is still a great deal of work to be done. We must forget young Pugin.'

'Did you mean to say we *mustn't* forget Pugin?'

'That's what I said, didn't I?'

Habershon lowers his voice to a whisper. 'Well, you know my concerns about the Catholic Church, Charles. I can't believe the Pope has made Wiseman the Cardinal Archbishop of Westminster. Apparently, Her Majesty asked the Prime Minister if she was still the

Queen of England. I've done my little bit...'

'What do you mean?'

'I've helped Mr Bing to block in Pugin's new Catholic church in Ramsgate.'

Barry looks Habershon in the eye. 'Is that really necessary? Don't be too hard on Pugin. He is headstrong, but his heart's in the right place, and he is talented. He's not unlike you in his religious zeal, even if he is on the other side.'

Habershon seems a bit put out. He scratches the back of his head. 'Rome is Babylon, Charles.'

Barry winces, 'Why are you religious chaps always so extreme?'

Habershon continues, unabashed. 'Have you heard that Henry Cole is going to give Pugin the best pitch in the Great Exhibition?'

Barry frowns. 'No, I haven't heard that. What else do you know?'

'Pugin's got John Hardman doing all of the negotiations for him.'

'Oh, I know Hardman, he does the glass for us at Westminster. Do you know what Pugin's planning to exhibit?'

'I do and I'm very concerned about it. Henry Cole has given Pugin a special dispensation. He's going to be allowed to show off the full range of his work. His stand is going to be called the Medieval Court, or some such nonsense. I wouldn't be surprised if it was a Catholic chapel. Pugin will be designing everything, from jewellery to carpets.'

Barry looks worried. 'I've enough trouble getting drawings out of Pugin as it is. The last thing I need is for him and Hardman to be distracted by the Great Exhibition.'

Habershon nods and his eyes narrow. 'Why does Henry Cole show Pugin such favour? Do they think he's the only one to have a coherent theory of design?

Is he the only one to make a connection between design and manufacturing? I think it's a great insult to you, Charles.'

'Well, there's nothing I can do about it.'

'You don't have to take it lying down. Don't let Pugin steal the world's biggest show from under your nose. Remember, he's your assistant.'

Barry nods thoughtfully. 'What do you suggest?'

'Apparently, Pugin wants to suspend a giant crucifix above his stand. It will make his pitch the most visually prominent in the hall. I'm convinced it's going to be a Catholic chapel. We need to talk to the Prime Minister.'

'No, better still, we'll get a Bishop to talk to the Prime Minister.'

'Oh, yes, that's better. There's one other thing.'

'What's that?'

'You're on the awards committee aren't you?'

'Yes, I'm the chairman.'

'Make sure there are no awards for designers, just for manufacturers, and only let manufacturers have their names displayed on the stands. I don't see why Pugin's name should be on any plaques. I think that's only fair since you've been excluded.'

Eighteen

Friday, 28th March 1851. The morning sun rises above trees in Hyde Park and glitters upon a magical palace that has appeared almost overnight, upon a sea of green grass. Amongst the waves of sightseers is William Morris, a young teenager, who is now busy sketching the Crystal Palace. He rises to his feet and stands open-mouthed as an elephant, the gift of an Indian prince, plods over the dewy lawn. It is carrying a small, brown man upon its shoulders and it is waving its trunk in the air. Morris leaves his drawing and rushes over to inspect the enormous round footprints left in the soft earth.

There are thirty-three days to go before the grand opening of the Crystal Palace. The vast structure is still covered in scaffolding. Hundreds of police officers are on duty. Inside the Crystal Palace, there are already thousands of things to see. The world's new manufacturing and artistic innovations have been gathered in one place. There are machines, fashionable clothes, carriages, sculptures, plants, pottery, heaters and coolers. It is a bizarre and wonderful amalgamation.

Many exhibitors from around the world are assembling their stands under national flags that hang down from the soaring, vaulted roof.

Over two thousand builders and decorators should be at work, but they have gone on strike. Whistles are being blown in different parts of the site. It is a sign for the exhibitors to stop what they are doing. Queen

Victoria and Prince Albert will soon enter.

At the far end of the structure, in a small office, Henry Cole sits at a desk, holding his head in his hands. He is dressed in a morning suit. He takes a deep breath and runs his hands through his thick, untidy, grey hair.

His assistant enters. 'There's quite a crowd waiting for you out there. The royal couple have probably left Buckingham Palace now. Did you hear the whistles? The Prime Minister is already here.'

'Right! Where is he? I mean the Prime Minister?'

'He's at the Medieval Court. Mr Pugin's haranguing him.'

'Will you go and rescue him, please? Ask him to meet me at the front entrance. We should both be there to greet Her Majesty. I must go!'

Henry Cole steps out of his office and he finds a huddle of angry foreign exhibitors is waiting for him.

'Mr Cole! I have been waiting for you all morning!' says a Spanish diplomat.

'My space is far too small!' says another.

'My space is too dark!'

'Nobody can find my space!'

Cole raises his hand. 'Not now, gentlemen! The Queen is about to arrive! Didn't you hear the whistles?'

'What! Queen Victoria is here?'

'Yes! Please return to your stands, immediately!'

At the Medieval Court, the Prime Minister, Lord John Russell, stares up at the great crucifix. Standing beside him is Pugin, Hardman, and Minton. George Myers, the master builder, is sitting beside the podium finishing off a steak and kidney pudding. He is also looking up at the crucifix. It was his men that erected it, a little higher than Pugin instructed.

The Medieval Court displays a wide range of Pugin's Gothic designs. It includes wallpaper, vestments, stained glass, carpets, curtains, ceramics, jewellery, chandeliers from Alton Towers, a memorial sculpture for Bishop Walsh, and an even grander monument that is over thirty feet tall. It is the first time such a dazzling display of interior design and architecture has been integrated together at an exhibition. Journalists from New York and Paris have already visited and written articles about it. It is being described as a vision, not just for the house of God, but also for the domestic setting.

The exhibits did not look quite right seen against the glass of the Crystal Palace, so Pugin has brought a team of sailors up from Ramsgate. They have erected canvas screens, like sails, to provide an appropriate backdrop. A couple of them are still up in the rigging. 'Get those men down now, please, Mr Myers!' instructs Pugin, sounding like a sea captain.

'Very good, Mr P,' mumbles Myers, swallowing the remains of his pie.

Behind the sails, Powell is getting annoyed with a small man dressed in a top hat and tails; he also has a monocle. Powell's heartbeat quickens. 'Look, sir, here is the boundary, your equipment has crossed into our area!'

The small man tuts and rolls his eyes.

Powell raises his voice. 'Well, if you won't move it, I'll move it for you.'

There is no response. Powell grabs hold of the man's machine and shoves it back over the line. Powell's face lights up with a triumphant smile. He wipes his forehead leaving behind black oily smears.

The Prime Minister cringes. 'It's just too high up, Mr Pugin. You don't want it to dominate the whole exhibition do you? It's even higher than the national flags.'

Pugin maintains a poker face. Now Hardman interjects, raising another subject that is bothering him. 'Do you see here on the podium, Prime Minister?' They have put my name, and the names of our colleagues, Mr Myers, Mr Crace, and Mr Minton, but they say Mr Pugin cannot be included because he's not a manufacturer. Isn't that nonsense? He has designed everything!'

To everyone's surprise, Queen Victoria and Prince Albert have arrived early. This is an unofficial visit, to check on progress, but even so there is protocol to follow. The royal couple are now making their own way down the main aisle. The Queen floats along in a blue chiffon dress. She is delighted by what she sees. She holds onto Prince Albert's arm and points at one of the mature trees that stands within the Crystal Palace.

'Look, dear. There's your Prime Minister. He's speaking to Mr Pugin,' says Prince Albert.

'Oh, shall we hide,' whispers the Queen, with a giggle. She continues. 'I must see Mr Pugin's jewellery, before I see anything else.'

'Well, there is the Medieval Court. That's where you'll find all of Mr Pugin's work.'

'Good gracious, Albert, I never imagined it would be so spectacular, look at the height of that monument. I feel as if I'm stepping into the court of Elizabeth I.' The Queen begins to inspect Pugin's work.

Henry Cole arrives at the front door of the Crystal Palace, breathless. He looks bewildered. He turns to a police officer.

'Where has everyone gone?'

The police officer speaks imperiously. 'Her Majesty is within the building, sir. If you can call it a building.'

'Oh, my, Lord! Which way did they go?'

'I think there was mention of the Medieval Court, sir.'

Cole rushes off to find them.

Lord John Russell raises a hand to stop John Hardman from rambling on. The Prime Minister can hear a familiar female laugh, coming from behind the

Bishop Walsh memorial. He takes a few steps and peeps around the sculpture. He gasps when he sees Queen Victoria is joking with a grimy faced young man from Birmingham.

'And are you married, Mr Powell?'

'Yes ma'am, I'm expecting a baby too.'

The Queen laughs out loud. 'I see and is this your first?'

'Yes ma'am, Mr Pugin's expecting another one too.'

'Well, children are such a blessing, Mr Powell. I have seven.' The Queen leans forward to admire a piece of stained glass. 'Who designed this beautiful window?'

'I did ma'am.'

'You're very talented, Mr Powell. Did you design the new stained glass windows for Parliament?'

'I helped, ma'am. I'm Mr Pugin's apprentice. His one and only apprentice I should add, ma'am.'

'Prince Albert should meet you.' The Queen glances around to find her husband. The Prime Minister catches her eye. 'Ma'am, I do humbly apologise, I missed your arrival.'

'Oh, don't worry Prime Minister, this is an informal visit.'

Pugin, Hardman, and Minton, are still standing on the other side of the Gothic monument, looking up at the crucifix. Now the Queen is looking up at it too.

'Don't worry ma'am, they're going to lower it, beneath the flags,' says the Prime Minister.

'Oh, what a pity, the cross is the secret of Britain's success, Prime Minister.'

Lord John Russell scratches his head. 'Ah, yes, quite, ma'am.'

The Queen joins Prince Albert who is reading the information on the podium. All heads turn to follow the progress of Her Majesty. The Prime Minister follows her like a shadow.

The Queen and Prince Albert approach Pugin,

Hardman, and Myers. The three men stand to attention. They look like three soldiers, bobbing up and down, giving little bows every time the Queen looks their way. Prince Albert shakes Pugin's hand. 'It's very good to see you again, Mr Pugin, but why isn't your name on the podium? Didn't you design all of this?'

'It's very good to see you again, your Royal Highness.' Pugin bows and then he turns to the Prime Minister. 'I think my name is going to be added, isn't it?'

Henry Cole arrives, breathless. He bows towards the Queen and then to Prince Albert. The Queen is distracted by the glimmer of rubies and she goes to investigate. The Prime Minister turns to Henry Cole. 'Ah, Mr Cole, you've arrived, at last. Will you make sure Mr Pugin's name is added to his podium?' He adds, surreptitiously, 'After his crucifix is lowered.'

Cole is perspiring. 'Yes, of course.'

Prince Albert narrows his eyes and he turns to Cole. 'Will everything be ready for the May Day opening ceremony, Mr Cole? We are most concerned about this strike.'

Cole grits his teeth. 'Yes, sir, everything will be ready,'

'When Her Majesty takes her seat, will the choir be singing the *Hallelujah Chorus* from Handel's *Messiah*?'

'Yes, of course, sir, all as agreed.'

'Excellent. How big do you think the crowd will be?'

'The police expect 300,000, sir.'

Prince Albert nods approvingly. He turns back to Lord John Russell. 'It's going to be a moment in history isn't it, Prime Minister?'

'Without a doubt, sir.'

The Prince turns to Pugin. 'Do you think this international exhibition will mark a new era, Mr Pugin, with the nations coming together?'

Pugin looks thoughtful. 'A new era, sir?'

Lord John Russell is wearing a face of calm endurance. 'Excuse me please, gentlemen, I should accompany Her Majesty.'

Pugin looks Prince Albert in the eye. 'If it's a new era, sir, I'd say it's one of social conscience, and you have helped to usher it in.'

'How do you mean, *social conscience*?'

'You have insisted that this exhibition is open to everyone, rich and poor, and that public facilities be provided for their comfort. That is a significant advancement, sir, and you have made it possible.'

Prince Albert smiles warmly. 'You are very kind. I hope you don't mind me asking, Mr Pugin, but how is your health? You seem to have lost a lot of weight.'

'I'll pull through, sir, thank you for asking.'

Myers suddenly interjects, wagging his finger at Pugin. 'I've told you, Mr P, you need to eat continually, throughout the day.' He bows to Prince Albert. 'Begging you pardon, Highness.'

The Prince turns back to Pugin. 'I admire your Medieval Court, very much. Your work shows how the industrial revolution can be about truth and beauty, not just mass production. I have an idea to take this vision forward.'

Nineteen

Tuesday, 7th October 1851, it is a quarter past eleven o'clock in the morning. Winter has arrived early and there is thick, grey cloud over London. A stooped figure, wrapped in a black cape makes his way through the gates of Buckingham Palace.

Pugin looks like a medieval monk. He has been very ill and he is finding it difficult to stay awake. Jane has also been ill and is too weak to breast-feed their new baby boy, Edmund.

Somehow, in his weakened condition, Pugin has managed to drag himself to London from Ramsgate. His attendance is required by royal command. A very polite equerry, dressed in red and gold military uniform, meets Pugin in the inner courtyard. He escorts him up several flights of steps and then they are walking along a wide, picture gallery. There is a clerestory window that runs above the walls, for the length of the gallery. Below are heavy, ornate cornices, dripping with gold. The window provides a perfect down light for the display of the enormous paintings, most of them by Dutch masters.

The thick, crimson carpet gives way beneath Pugin's feet. He keeps his eyes down. The Palace is not to his taste. In fact, he considers Nash's creation to be a monstrosity. A footman opens a door and the equerry shows Pugin into a large, elegant room, with French windows overlooking the golden-brown trees of Saint James' Park. A large white marble chimney-piece contains a crackling fire.

On the wall above the fireplace is a stunning watercolour by Turner. Set within the wide, gilt frame is a yacht, riding the crest of a wave in a gale. Pugin recognises the Kent coastline. He can't take his eyes off this painting. Turner has used washes of paint to capture the raw power of sea, sky, and sunlight. Pugin is captivated. He would love to be sailing in that yacht.

In front of the fireplace is a luxurious, hand-woven rug. Ornate patterns of green foliage radiate out from the middle of it. Hanging down from the ceiling above the rug is a crystal chandelier with all the colours of the rainbow flickering about it. Either side of the fireplace, facing each other, are two green settees. Ensconced between pink cushions is Henry Cole. Two men are sitting opposite him. Richard Redgrave is a talented artist, in his late forties. He is on friendly terms with Pugin. He is one of Henry Cole's best friends and they have championed design reform together. The other man, Owen Jones, is an architect, a few years younger than Redgrave. He was the superintendent of works for the Great Exhibition. He is also a friendly acquaintance of Pugin.

Henry Cole rises to his feet and walks over to shake Pugin's hand. 'It's a wonderful painting isn't it, Mr Pugin?'

'Hello, Mr Cole, yes, it's splendid.'

The door opens again. Prince Albert enters, alone. He is wearing a tailored grey suit and a long black jacket. All the men now stand to attention. 'Are you admiring the painting, gentlemen?'

Henry Cole answers first. 'Yes, your Royal Highness, Turner is a fine, modern artist isn't he?'

'Indeed, Mr Cole, but have you heard the sad news?'

'No, sir, what's happened?'

'I'm afraid Mr Turner is dangerously ill.'

All of the men look genuinely concerned. Pugin steadies himself, placing a hand on the back of the seat.

He turns to Prince Albert. 'I'm very sorry to hear that, sir.' For a moment both men stare at each other. On the few occasions they have met, they seem to connect in some unspoken way. Perhaps it is their radicalism that gives them some affinity; their common cause for social justice, or today it might just be their sadness at the illness of a remarkable artist. In spite of their successes, Prince Albert and Pugin both feel like outsiders. Many parliamentarians frown upon the fact that the Prince is German, and Pugin, the son of French émigré, is not of the pedigree they would seek for an architect working on the Palace of Westminster.

Prince Albert's once handsome face has become slightly bloated. His hair has receded, revealing a high forehead. He has very long, bushy sideburns, which are not as stylish as they used to be. The Great Exhibition has placed a great strain upon him. He looks tired. He manages to raise a smile and Pugin recalls the youthful vigour he admired when they first met, ten years ago, almost to the day.

Prince Albert holds onto Pugin's hand after he has shaken it, as if he is giving him a transfusion. 'It's very good to see you again, Mr Pugin. I seem to have put on all the weight that you have lost.'

Pugin laughs out loud. He is beginning to revive. The Prince turns to the others and gestures towards the settees. 'Gentlemen, please do sit down.' Pugin sits beside Henry Cole. The Prince remains on his feet and he positions himself in front of the fire. He speaks in an engaging tone and most of the time he is looking at Pugin. 'So, gentlemen, the Great Exhibition is now closed, but we must ensure its spirit lives on. You may have heard Mr Cole is planning a new campus in South Kensington, which will include a national industrial museum.'

'I did hear about that, sir, but what will be in it?'

'It will show exhibits that integrate art with industry,

Mr Redgrave. It will include the finest exhibits from the Great Exhibition.' The Prince turns to Cole, looking for support. Cole picks up the thread. 'The South Kensington campus will also include a new school of art. It will become a cultural centre.'

'Thank you, Mr Cole, now, I would like you gentlemen to form a committee to decide which items from the Great Exhibition should go into the new museum.'

For a moment there is stunned silence. Richard Redgrave turns to the others to gauge their response. They are all nodding. 'Thank you, your Royal Highness, that is a great honour for us all, I'm sure.'

'May I ask, sir, is there a budget to acquire this collection?' asks Pugin, bracing himself for a negative answer.

'Yes, Mr Pugin, the Great Exhibition made a healthy profit under the direction of Mr Cole, so there is a budget.' Prince Albert turns to Cole again. 'Could you remind us of the budget, Mr Cole?'

'Yes, sir, it is £20,000.'

Prince Albert turns back to Pugin. 'Will that be sufficient?'

Pugin nearly chokes. 'Oh, yes, sir, quite sufficient.'

'The Queen and I were very impressed with your Medieval Court, Mr Pugin. It demonstrates a relationship between art and manufactured goods, and that is what South Kensington will be all about.' He turns to Cole, 'Is there anything else you'd like to add?'

'Well, I don't want to be presumptuous, sir, but I expect a significant part of the budget will be used to acquire the items designed by Mr Pugin. He seems to have reformed the nation's taste, almost singlehandedly.'

'Quite, so,' adds Prince Albert. 'It was quite wrong that you didn't win a prize at the Great Exhibition, Mr Pugin. I noted that all of your team won, individually.'

Everyone turns to Henry Cole, who shrugs his shoulders. 'I didn't write the rules.'

'Who did?' asks Redgrave.

Prince Albert looks at his pocket watch. 'Oh, would you please excuse me now, gentlemen? I have a meeting to attend with the Prime Minister. Today we're trying to reform housing for the poor.'

Twenty

Thursday, 5th February 1852. The English saints are luminous red, blue and green in the stained glass top lights within the drawing room bay window. Through the clear glass there is a vision of the morning sunshine dancing upon the sea.

Pugin and Jane were up early for prayers and breakfast. Now Pugin is sipping coffee, in his favourite green armchair. Something is not right though. It is the calm before the storm.

Pugin's heath has deteriorated. When he visited Hardman in Birmingham a few days ago, he collapsed. Hardman had to bring him all the way back to Ramsgate. Pugin is now under doctor's orders not to leave the house. He has had a bad night with terrifying dreams, and a vision from the Book of Revelation. Jane sits on the edge of the red settee, surrounded by newspapers. 'It's two days since the Queen opened the House of Commons and I've read every newspaper, all the way through. I'm sorry, darling, but your name isn't mentioned, not once.' Now she whispers and points up at the ceiling. 'He's done it again. It's as if you don't exist.'

Pugin is also whispering. 'Don't worry, Jane. Great men do away with their affiliates when a project nears completion. I'm fortunate not to have been dismissed. You didn't really want to go to the opening, did you?'

Jane takes a deep breath. She places the newspaper on the floor, and rises to her full height. 'You're a great man, Augustus, and yet he pays you £2 a week. This cannot go on. You're not well and you told me you owe George Myers money.'

Pugin raises one hand for Jane to stop. With the other hand he cups his ear. 'He's coming down.'

The drawing room door is ajar. The floorboards on the stairs creak as a large body descends. The door opens. A deep, male voice roars. 'Ah, there you both are! Good morning. It's so kind of you to give me board and lodgings. I slept like a baby. I can see the coast of France from my window, quite clearly. There's such a wonderful light. Now, I have an announcement to make.'

'Good morning Mr Barry,' says Pugin, 'do take a seat, what do you have to announce, sir?'

'Her Majesty is to confer upon me a very great honour. I'm to be awarded a knighthood, next week at Windsor Castle.'

'Oh, congratulations, well deserved, sir!'

Jane looks perplexed. 'Oh, yes, congratulations, Mr Barry. Forgive me for asking, but why is it that all of my husband's suppliers are praised in the press reports for the opening of the House of Commons, but his name is not mentioned once?'

A look of fear flashes across Barry's face. 'My dear, Mrs Pugin, is that true? I rarely read the newspapers, they're full of title-tattle.'

'It was just the same when the House of Lords was opened.'

'Was it?' Barry caresses his sagging jowls. 'Well, you can't tell these newspapermen what to write, I'm afraid. They're very independently minded.'

'Please excuse me, Mr Barry. I have things to be getting on with.' Before Jane leaves the room she turns back and looks Barry in the eye. 'May I remind you, sir, that my husband is very ill. The doctors have given strict orders that he is to rest. Please do not agitate him.' She leaves the room.

Barry takes a seat opposite Pugin. He rubs his hands together and smiles. 'Thank you, once again, for all your efforts with the House of Commons. There's still much work to be done though in the Palace of Westminster. I thought you might find it amusing to design the clock tower. It needs to be full steam ahead.'

Pugin does not look happy. 'Full steam ahead, sir? For steam you need heat, and for heat you need fuel. I'm running out of fuel, Mr Barry. I've produced ten thousand drawings for you already, largely at my own cost, with no recognition. You may have to finish the Palace of Westminster without me.'

'Oh, my dear fellow, I shudder at the thought, but do you recall, at the beginning of our enterprise, you said you didn't want to be centre stage on this project?'

'Yes, sir, but I didn't know it would become all-consuming. If I design the clock tower, I must ask you to respect my judgment and not seek so many revisions.'

Thursday, 26th February 1852. The Kent countryside is passing by at thirty miles-per-hour. Far away, a sliver of the River Thames looks like a silver eel, and then it is gone. Flashing by is an oasthouse with a crooked chimney, a naked orchard, and then a long forested hill. The landscape opens up into great folds and troughs. Roman legions, adventurers, merchants, and battalions headed to France, have all passed through these valleys.

Teddy is nearly eighteen. He is a pleasant, ruddy-faced youth, who has already been working for his father for three years. He glances at his pocket watch. He smiles and runs his fingers through his mop of thick, black hair. 'It's just gone eleven, Papa. We should be in London for one o'clock.'

Pugin is staring out of the window, in a world of his own.

'Are you all right, Papa?'

'Eh? What? It's so cold. I can't get warm.'

'Here, take my scarf, Papa.'

'Aunt Selina was a good, holy woman. Have you been to her tomb?'

Teddy furrows his brow. 'No, Papa, you know I haven't, that's where we're going, to see Aunt Selina's tomb. You said you wanted to see it. Don't you remember?'

'Your grandparents are buried there too. It will be good for you to see them. The tomb might need some repairs. We can do it together.'

'Yes, Papa, I'm looking forward to seeing it.' Teddy turns away and frowns. He looks out of the window at the passing countryside. He scratches his head. His father was very ill before Christmas, but then there was a significant improvement after the Bishop of Southwark visited and placed a relic of the Holy Cross on his forehead. Over the last couple of days his health has been failing again.

Three hours later, Pugin and Teddy are in a Hansom cab driving at a steady trot towards Islington. Palatial terraces in white Portland stone pass by along The Strand. The street is busy and noisy. There are lots of carriages, pedestrians, riders on horseback, and bicyclists. Pugin has been in an odd mood all day, but now he is behaving very strangely. He keeps rubbing his hands and looking about the cab with jerky head movements. He stares at Teddy with a blank expression. 'Where are we going?' he snaps

Teddy is becoming distressed. 'What's wrong with you, Papa?'

'Eh? Where are you taking me?'

'We're going to Islington, Papa, to see Aunt Selina's tomb. You know that.'

'What do you want with me? I've got to get out of

here!' Pugin lunges for the door handle but Teddy is stronger than him. He grabs his father's arm and pushes him back. 'Wait there, Papa!' Tears are now streaming down Teddy's face. He needs to get help. 'Driver! Stop the cab!'

The cab pulls up at the kerbside. Frantically, Teddy searches in his pocket for money to pay the cabby. Pugin breaks free and opens the door. He is out, hurrying off down the street. Teddy pays the cabby. 'Keep the change!'

A pink mist descends over Pugin's eyes and his legs buckle under him. He is falling. His head hits a granite kerbstone. Teddy sees his father drop. "Papa!" He sprints over to Pugin who is sprawled over the pavement. The blood is flowing freely over his forehead, through his matted hair, and into the gutter. Teddy squats down and cups his father's head in his hands. He presses his clean handkerchief against the wound.

'Papa! Papa! Can you hear me?' There is no response. A small crowd of onlookers gathers around.

'Is he dead?' asks a wide-eyed old man.

'Nah, he's just out cold, ain't he?' replies another.

'Probably been on the gin.'

'It's a bit early for that ain't it?'

'Look at all that blood!'

'That's a nasty wound, oh, no, don't look.'

'Put my scarf around is 'ed, it'll stop the bleedin,' says a young maid, who should be on an errand. 'Do you want me to do it for you, lovey?'

Teddy nods, 'Yes, please, miss.'

While the maid ties her scarf around Pugin's head, Teddy looks around, trying to get his bearings. This bit of The Strand is familiar to him. He recalls the Golden Cross Inn is nearby. Pugin and Teddy have stayed there. The proprietor might remember them. Teddy girds his loins, takes a deep breath, and places his arms under his father's body. 'God, give me strength!' He lifts his father up in his arms and staggers down the street. He is surprised by how light his father is. He is all skin and bones, but he is still very difficult to carry. After a few steps, the maid joins him. "Ere, lovey, it'll be easier with two of us.'

'He's a dead weight, miss, are you sure?'

'I'm quite strong you know,' she flexes her muscles, 'ere let's hold him like this.'

The maid helps Teddy carry his father all the way to the Golden Cross.

'This is it,' says Teddy. 'Let's put him down here, on the step, careful now.'

'It looks like it's closed,' says the maid, gasping for breath, 'I'll ring the bell for you.'

Teddy is relieved when the innkeeper answers the door. He is an enormous man with a beard. His shirt is stretched around his wide stomach. He stands there for a moment, trying to comprehend the situation. 'Heavens above! Has this man been assaulted? Is he unconscious?'

'He's my father, sir, Augustus Pugin. He's fallen and hit his head. He's out cold.'

'Oh, it's Mr Pugin is it, the architect? Well, let's bring him in then. I recognise him now, sir. Here let me lift him up. Oh dear, poor Mr Pugin, what a state you're in.'

The innkeeper, the maid, and Teddy, struggle to get Pugin up the stairs and into one of the first floor guest bedrooms. They position the unconscious Pugin onto the bed and then they catch their breath. The innkeeper rests his hands upon his bulging stomach. He turns to Teddy. 'I'll fetch the doctor, sir, your father will need the wound to be attended to.'

'Thank you, sir.'

'Will it just be the one night I'll book you in for?'

'Yes, I think so, we'll share the room.'

'Right you are, just call if you need anything.'

Now Teddy turns to the maid. He gives her a heartfelt smile. 'Thank you for your assistance, miss, you're right, you are strong.'

'That's quite all right, lovey. Listen, I'll get off now. I've gotta deliver a letter. Do you want me to get a message to anyone? I'm quite 'appy to do that, if it ain't too far.'

'Where are you going?'

'Westminster.'

'Anywhere near Parliament?'

'Yeah, just around the corner, my employer works on Bridge Street.'

'My father's colleague, Mr Hardman, is working in Parliament. If you could ask him to come here, to the Golden Cross, and tell him Mr Pugin is very sick. I would be so grateful.'

'Do you wanna write that down for me, lovey, so I don't forget naffin?'

'Yes, of course,' replies Teddy reaching for the pen and paper on the desk. If Mr Hardman isn't there, please ask for Mr George Myers, or Mr Herbert Minton, or Mr John Crace. One of them is sure to be there. If none of them are, then give the message to Sir Charles Barry.'

The maid places a hand on the desk to steady herself. 'Write it all down, lovey, I'd never remember any of 'em names.'

George Myers is the first to arrive. Teddy shows him into the room at the Golden Cross. A doctor has dressed Pugin's wound, but it is still bloody and he is a frightful sight. Myers recoils when he sees him. Pugin groans. 'I think he's coming around, Mr Myers,' says Teddy.

'You're right.' Myers cautiously leans over the bed and examines Pugin's face. Pugin's eyes suddenly open. Myers is startled. The eyes are bloodshot and lifeless. Now Pugin pulls himself up in the bed. His terrified eyes dart around the room.

Myers speaks falteringly. 'You have been in the wars, Mr P.'

Pugin suddenly lunges forward with his fist and he smacks Myers in the face.

'Papa!' shouts Teddy. Myers hardly notices the strike. Pugin lunges out again. Myers ducks and then he uses his considerable bulk to pin Pugin down on the bed. Pugin struggles for a while and then he cries like a baby.

Teddy is distraught. 'What should we do?'

Myers is breathing heavily. 'He's had a mental collapse, Teddy. We need more help. Hardman and Minton are on their way. We'll work out what to do when they get here. Don't worry, my boy, everything will be all right.'

Half an hour later, George Myers, John Hardman, Herbert Minton, and Teddy, are discussing what to do with Pugin. He has had another violent fit with a lot of shouting. George Myers is sitting on top of him. Somebody is knocking at the door. Teddy is aware that the three men are staring at him, as if he is in charge. 'What shall I do, Uncle John?' he whispers.

Hardman whispers back. 'Ask who it is.'

'Who is it?'

'It's the innkeeper, sir.'

'What is it?'

'Is everything all right? There have been reports of a disturbance.'

'Everything is fine, sir. My father just had a bad dream.'

'Well done, Teddy,' whispers Hardman.

'I see,' replies the innkeeper, doubtfully. 'I have Sir Charles Barry waiting down stairs for you, sir. Shall I show him up?'

Teddy turns to Hardman with a questioning look.

'What's Sir Charles doing here?' snaps Hardman.

'My messenger the maid must have spoken to him. I'm sorry.'

'Don't worry, Teddy,' says Herbert Minton. He turns to Hardman. 'We might as well get him up here. What harm can he do?'

'Is everything all right, sir?' asks the innkeeper on the other side of the door.

'Yes, one moment, please,' replies Teddy.

Hardman is thinking. 'Oh, yes, let's have him up here.'

Teddy speaks up. 'Show Sir Charles up, please, innkeeper.'

'Very good, sir.'

Sir Charles Barry bursts into the room. He sees Myers sitting on top of Pugin and surmises what has happened. 'Has he gone mad?'

Hardman is mute but his head is nodding.

Sir Charles takes control of the situation. 'A lot of reputations are at stake here!' He looks around the room. Hardman, Myers, and Minton all look pensive. Teddy holds his gaze. 'What should we do, Sir Charles?'

'We need to get your father to Kensington House.'

'What's at Kensington House?'

'It's a private asylum, on Kensington High Street.'

'An *asylum*, what will they do to my father?'

'They will take care of him, Edward. They're very discreet. I know the doctors. We need to keep what has happened quiet. We need to protect your father's reputation, and your reputation, and all of ours, too.'

Teddy turns to Hardman. 'What do you think, Uncle John?'

Hardman scratches his head. He looks down at Pugin, who is fast asleep. 'I think Sir Charles is right, Teddy. We need to make sure he doesn't hurt himself, or anyone else.' He turns to gauge the opinion of Myers and Minton. They both nod their heads, solemnly. Hardman turns back to Teddy. 'For the time being, we should tell nobody what has happened to your father.'

'What about my stepmother?'

Sir Charles interjects. 'They don't allow visitors at Kensington House.'

Hardman places a hand upon Teddy's shoulder. 'Look, I'm your father's closest friend, Teddy, and I'm the executor of his will. By your leave, I'll manage this situation. I think we should wait until your father has returned to his right mind. That'll be the right time for your stepmother to see him. It would be too shocking for her to see him like this. Is that acceptable to you?

Teddy looks lost. 'Yes, Uncle John, but what about all of Papa's work?'

'Don't worry about that for now. I'll explain everything to your stepmother.' Hardman now turns to Myers. 'George, will you come to Kensington House with us?'

'Yes, of course, I will.'

'Good, and you too, Sir Charles?'

'Yes, I will accompany you, in a separate cab.'

Minton looks distraught. 'I'll come too, John.'

Sir Charles interrupts. 'I don't think too many of us should go, Mr Minton. We do need to be discreet.'

Suddenly Pugin wakes up and starts yelling.

Myers raises his hand to restrain him; Pugin flinches as if he is going to be hit. Sir Charles grimaces. 'We'll need to bring the doctors here first. They can sedate him, then we'll take him to Kensington.'

Twenty-One

Monday, 1st March 1852. Jane Pugin walks alone down Kensington High Street, in her best bonnet and shawl. An umbrella shields her from the drizzle. She clutches a precious card close to her chest, against a necklace with a crucifix that Pugin made for her.

Jane stops and looks up at an imposing cream rendered villa. There is a plaque upon one of the columns supporting the portico entrance; it reads 'Kensington House'. She rings the bell and stares into the glossy black front door. There is a long wait. Jane is just about to ring the bell again when an angry looking fellow with ruffled grey hair and bulging eyes opens the door. 'Ah, madam, are you here again?'

'Yes, sir, I wish to see my husband, Mr Pugin,' says Jane in the most authoritative voice she can muster.

'As I told you last time ma'am, the guardians will not allow it.'

'But why, sir?'

'As I said last time, ma'am, visitors are not conducive to his recovery, not yet.'

Jane can feel her lips begin to tremble. 'How is he?'

'His doctor will be writing to you, ma'am. You really should spare yourself this unpleasantness.'

Jane's face crumples and she begins to weep. 'It's his birthday. He's forty today. I have this birthday card for him. Oh, please let me see him.'

'I will take the card, ma'am, but you really must depart now. You must trust us with his care.'

Jane hands the man the card. As soon as the man

closes the door he disposes of the birthday card in the wastepaper basket. Reluctantly, slowly, Jane walks away, turning back many times, in case they should change their minds, and have pity on her. She prays for Pugin, all the way back to Ramsgate.

Thursday, 17th June 1852. The Grange is strangely quiet. Jane sits alone in the dining room. Her elbows rest upon the table and her hands are cupped around her face. Her brown eyes stare out of the window and follow the shadows of clouds racing over the sea. She has been denied access to her husband for over three months. She feels utterly powerless and dejected, but a new fire is stirring within her.

Teddy and Powell have left the Grange. They are now working in John Hardman's drawing studio in Birmingham. Jane misses them. Without consulting her, they have taken all of Pugin's drawings and documents so they can continue his work. The Palace of Westminster remains the most demanding project, but there are also many others.

The doorbell rings. Jane jumps out of her seat. She pinches her cheeks and pats her hair. She listens as Charlotte, the maid, answers the door. A few seconds later, there is a knock on the dining room door. 'Come in!' It opens.

'Mr Samuel Sharwood to see you, madam.'

'Show him in please, Charlotte.'

Mr Sharwood is one of the governors at the public lunatic asylum. 'Ah, Mrs Pugin, good morning, if I may say, your house glows with warmth, such colours, and what a fine view of the sea.'

'You're very kind, Mr Sharwood. Please do take a seat.'

'Thank you, Mrs Pugin, now, everything has been arranged. I have the papers for you to sign.'

Jane takes a deep breath and then she sits down

beside Mr Sharwood. She notices, with considerable annoyance, that Charlotte is still standing beside the door, hanging on every word.

'That'll be all, thank you, Charlotte,' she snaps.

'Thank you madam,' replies Charlotte, with a little curtsy and a roll of her eyes. On leaving the room, she mumbles under her breath, 'I was only waiting to be dismissed.' She closes the door, loudly. Jane flashes an angry look towards it.

Mr Sharwood places his case upon the dining table. He retrieves an official, medical paper and passes it to Jane.

'I just need you sign at the bottom, if you please, Mrs Pugin.'

'So, I'm signing for my husband to be certified insane, is that right?' Jane tries to maintain her composure but she cannot. Tears fall down her cheeks.

'Oh, my dear, Mrs Pugin, please don't lose hope. He will get the best treatment that is available. I can assure you of that.'

Jane turns away and stares out of the window, where the clouds are still racing by. She speaks as if in a trance. 'Bedlam… is a dreadful place. I've seen what they do to people there, the exercise yard is beside the church I was married in.'

'Well, Mrs Pugin, the hospital is now called Bethlem. Bedlam is all in the past. As I said in my letter, it is much improved since Doctor Hood took over. He is a good Christian man. Now, I just need you to sign here, if you would be so kind.'

Jane signs her name. 'When will he be taken to Bethlem?'

'He will be there on 21st June, madam.'

'My birthday.'

Friday, 2nd July 1852. Lord Shrewsbury sits on a

private terrace outside his sumptuous apartment at the Neo-Classical palace, the Villa Belmonte, in Palermo, Sicily. It was once the home of the Prince of Belmonte, but it is now an exclusive hotel favoured by the English aristocracy. Lord Shrewsbury has turned sixty. The loss of a daughter, and grandchildren through illness, has taken a great emotional toll on him and Lady Shrewsbury. Physically, he has become portly, has a double chin, and receding hair, but the light still flickers in his eyes.

Lord Shrewsbury has found peace in his faith and he potters around Sicily's Norman churches. He also walks amongst the wild hills and sits for hours on this terrace, overlooking the turquoise sea, following the progress of boats under the great dome of the sky.

It is very hot. The Earl sips his iced lemonade. Lady Shrewsbury has left him a copy of *The Times*, which he now casually thumbs through. It falls open, randomly, at the *Letters* page. One sentence immediately stands out, '*Pugin admitted to asylum*'. It is a letter from Lord John Russell, who is no longer the Prime Minister. In his letter he pledges to donate £10 to support Mr Pugin in his recuperation. He is encouraging others to do likewise.

There is a sound from within the apartment. Lady Shrewsbury has returned from her walk. She has been seeking solace in the romantic gardens and walnut groves that surround the palace.

'Maria, is that you?'

Lady Shrewsbury appears at the wide-open French doors. She is still attractive. Her cheeks are flushed. 'Yes, darling it's me.'

'There's terrible news from London. Pugin is unwell,' says Lord Shrewsbury, grimacing.

'Yes, I know.'

'You know?'

'A letter has just arrived, from Jane. I have it here.'

'Bring it over. I must read it. Apparently, he's in Bethlem. Do they mean Bedlam? That's a pauper's hospital isn't it? We must go to him.'

Lady Shrewsbury takes a chair beside her husband and hands him the letter. 'I'm not sure that's wise, John, not with your health, and he's been certified insane.'

Lord Shrewsbury looks aghast. 'Insane? Pugin? More like a breakdown caused by overwork. We must pay for him to come here, for a holiday, for as long as he needs. Sicily will help to restore him. Here, let me read Jane's letter.'

Wednesday, July 21st 1852. It is a close, humid morning in London. Jane is walking beside Father John Glennie, the wiry priest who has been a friend of Pugin for many years. They come to a halt. They both look down at the pavement and mentally prepare themselves. Jane takes a deep breath. She gives Father John an encouraging smile. He smiles back. 'Come on, Jane, let's not be intimidated. This time I have a feeling you will get to see him.'

They walk past the wrought iron gates of Bethlem, Jane's pulse quickens. They pass through a small park and then under a very grand pedimented gable, resting upon Ionic columns. They have arrived at the asylum's entrance. Father John rings the bell. They wait.

'I don't like this place,' says Jane. 'This is as far as I got last time. They wouldn't let me over the threshold. Thank you again for coming, John.'

Father John smiles. 'You should never have come here alone, Jane. This place is enough to make your blood run cold. Just think, thousands of people queued up here, to mock the inmates. The only treatment those poor souls got was bleeding, purging, and the lash.'

'Oh, Lord, don't say that, John!' Jane leans against a column for support. 'I can't bear to think of Augustus suffering.'

'I'm sorry, Jane. What am I saying? It's not like that now. It's not Bedlam any more, it's Bethlem.'

Jane wipes away her tears. 'Augustus is so sensitive. He cried profusely when he read *Oliver Twist*. He couldn't stand to think of anyone living in a workhouse, and now he is somewhere much worse.'

'I shouldn't have spoken like that, Jane. It's my nerves. I'm sure this place is much improved. I pray God it is.'

The door opens. Before them stands a tall man, in a uniform. He turns to Father John, 'Good morning, sir, how may I help you?'

Father John opens his mouth to speak, but Jane gets her words out first. 'Good morning, I'm Mrs Pugin and this is Father John. We have an appointment with Doctor Hood, at ten o'clock.'

'Ah, yes, Mrs Pugin, it's you again. Follow me, please.'

Jane and Father John are escorted through a spacious central hallway with a very high ceiling. They are then ushered into a comfortable waiting room. It is well furnished in a traditional style, like the parlour of a country house. After a couple of minutes, a tall man enters. He is very well spoken. 'Good morning, I'm Doctor Charles Hood, Mrs Pugin I presume?'

'Yes, good morning, Doctor Hood; this is Father John.'

They all shake hands. 'Please do take a seat and make yourselves comfortable. Would you care for tea?'

Tea is declined. Doctor Hood is dressed in a black suit, with a smart black silk cravat around his neck. He has jet-black hair, parted to one side, sideburns, and a long, slender nose.

'I've come to see my husband, Doctor Hood.'

'Augustus Pugin, the architect, we're honoured to have him staying with us. You might be surprised to know that we have several famous persons in residence.'

'Will you please let me see my husband, Doctor Hood?'

The doctor strokes his chin. 'Well, Mrs Pugin, I don't think the time is quite right, not just yet. '

'Why not?' interjects Father John.

'Mr Pugin must not be agitated or excited in any way.'

'Why not?'

'It may provoke another seizure.'

'What is the cause of these seizures?'

'Well, sir, the honest answer is that we don't know. The brain is a very complex organ. However, it seems that Mr Pugin has been accelerating through life at such a very rapid pace it has caused a fever in his brain. The mercury prescribed by his doctors, in my humble opinion, has not helped his condition.'

Jane puts her hand to her brow, 'Oh, my Lord, what my poor Augustus has endured.'

Father John continues. 'Mrs Pugin surely has a right to see her husband, is that not the case, Doctor Hood?'

'I'm recently in post, sir. We're undergoing a transformation here. A new regime of kindness and purposeful activity will improve the quality of the lives entrusted into our care. Not everything is as I would wish it to be, at least not yet, and Mrs Pugin appears to be upset. I don't think this is the right time for her to see her husband.'

Jane tries to pull herself together. She continues in a faltering voice. 'I sympathise with you, Doctor Hood, and with your cause. You seem to be a kind man, but I must insist, I'm here to see my husband. I have been denied access to him for five months. I will wait no longer.'

Doctor Hood gives Jane a sympathetic look but he remains silent. Jane is physically shaking. She has had enough. To the shock of both men she retrieves a metal object from her bag and dangles it in front of Doctor Hood's face.

'Do you know what these are, Doctor Hood?'

'They look very much like handcuffs to me, Mrs Pugin.'

'If you don't allow me to see my husband, I will chain myself to the railings at the front of your asylum. I will stay there until you let me see my husband. Father John will be notifying *The Times*.'

'So I will,' adds a wide-eyed Father John.

Doctor Hood is looking down at his desk. He sighs. 'Very well, Mrs Pugin, I will ask George to take you to your husband, but please remember, not everything is as I'd like it to be, not yet.'

As soon as they leave the main hall they hear unnatural wailing and howling. It is a terrifying sound. Jane clings onto Father John's arm. He is praying under his breath. They follow the gangling frame of George, who lights the way with a swinging lantern. In his other hand he dangles an enormous set of keys. They progress down a long dark, corridor. There is a strong smell of chlorine disinfectant, but it does not disguise the smell of sewage and vomit.

'This is where the male patients are kept,' growls George. 'Doctor Hood lets them out of their cells. It's not a good idea. Watch where you step ma'am, they're all around us.'

Jane moves even closer to Father John. In the shadows she can see figures on the floor, swaying back and forth. Some of them are gathered around flickering lanterns. Their ghostly, contorted faces turn towards her. As she gets closer she sees they are dressed in sacking.

A strange figure crawls along the floor behind them; it is not quite a man. It has an enormous head and an iron ring around its neck. It emits a disturbing cackling sound. Suddenly, it lunges forward and grabs hold of Jane's ankle with a wet hand. 'I've got you!' it snarls.

Jane puts her hand over her mouth to smother a scream. George kicks the creature off her. 'Get back, cannibal! You'll be hanged, drawn, and quartered, when I get my hands on you!'

The cannibal recoils, snarling.

'That one should not be loose,' snaps George.

Father John puts his arm around Jane's shoulder. He can feel her shaking. They continue walking. George holds his lantern up to check the numbers on the cell doors. He is muttering to himself. 'Pugin... Pugin... Pugin...'

The large headed cannibal creeps through the shadows behind them, sniffing the air. It is following Jane's scent, like a wolf locked onto its prey. It cannot help itself.

'Ah, this is the one, Pugin!' exclaims George, sliding back a view hole.

Jane gently pushes George out of the way and she presses her face against the mesh.

'Augustus! Augustus! Are you there, my darling?' She is staring into a dark, silent cell. She squints and waits.

'What do you see, Jane? Is he there?' asks Father John.

'I think this cell is empty,' she says, but she continues to look. Her eyes adjust to the darkness. The faint outline of a little old man becomes discernable. 'Oh, there is someone in there. He's got a shaved head. The poor thing is strapped to an iron bar on the wall. It's not Augustus though.

'Tis ma'am,' says George, 'tis Augustus Pugin.'

Jane squints again. 'Oh, no... it is Augustus, oh, no... what have you done to him?'

Jane supports herself against the wall. Her head is spinning.'

'Steady ma'am, you mustn't get him agitated now. This is why Doctor Hood didn't want you to visit.'

Jane tries to steady her breathing. 'George, open the door, please. I'm going in!'

'Oh, no, I don't think Doctor Hood said you were to go in ma'am, you were just to see him, begging your pardon, but I don't think you're in a fit state.'

'I am going in, George! Doctor Hood said I could go in, didn't he Father John?'

Father John nods his head, 'Quite so, quite so.'

'Well, perhaps, if the Father here escorts you, ma'am.'

'Of course he will, that's why he's here. Please open the door, immediately!'

George fumbles with his keys. He finds the right one and turns the large lock with a clunk. He opens the door slightly. There is a foul smell. Jane grabs the side of the door and opens it further. George bars her way with his arm. 'Steady now, ma'am, steady now…'

'Jane, let me go first, please,' says Father John. Then he whispers, 'Are you going to be all right, do you feel faint?'

'I'll be all right, John, but, yes, you go first. See if he recognises you. I'll wait here.'

Father John turns to George. 'May I take the lantern?'

'No, I'd better keep that, sir. Mrs Pugin won't want to be in the dark. I will light a candle for you.'

Father John clutches the candle with both hands. He disappears into the cell. George slams the heavy metal door behind him. Father John's voice is shaky. 'Hello Augustus, it's Father John here, your old friend. Do remember me?'

A high-pitched, strangulated voice is heard in the darkness. 'Can I have some paper?'

Father John rummages in his pockets. He finds an old envelope and a pencil. He can see a human figure now, lying on a metal bed. With an outstretched arm he offers up the envelope and the pencil. A hand comes out of the darkness and grabs it.

Father John holds the candle up. Now he can see that Pugin is drawing. 'Do you mind if I sit on the end of your bed?' There is no answer. Father John sits down. The metal is cold. 'I think it's safe to come in, Jane.'

George opens the cell door. Jane wipes the tears from her face and she enters. The metal door is slammed shut behind her. Father John gets up so Jane can sit on the bed. Pugin glances at her momentarily. His face is pale and gaunt. He looks seventy years old. He doesn't recognise Jane. He turns his head down and continues with his drawing. Jane strokes his head. He seems to find this comforting. There is some commotion going on outside. The cell door opens again. George pops his head in. 'Can you finish up now, please? I need to deal with this disturbance.'

Somebody is shouting from down the corridor 'George! George! George!'

'Just one moment, I shall be back presently…' George disappears. He has left the cell door ajar.

Jane turns to Father John. 'Would you leave me alone with him, just for a minute?

Father John hesitates. 'Are you sure?'

'Yes, please, John, just for one minute.'

'Very well, I'll wait for you, right by the door. Here, you take the candle.'

'No, you take the candle you will need it. George has taken the lantern.'

'All right, just call out if you need me.'

At last, Jane is alone with Augustus. She kisses his cheek and presses her arm against his. They just sit there for a moment.

Jane senses the temperature in the cell has fallen. It is definitely colder. There is a rasping, heavy breathing. An evil presence has entered. Jane moves closer to

Pugin. The sound is not coming from him. Suddenly, Jane feels a cold, wet hand clasped around her leg. She screams. Pugin kicks out. Something goes flying across the room and hits the wall with a thud. There is another scream. The cell door opens. George and Father John are standing there with the lantern. Cowering from the light, curled up in the corner of the cell, is the creature, blood trickling down its ear.

'Cannibal! Get out of here, you vermin!' yells George.

On all fours, the cannibal scampers out of the cell, brushing against their legs. Father John shudders with disgust. Jane is gasping for breath. Pugin continues drawing peacefully.

Jane pulls herself up. 'I'm going now, Augustus, but I'll be back for you, very soon.' She kisses him on the forehead. There seems to be a flicker of recognition in his face. He smiles and hands Jane the piece of paper. He has drawn a church upon it.

Pugin snatches the paper back. 'It's not finished yet.'

Jane fights to hold back the tears.

Back in the waiting room, Jane paces back and forth and fidgets anxiously. Father John returns from the lavatory. 'My dear, Jane, I'm so sorry. This must be such an ordeal for you.'

'We can't leave him here, John. Not with that cannibal creature on the loose.'

Father John frowns. 'I don't want to leave him here either, Jane. Perhaps there's another doctor who can help us.'

'Who? Tell me, do you know of someone?'

'Well, there is Doctor Samuel Dickson; he's an expert on mental fever. He applies something of a new approach. I must confess, I have taken the liberty of speaking with him already. I hope you don't mind?'

'Of course I don't mind. What did he say?'

'He thinks Augustus is curable.'

Jane's face lights up. 'Really? Would he take Augustus on?'

'I think he might. We would have to rent a safe house for Augustus to stay in. Doctor Dickson said he could recommend somewhere. I'd be happy to manage things for you, Jane. Shall we go and speak to him?'

'Yes, I can't believe you haven't told me this. We must go to him immediately. Where is he based?'

'In Piccadilly, it's not far away.'

Friday, 23rd July 1852. Washes of paint show the conflagration consuming Parliament. Flames reach high into the sky, across the river, and lap against Westminster Bridge.

There is a tap on Powell's shoulder. 'How on earth did Westminster Hall survive that inferno?'

'Hello, Uncle John, it was a miracle wasn't it? It's good to see the hall restored.'

'It certainly is, and that's a fine painting by Turner. I'm glad it's hanging here in Parliament. Sometimes we need reminders of past events.'

'He was a remarkable artist.'

'Come along, we shouldn't keep Jane waiting.'

There is a gentle hum of chatter in the Royal Gallery of the Palace of Westminster. It is the ceremonial space through which the monarch passes after leaving the Robing Room. Jane Pugin is sitting at the head of a beautifully crafted table, designed by her husband. A cream shawl covers her shoulders.

Pugin has designed almost everything that can be seen in the Royal Gallery, and either John Hardman, John Crace, Herbert Minton, or George Myers, has made it. One exception is the spectacular paintings, commissioned by Prince Albert, which depict Britain's military and naval victories.

Jane has called this meeting of family and friends to

discuss Pugin's care. Seated around the table is the enormous figure of her uncle, John Knill, the bespectacled John Hardman, the debonair Herbert Minton, Father John, dressed in a black cassock, and Powell, who is fidgeting nervously.

A number of other private meetings are being conducted at tables in close proximity. Peers, thumbing through parliamentary bills, occupy the settees upholstered by John Crace.

'Do you want to begin, Jane, my dear?'

'Yes, uncle, I will.' Jane coughs delicately and then she rubs her finger and thumb around her wedding ring. 'Thank you for coming today gentlemen, and at such short notice. We're the guests of Lord Shrewsbury, but sadly, he has written to say due to poor health, he cannot attend. I have also received a letter of apology from George Myers and from John Crace. They are both away on business.'

The men listen intently. Jane continues. 'After five months of trying, I have at last seen Augustus. As you know, he is in Bethlem, the asylum. It is a very disturbing place. I don't want Augustus to stay there for a minute longer than is absolutely necessary.'

Hardman removes his spectacles. He polishes them with his handkerchief. He looks up. 'Jane, I've also met with Doctor Hood at Bethlem. I wasn't allowed to see Pugin, but I don't think the place is as bad as you make it out to be.' He puts his glasses back on and fixes Jane with a concerned look.

'Mr Hardman, please let Jane finish!' snaps John Knill. His bushy eyebrows are raised high.

'I'm sorry, please continue,' replies Hardman, admonished.

'I've been to see Doctor Samuel Dickson.'

Hardman shifts uneasily in his chair and coughs. 'I'm sorry, do continue.'

'Doctor Dickson believes he can help Augustus. He

is keen to try and help. He has already identified a safe house in Hammersmith that Augustus can be moved into. His methods are, somewhat controversial.'

'Controversial?'

'Yes, Mr Minton.'

'I would say that is an understatement,' interjects Hardman.

Minton ignores him. 'In what way, Jane?'

'Well, he wants to use chloroform to relieve the fever in Augustus's brain.' Jane turns to Hardman. 'Look, I want to take counsel from all of you, before I make my decision on whether to send Augustus to Doctor Dickson.' Jane suddenly gasps. 'Oh, no!'

'What is it, Jane?'

'Don't look now, Sir Charles Barry has just walked in.'

Sir Charles is with Lord John Russell. Both of them are puffing on cigars.

'You've done a splendid job, Sir Charles. This is one of the finest galleries in Europe,' says Lord John Russell in a loud voice.

'You're too kind, my Lord,' replies Sir Charles.

'Oh, did you hear the dreadful news about Matthew Habershon?'

'No, my Lord.'

'He's dead.'

'Dead? Really?'

'Yes, and he wasn't all that old.'

Sir Charles lowers his voice. 'I say, look over there. Isn't that Mrs Pugin?'

'I wouldn't recognise her.'

'It is her, she's with John Hardman, Minton, and oh, what's his name. It looks as if they're having a family meeting. How odd. Oh, she's seen me. Would you please excuse me for a moment, my Lord? I'd better go and pay my respects.'

'Yes, do go over, Sir Charles. Please pass on my

regards, too.'

Jane looks aghast. 'Oh, no, Sir Charles is coming over.'

Powell nudges Hardman with his elbow. 'This could be trouble, Uncle John.'

Hardman replies, 'Leave this to me. Just a moment, I'll ask him to leave us alone.'

'Thank you, John, I really don't think I can face him right now.'

Sir Charles Barry raises a hand and waves to Jane as he approaches, but she looks away. Hardman is quick on his feet. He intercepts Sir Charles. They become engaged in a brief, intense, conversation, in the middle of the Royal Gallery. Both men are gesticulating. Hardman has to be quite firm before Sir Charles will depart.

Hardman returns to his seat.

'Thank you John,' says Jane.

'What was all that about, Uncle John?' asks Powell.

'He's changed his mind about a fanlight.' Hardman turns to Jane. 'Now, you know my thoughts. I believe Augustus will receive the best care where he is, in Bethlem.'

Jane's uncle nods his head. 'I agree with Mr Hardman on this, Jane. They know what they are doing. Doctor Dickson's methods are unproven, but it's your decision, my dear. I will support you, whatever you decide.'

Jane steadies herself. 'Thank you, uncle.'

Father John interjects. 'Doctor Dickson is well qualified. His books have changed medical practice. It's just that he challenges the established practice of blood letting, that's why he gets criticised. He served as a medical officer in the British army.'

Jane nods. 'Thank you, Father John.' She turns to Powell and smiles in a reassuring way. 'What do you think, Mr Powell?'

'Well, from what you've said, Mrs Pugin, it isn't right for the gaffer to stay where he is. If he goes to Doctor Dickson, could it be any worse than Bethlem?'

'It couldn't be any worse, Powell.'

'Could it be any better?'

'It could be.'

'It's worth taking a risk then, Mrs Pugin.'

John Hardman scowls at his nephew.

Herbert Minton gestures with an outstretched hand. 'Well, whatever you decide, Jane. I will assist in any way I can. I'm sure that goes for all of us.' There are nods of agreement around the table.

'Thank you, all of you, thank you very much. I know you all love Augustus, and that you want the best for him. I have made my decision. If he stays in Bethlem, he will not last long. He will die in misery. I shall instruct Doctor Hood that Augustus is to be moved to a safe house, under the care of Doctor Dickson.'

Friday, 30th July 1852. The sun has been up for half an hour. Three men clamber awkwardly out of a Hansom cab, in front of Number 16, The Grove, Hammersmith. The men stand for a moment at the roadside. The man in the middle is handcuffed to the other two.

Pugin breathes in deeply. The sensation of cool, showering drizzle upon his face is tantalizing. 'Wait,' he says to his captors. He is savouring the scent of the sweet white flowers upon the privet hedge, the river, and the summer rain. The tide is coming in fast, bringing fresher water. Number 16 is a pleasant, three-storey, Regency villa.

'Come on, Father John, we'd better get him in, there's a cab coming down the road, we don't want to be seen,' says Herbert Minton, looking incongruous in workman's clothes.

The first cab pulls off and another takes its place. A

servant woman gets out. She is wearing a black dress, white apron, and a white mop cap with a frill that covers her brow. She is also wearing a light brown, curly wig.

Doctor Dickson has forbidden Jane to see Pugin in case her presence excites him and brings on a seizure. Now that Jane has taken matters into her own hands, she has become more resourceful. She is finding solutions to problems. It was her idea that she should serve as Pugin's housekeeper, appropriately disguised.

The dark-skinned attendant stands aside. 'Good morning ma'am.'

'Good morning, Aladdin, remember, you are to call me Mrs Knight. I'm the housekeeper.'

'Very good, ma'am.'

'Where is Mr Pugin? I'd like to see him straight away, please.'

'Of course... Mrs Knight, he's in with Father John and my brother in the secure room.' On the inside, Number 16 contains a prison cell.

Jane walks briskly through the hallway and knocks upon a metal door.

'Come in,' says Father John, sounding a long way off.

Jane enters the secure room. Enough sunlight enters through cracks in the wooden shutters and between the metal bars to reveal Pugin sitting on the floor, swaying back and forth. He looks up at Jane. He opens his mouth. His voice is still strangulated. 'Are you Mary Amherst? Have you come back from the convent?' Now he is screeching. 'Mary! Mary!'

Jane clutches her chest; she is fighting back the tears.

Minton puts his arm around Pugin. 'No, this is Mrs Knight, the housekeeper.'

Pugin looks downcast, 'You look like Mary... or Anne, my wife.'

A tear escapes from Jane's eye. She wipes it away

quickly.

Pugin grunts. 'Is there food?'

'I'll prepare a meal,' says Jane. She leaves the room and makes her way downstairs, to the kitchen. As soon as she is alone, she falls to her knees upon the terracotta tiles and sobs.

Several hours later, Jane is at the kitchen sink washing up crockery, in a much better mood. She looks out over the colourful garden and indulges in a small smile. She is so relieved to have secured Pugin's release from Bethlem. Father John appears at the door, behind her. 'Doctor Dickson has just arrived, Jane. He's upstairs with Aladdin.'

'Oh, already? I didn't hear the doorbell. I'll come up.'

'I'm already here, ma'am,' says Doctor Dickson, appearing in the doorway, behind Father John. His jacket is thrown over his arm. 'Don't worry I'm quite happy to be in the kitchen, it's nice and cool in here.' He shakes hands with both Father John and then Jane. The doctor has thick black hair and a long face. He places his bag down upon the tiles and stands upright in his shirtsleeves. 'I'm so pleased you've managed to get your husband here, Mrs Pugin. Well done!'

'It's certainly been a struggle, doctor, but he's here now.'

'How is he?'

'He seems to be quite comfortable. He was absolutely ravenous when we arrived. He hasn't stopped eating. I'd say he has an unnatural appetite. I was worried that perhaps we shouldn't have fed him, before you apply your treatment.'

'Oh, that's quite all right, abstinence engenders maladies, isn't that what Shakespeare said?'

'Is it?'

'Well, I'd like to see your husband now if I may.'

'Of course, doctor. Oh, do you recall, I'm Mrs Knight, the housekeeper.'

'Yes, of course you are.'

'Doctor…'

'Yes, Mrs Pugin, sorry, Mrs Knight.'

'Will you be treating Mr Pugin with chloroform this evening? Please forgive me, I can't remember everything you said when we last met. I think it's the pressure I've been under, it's effected my memory.'

Doctor Dickson smiles, sympathetically. 'You're doing very well… Mrs Knight. Let me explain again, the chrono-thermal system of medicine identifies that external agencies are the cause of Mr Pugin's malady. My treatment may change depending upon his condition, day to day, but I believe the regular application of chloroform will relieve the fever. I will apply this now, if he is strong enough to receive it. I might also prescribe some silver nitrate to begin with.'

Jane looks overwhelmed. 'And there will be no blood letting.'

'Certainly not! Bloodletting has worsened your husband's condition. There will be no blood letting and no mercury.'

Father John interjects. 'I heard that Lord Byron's mania was actually caused by his blood letting.'

'Precisely, sir, can you imagine being left to wallow in your own blood? It is quite disgusting. I don't think many doctors under the age of fifty bleed their patients any more.'

Jane shudders. 'I'll show you through to Mr Pugin, doctor.'

Wednesday, 11th August 1852. It is a beautiful summer's day. John Hardman bites his lower lip and braces himself. He fixes his spectacles in place. He glances down the long, leafy grove. The air is so warm and thick it mutes the hustle and bustle of the high street, which is not far away. Hardman is relieved that nobody has seen him. He snatches a look at his pocket watch. He is a few minutes early. He has been dreading this visit all day, he is anxious to get it over and done with. He walks up to the front door of Number 16. From within the house there is the muffled sound of men shouting. Hardman scratches the back of his grey head. He wonders if there might be intruders. He knocks at the front door, firmly.

After a short delay, Jane opens it, in her disguise. 'Oh, it's you, John.'

'What on earth's going on in there, Jane? Why are you dressed as a maid?'

'Shush,' replies Jane putting her finger to her lips. 'I'm Mrs Knight, the housekeeper. It's not a good time for you to come in, John. We're having a bad time at the moment. Could you come back in an hour?'

Suddenly there is another crash from within followed by an unearthly scream.

'Jane! I insist that you let me in, immediately!'

'Oh, very well, but please stay calm. You mustn't interrupt the men.'

Hardman follows Jane into the house. 'What are they doing?' he asks.

'They're restraining Augustus. It's horrible, I know, but they have to do it. Please come down to the kitchen, we can talk in there.'

Hardman ignores Jane. He opens the metal door behind which the hullabaloo is coming. He stands there aghast. A smashed table is in the middle of the room and two burly men are pinning Pugin down. Aladdin has him in a headlock. Father John is watching on, anxiously, from the corner.

'Mr Hardman! Close that door immediately and follow me into the kitchen!' bellows Jane.

Hardman pulls a chair up at the opposite side of the kitchen table to Jane. The air is tense. They are like a separated couple forced together to discuss the wellbeing of their child. The door leading from the kitchen to the garden is open, providing a light breeze. The sound of a blackbird can be heard, giving a piercing, distress call.

'Does Doctor Dickson approve of this rough treatment, Jane?'

'He's abroad on business. Augustus has been getting better...'

'Better? You call this, better?'

'He's only been having these violent fits since the chloroform treatment stopped. We have to employ Aladdin and his brother to restrain him. I have to pay them of course. Did you get my letter about releasing more of the money?'

'I did, Jane, but you need to go steady. You've been spending a lot of money. Isn't it time you went home? The children will be forgetting they have a mother.'

'My duty, at this time, John, is to stay here. I need to be with Augustus. I know you don't approve, but he has been making progress.'

'Progress, really?'

Jane's lips begin to tremble. She puts her hand over her mouth and steadies herself. 'It's a shame you arrived when you did. You see, when he has these violent fits, we've found that I can calm him down.'

'How?'

'If I lie down beside him and put my head next to his, he falls asleep like a baby. The men say I get in the way, but I think progress is being made, and after all, love conquers all, doesn't it?'

Hardman can't hold her gaze. He smiles, nods, and looks down at his feet. Now he lifts his head and looks at Jane directly. 'I don't like that man, Aladdin, or his brother.'

'Neither do I. They talk about me, unpleasantly, behind my back. Doctor Dickson appointed them.'

'We'd better get rid of them. Why don't I send a couple of men over from Ramsgate?'

'Oh, yes, that would be helpful.'

Monday, 30th August 1852. Jane is in the back garden at Number 16, picking blackberries. She has put some flowers in her hair.

'Hello! Mrs Knight! It's me, Doctor Dickson. Father John let me in.'

'Ah, doctor, you're back from Ireland, would you like to join me? There's a bench over here.'

'Of course! You've made the garden delightful.'

They sit together and take a moment to exchange a few pleasantries.

'Now, then, how are things here?' asks the doctor. 'I'm not sure if I should call you Mrs Knight or Mrs Pugin. Why are you not wearing your disguise?'

Jane is beaming. 'Well, doctor, something wonderful has happened. Augustus has been so much better. He's been saying his daily prayers. He's started to laugh again, and yesterday... Oh! Yesterday, we went for a walk together, as afar as the field by the river.'

'Mrs Pugin, that is not wise, that is not at all wise.'

'But, doctor, he recognised me.'

'How do you know that?'

'He said, are you not my wife, Jane? I said, yes, I am dearest. I then took off my disguise.'

The doctor looks shocked. 'How did he respond?'

Jane is taking short, sharp breaths. Her lips are trembling. She doesn't want to break down crying.

'Take your time...'

After a moment she continues. 'He said to me, how kind you are to come and take care of me. I will never leave you again. Oh, doctor. He also remembers that we have a home in Ramsgate. He asked me, why do we not go there? Do let us go back, he said. Isn't that remarkable? He wants to go home. I'm afraid I cried for joy.'

'That is quite remarkable, Mrs Pugin. What do the men think of this change?'

'The men?'

'Yes, Father John, Aladdin and his brother.'

'Oh, Father John is overjoyed. I sacked Aladdin and his brother. They were too rough. Mr Mayman has come over from Ramsgate to help out. He's an excellent man. Augustus recognised him immediately.'

'Really?'

'Yes, I was so pleased. They always got on well together.'

'I see. There was another man upstairs, is he from Ramsgate too?'

'Oh, yes, he's a lovely old man who works with Mr Mayman. Augustus thinks he looks like Hogarth, the famous painter, so that's what we all call him.' Jane looks hesitant. 'There's one other thing, doctor.'

'Oh, yes.'

'My husband and I spent the night together.'

'Now that was strictly forbidden wasn't it?'

Jane blushes. 'He fell asleep almost immediately.' She quickly changes the subject. 'He's stopped taking his medicine too.'

Doctor Dickson scowls. 'Well, you seem to be taking over my role, Mrs Pugin.'

'I'm sorry, doctor, and I'm very grateful to you, but I'd like to take Augustus home. Would you agree to that?'

'Well, there's a big risk there, Mrs Pugin, but…'

'But what?'

'Well, strangely, sometimes travel can be a benefit. It seems that new scenery stimulates the brain, but under no circumstances should he become agitated. May I suggest that if he continues with this progress over the course of the next two weeks, then I will decide if he is well enough to go home?'

Jane claps her hands. 'Yes, doctor, we can wait for two weeks.'

Twenty-Two

Saturday, 11th September 1852. The South Eastern Railway Terminus is heaving with people anxious to leave London for a day on the coast. On Platform 1, a priest dressed in a black cassock gives a nun, in a full black habit, a kiss on the cheek. There are curious looks from the crowd.

'We've said goodbye now, Kerril, so please don't wait. Go on, dear, get on your own train, I don't want you to miss it.'

'All right, Mary, it's been lovely to see you.'

'And you too, my dear little brother, now off you go. Have a lovely rest in Ramsgate.'

'I will. God bless you, Mary.'

'God bless you, Kerril.'

Kerril Amherst is now in his thirties. He gives his sister one last wave and then he turns to leave. A beautiful lady remonstrating with the stationmaster immediately takes his attention. She is clearly in some distress.

'For pity's sake will you please find me four seats. My husband is not well.' Jane is pointing towards Pugin who is slouched upon a bench. Mr Mayman and Hogarth are keeping him upright. Kerril's eyes follow Jane's pointing finger. He squints at the seated man for a couple of seconds and wonders if he is intoxicated. Even though Pugin's appearance is much altered, he recognises his old teacher.

'This train is full madam,' asserts the stationmaster, 'and anyway, if your husband is sick, he may not board

252

the train.'

The stationmaster walks off. Jane is close to tears. Kerril walks over to her. 'Excuse me madam, are you Mrs Pugin?'

Jane looks at Kerril blankly, she can see he is a priest but she cannot speak.

'It's just that I'm an old friend of his, from Oscott. I'm Kerril Amherst.'

'From Oscott? Oh, please, Father Kerril, if there's anything you can do to help me. My husband is very sick. We need to get home to Ramsgate, but the train is full!'

'I'm also travelling to Ramsgate, Mrs Pugin. I'll have a word with the stationmaster.'

Within minutes, another carriage is taken out of a shed and it is connected to the back of the Ramsgate train.

Jane is soon sitting in the carriage next to Kerril Amherst. Opposite them sits Pugin, wedged between Mayman and Hogarth. There is a loud, rattling whistle, and the train chugs into motion.

'Oh, Father Kerril, the angels must have sent you,' says Jane.

'I heard the news about your husband, but it's such a shock to see him like this.'

'I know, Father, he has aged terribly. He was so distressed when we arrived at the railway station.'

'What happened?'

'When he saw all of the people at the station, he became very afraid. He wanted to go back to Hammersmith, but I had already handed over the keys to the new tenants.'

'So, what did you do?'

'These gentlemen had to apply chloroform, as a sedative. I do hope he's all right. I pray I'm doing the right thing, bringing him home. He has become so frail. The doctor wasn't happy to discharge him.'

'I'm sure you're doing the right thing, Mrs Pugin. Oh, look, I think he's coming around.'

Charlotte, the maid, is waiting outside the Grange, on the roadside. She spots the cab as soon as it turns the corner. She lifts her skirt and hurries back into the house. All of the children are away. They are either staying with their friends, or they are with Jane's family in London. Teddy is due back from Birmingham, tomorrow, after he has fulfilled a critical deadline for the Palace of Westminster.

The cab pulls up. The door opens. Jane gets out first. Mayman and Hogarth follow. They hold out their arms to assist Pugin. He climbs out of the cab and walks into his house, slowly, but unassisted. Once over the threshold, he looks overjoyed. His voice sounds clearer. 'I remember, I have a beautiful family. I must see the children. I have such a lovely home.'

He falls to his knees under the crucifix in the hallway. After praying he manages to get to his feet and he stumbles into the drawing room, followed by Jane. Pugin leans against his empty desk. Like an old captain that has weathered a great storm, he looks out of the window, over the grey sea, to where the fiery sun is setting.

'Where is all of my work, Jane?'

'It's all gone to Birmingham, darling, for safekeeping.'

'I see. Where is Hogarth?'

'I think he's gone home, he's got a long way to go.'

'He must stay over. I want him to see this sky.'

'Let me go and check.' Jane manages to call Hogarth back. He had already left and was walking down the lane.

Pugin and Hogarth stay up together most of the night, talking about paintings, light, and the sea. They go into the garden, and stare up at the bright stars.

Sunday, 12th September 1852. John Hardman arrives at the Grange at lunchtime. He sits next to Pugin, in silence, in the drawing room. They remain like this, next to each other, for a long time. Later on in the evening, Jane joins them. Pugin produces a drawing. When Jane hands him a cup of tea, he gives her the drawing. It is of a beautiful rose. There is an inscription. *Drawn in the presence of my dear wife Jane, the XII Sept 1852.*

Monday, 13th September 1852, it is five o'clock in the afternoon. The day has been very fine with a gentle sea breeze. The sky is blue and cloudless. The last of the swallows are swooping down, all around. Pugin and Jane are walking back across the fallow field, looking towards the Grange. There is a vast expanse of green sea behind the house and the rugged flint church. A faint grey line on the horizon marks the coast of France. In the middle distance, there are three ships of the line anchored off the headland, each has three masts.

Jane smiles as a swallow swoops down close. 'They're fattening up before their departure.'

The wind changes direction and they hear the happy sound of end of season holidaymakers on the beach in Ramsgate.'

'I can hear the band playing,' says Pugin.

'Yes, dear, I can too. They are fortunate to have this sunshine.'

Pugin squeezes Jane's hand. 'My dear, it is beautiful, isn't it, all of this?'

'Yes, darling, it is.'

'I'm so blessed. What a good wife you've been to me.'

Jane tries to hold her smile but her lips tremble.

Pugin continues. 'How can I thank you, for all you've done for me?'

He touches Jane's cheek, tenderly, and kisses her lips. They both just stand, crying, holding onto each other.

After a few minutes, Jane says, 'Shall we get back now?'

'Yes, I want to give thanks in the chapel.'

The Kent soil retains the heat of the sun well into the evening. Pugin and Jane eat their supper in the garden.

'That was delicious, Jane,' says Pugin, placing his knife and fork down.

'Yes, Charlotte wanted to cook something special for you.'

'What time is it now?'

'It's just after eight o'clock.'

'Do you mind if I go to bed?'

'Of course not, Augustus, dear, I will be up shortly myself.'

Later that night…

'Jane! Jane! Jane! I'm going, Jane!'

For a moment Jane doesn't know where she is. She struggles up in the bed. 'What? What? What is it, Augustus?'

Pugin is sitting bolt upright in bed. He has his eyes fixed on some invisible thing above him.

'What is it Augustus? Do you feel sick?'

'It's time, Jane. I'm leaving.'

'Should I call the doctor?'

There is no answer. Jane rushes out of the bedroom. She runs along the landing and knocks on Teddy's door. 'Teddy! Teddy! Teddy! Fetch the doctor from town! Send a message for Doctor Dickson to come, immediately!'

Teddy springs out of his bed. He is quickly down the stairs. He puts on his father's raincoat, over his nightshirt. He is out of the door.

An hour later, Pugin is in exactly the same position in his bed. He is fixedly staring at the same spot. Two elderly doctors are now prodding and poking him. They have asked Jane to wait outside. She is standing on the landing. The bedroom door opens. The doctor, with a long, grey beard, speaks to her in a conspiratorial whisper.

'Mrs Pugin, we will have to bleed him.'

'Oh, no, doctor, that's out of the question.'

The doctor is insistent. 'Madam, your husband's life depends upon it.'

'My husband's doctor in London has forbidden him to be bled.'

Now the other doctor appears, with a craning, vulture like neck. 'Mrs Pugin, you have the opinion of not one, but two learned doctors here, if your husband is not bled, immediately, there will be very serious consequences. Frankly, madam, you will have only yourself to blame.'

The first doctor adds, caustically, 'Doctor Dickson has some controversial ideas, ma'am. It is not judicious to throw out the learning of centuries, based upon the opinion of one man.'

Jane clutches hold of the wooden balustrade to steady herself. Her head is spinning.

'Madam, we must bleed him now. Do you consent?'

Jane gasps. 'Oh, Lord, have mercy, do what you must.'

The doctors disappear back into the bedroom and the door is closed behind them. Now they unravel their instruments and their leeches. They practise their medicine upon Pugin's emaciated body.

The following day...

Tuesday, 14th September 1852. The hallway clock chimes three times. It is three o'clock in the afternoon. Charlotte is opening the front door to Doctor Dickson.

'Oh, doctor, thank the Lord you're here! Mrs Pugin says I'm to take you straight up to the bedroom. Teddy is in the chapel, shall I get him?'

'Just take me to Mr Pugin, please.'

Doctor Dickson finds Pugin lying on his bed, unconscious. The sheets are covered in blood. Jane is kneeling beside him, sobbing. Charlotte remains standing by the door, her hands cover her mouth, holding back a scream. Doctor Dickson reaches out to touch Jane's shoulder. 'Oh, Mrs Pugin, you shouldn't have let them do this.'

Jane lets out a terrible cry. Charlotte rushes to her side. Jane buries her face in Charlotte's arm. 'Oh, Charlotte, what have I done?'

'You've only done good ma'am, you're the one that saved him.'

'Take deep breaths, Mrs Pugin, breath deeply,' says Doctor Dickson. He then undertakes an examination of Pugin. After listening to his heart beat, he sits down on the edge of the bed and sighs. He looks Jane in the eye. 'It's time to say goodbye to Augustus now.'

Tears are streaming down Jane's face. Charlotte takes a few steps back.

The doctor continues. 'Have you called for the priest?'

Jane cannot talk. She just shakes her head.

'Would you like Charlotte to fetch him?'

Jane nods her head. Charlotte acknowledges the instruction and leaves the room.

The priest reads Augustus Pugin the last rites.

The sun is rising and Pugin is at the helm of the *Elizabeth*, his little sailing boat. The sea spray is fresh on his face. He looks towards the eastern sky and sees a crimson dawn. Clouds rise several miles high amid shafts of light. It is the kind of sky that Turner would paint. Suddenly, an enormous wave washes over the boat and Pugin is swept overboard.

He opens his eyes to find himself in bed at the Grange. He does not move. His eyesight is suddenly sharp. Through the window he can see sunlight glittering on the sea. He feels himself sinking into the mattress. All of his muscles are relaxed and he is calm. Pugin knows what is happening. He decides not to struggle, but to trust that all will be well.

A breeze brings the sound of his father's voice, young and strong, and the boys are laughing in the drawing school. There is joyful singing from his mamma and aunt, then a crescendo and the whole world is singing with them. Higher voices join in, a holy choir, and then a beating sound and a rushing of air. Pugin wonders if it is his heart. He smiles and closes his eyes. There is a surge of power and his spirit is taken up.

Acknowledgements

I am grateful to the editors, designers, and reviewers of this book, including Catriona Blaker, Michael Blaker, Wendy Greenberg, Jennifer Corbett, Jerina Phillips, Sarah Wicker, and the artist Winnie O'Brien.

Thanks also to Joe Treasure, Jane Bailey, the Millers, the Goodlets, the Winmills, the McDonalds, Father Gerry Breen - Dean of Saint Chad's Cathedral, Monsignor Mark Crisp - Rector of Saint Mary's College, Oscott, the Landmark Trust at the Grange, officials at the Palace of Westminster, and members of the Pugin Society, for helpful feedback, encouragement, and access to Pugin buildings.

I am also grateful to the writers who have inspired me, including Rosemary Hill, author of *God's Architect* (Penguin Books, 2007); Margaret Belcher, editor of *The Collected Letters of A.W.N. Pugin* (Oxford University Press); Henry Vaughan, editor of *The Memoirs of Francis Kerril Amherst, Lord Bishop of Northampton*; Caroline Shenton, author of *The Day Parliament Burned Down* (Oxford University Press, 2012); Jane Pugin, author of *Dear Augustus and I: The Journal of Jane Pugin*, edited by Caroline Stanford (Spire Books, 2003), the publications and broadcasts of Timothy Brittain-Catlin, and of course Augustus Pugin himself, author of several books, including *Contrasts*, and *The True Principles of Pointed or Christian Architecture* (Spire Books in association with the Pugin Society).

To the many others who have helped with this book, thank you. En Avant!

Printed in Great Britain
by Amazon.co.uk, Ltd.,
Marston Gate.